LYNNA BANNING

'...ny. Enjoyable. Adventurous. Banning has written ...er winning Western.'

—*RT Book Reviews* on
The Lone Sheriff

'...ning pens another delightful, quick and ...warming read.'

—*RT Book Reviews* on
Smoke River Bride

KATHRYN ALBRIGHT

'[A ...fast-paced, sensual and delightful read about lov...rs torn apart by duty and reunited by destiny.'
—*RT Book Reviews* on
The Gunslinger and the Heiress

'Fa...s of Western and marriage-of-convenience rom...nces have it all.'

—*RT Book Reviews* on
Texas Wedding for Their Baby's Sake

LAURI ROBINSON

'The Roaring Twenties come to delightful life.'
—*Heroes and Heartbreakers* on
The Bootlegger's Daughter

'Robinson delivers a sexy, engaging adventure.'
—*RT Book Reviews* on

Acclaim for the authors of

Lynna Banning combines her lifelong love of history and literature in a satisfying career as a writer. Born in Oregon, she graduated from Scripps College and embarked on a career as an editor and technical writer, and later as a high school English teacher. She enjoys hearing from her readers. You may write to her directly at PO Box 324, Felton, CA 95018, USA, email her at carowoolston@att.net or visit Lynna's website at lynnabanning.net.

Kathryn Albright writes American-set historical romance for Harlequin Mills & Boon. From her first breath she has had a passion for stories that celebrate the goodness in people. She combines her love of history and her love of story to write novels of inspiration, endurance and hope. Visit her at kathrynalbright.com and on Facebook.

A lover of fairy tales and cowboy boots, **Lauri Robinson** can't imagine a better profession than penning happily-ever-after stories about men (and women) who pull on a pair of boots before riding off into the sunset—or kick them off for other reasons. Lauri and her husband raised three sons in their rural Minnesota home, and are now getting their just rewards by spoiling their grandchildren. Visit: laurirobinson.blogspot.com, facebook.com/lauri.robinson1 or twitter.com/LauriR.

WESTERN SPRING WEDDINGS

Lynna Banning
Kathryn Albright
Lauri Robinson

Published in Great Britain 2016
by Mills & Boon, an imprint of HarperCollins*Publishers*
1 London Bridge Street, London, SE1 9GF

Western Spring Weddings

© 2016 Harlequin Books S.A.

ISBN: 978-0-263-91694-2

The publisher acknowledges the copyright holders of the
individual works as follows:

THE CITY GIRL AND THE RANCHER © 2016 The Woolston Family Trust
HIS SPRINGTIME BRIDE © 2016 Kathryn Leigh Albright
WHEN A COWBOY SAYS I DO © 2016 Lauri Robinson

Our policy is to use papers that are natural, renewable and
recyclable products and made from wood grown in sustainable
forests. The logging and manufacturing processes conform to the
legal environmental regulations of the country of origin.

Printed and bound in Spain
by CPI, Barcelona

CONTENTS

THE CITY GIRL
AND THE RANCHER

Lynna Banning

Dear Reader,

After winter—often a long, cold, bleak period in nature and in life—a miracle happens: Nature regenerates and lives change.

To me, spring signals the renewal of both living things and the human spirit. It's a time when growth is resumed, when hope is renewed, when fear turns into courage and when the seeds of new life are sown.

Lynna Banning

Chapter One

April, 1873

"Hey, mister! Mister? Are you awake?"

Something lifted the battered wide-brimmed hat Gray had pulled over his face. "Who wants to know?" he grumbled.

"Me!"

He opened one eye. "Yeah? Who's 'me'?"

"Me! Emily!"

Gray stared into a pair of wide blue eyes framed by a mop of bright red curls. A kid. A female kid, by the look of her ruffled blue plaid dress.

"Are you sleeping?" a high-pitched voice chirped.

"He— Heck, yeah. At least I was tryin' my da— darndest."

"Are you hungry? My mama's gone to get something to eat."

"Gone where?" He surveyed the other seats in the stifling passenger car. Three silver-haired ladies with big hats, two ranchers he thought he recognized and a preacher in a shiny black suit and stiff collar.

"Gone with the conductor man. To get a sandwich for me. I hope it's not chicken. I hate chicken!"

Gray stretched his legs across the aisle space. "What's wrong with chicken?"

A frown wrinkled the girl's forehead. "A chicken pecked me once. It hurt."

"Yep, a chicken'll do that sometimes." He resettled his hat over his face and closed his eyes.

"Mister? Mister, aren'tcha gonna talk to me?"

"Not if I can help it," he said. He'd just finished a four-hundred-mile cattle drive plagued by bad weather, rustlers and no sleep. He was desperate for some shut-eye.

"Emily!" The voice was stern and female. "What are you doing bothering that man?"

"I'm not botherin' him, Mama. I'm talkin' to him."

"Haven't I told you never to talk to strangers? Come away from there, honey. I've brought you a sandwich."

"It isn't chicken, is it?" the small voice inquired.

"I beg your pardon? Emily, what's wrong with chicken?"

Something swished past him. Something that smelled good, like soap. Maybe honeysuckle, too. "She doesn't like chicken," Gray said. He thumbed his hat back and opened his eyes. And then he sat up straight so fast his jeans rubbed the wrong way on the velvet upholstery. Holy—! The prettiest woman he'd ever seen in his life sat opposite him, a brown paper sack in her lap. She wore a stiff dark blue traveling dress and a silly-looking hat with lots of feathers on top. Partridge feathers.

She looked up and smiled. "Oh, good morning, sir. I trust Emily was not bothering you?"

"Uh, no."

"Would you like a sandwich? I wasn't sure how long it would be before the train made its next stop, so I purchased an extra one."

He shot a glance at Emily. "Is it chicken?"

"Well, yes, it is. You do not like chicken?"

"Nope." He winked at the girl who was sprawled on the seat next to her mother. "A chicken pecked me once."

Emily giggled.

"Oh. I also have, let's see…roast beef and egg salad. I trust a cow has not pecked you in the past?"

Gray laughed. "Not hardly, ma'am. Fact is, I've seen enough cows in the past month to last me a good while, so if it's all the same to you, I'll take the chicken after all. And thanks."

"You are quite welcome," she said primly. "I suspect my daughter has interrupted your rest." She looked straight at him with eyes so green they looked like new willow leaves and handed him something wrapped up in butcher paper. "Emily is quite skilled at interrupting."

Emily unwrapped her sandwich. "Mister sleeps under his hat!"

"I do hope you didn't wake—"

"Yes, I did!" Emily crowed. "And he talked to me and everything." The girl's bright blue eyes snapped with intelligence. He'd bet she was a real handful. He didn't envy her mother one bit.

Suddenly he remembered what manners he'd

managed to pick up over the past thirty-one years. "Name's Graydon Harris, ma'am."

"How do you do? I am Clarissa Seaforth, traveling from Boston. And this is Emily, my daughter."

He tipped his Stetson. "Emily and I met earlier, Mrs. Seaforth."

"It's *Miss* Seaforth."

That stopped him midbite. "Miss? As in not married?"

"That is correct. Emily is adopted."

"Yes, and I'm real special!" the girl sang. "Mama said she really, really wanted me."

Gray watched Clarissa Seaforth's face turn white as an overcooked dumpling and then pink and then white again. *Whoa, Nelly!* Something about Miss Clarissa Seaforth didn't exactly add up. He clamped his jaw shut and resolved not to ask. Not his business, anyway. He had enough on his mind getting back to the ranch after the drive to Abilene, paying Shorty and Ramon the salary he owed them, eating something besides beans and bacon, and finally getting a good night's sleep.

"Are you a cowboy, mister?"

"Emily," her mother admonished. "Eat your sandwich and don't bother the gentleman."

Jehoshaphat, nobody'd called him a gentleman since he was ten years old and helped old Mrs. DiBenedetti corral her runaway rooster. The train gave a noisy jerk and began to glide forward.

"Yeah, I'm sort of a cowboy. I just drove three hundred cows to the railhead in Kansas. Guess that makes me a cowboy."

"What's a railhead?"

"Emily..." the cool voice cautioned.

Gray bit into his chicken sandwich. "A railhead? Well, that's where a train stops to pick up cattle cars."

"You mean a train like this one? I've never been on a train before. It's kinda rumbly."

He couldn't help chuckling. "*Rumbly* is a good way to describe it."

"Doesn't it bother the cows?"

"This is a passenger train, honey. Cows ride on different trains."

Her red curls bobbed. "Where do they go?"

"Uh, well, they go...well, *my* cows are goin' to Chicago."

"What do they do when they get there?"

"Emily..." the woman warned. "Eat your sandwich."

Whew. He didn't relish explaining a slaughterhouse to little Emily. Or her mother. He devoured another mouthful of chicken sandwich.

Clarissa swallowed a morsel of roast beef down a throat so dry it felt like sandpaper. How her brother would have laughed about her discomfort. *What, sis? You riding the train all the way across the country? You won't last a single day.*

He was wrong. *I have lasted all the way from Boston, and I'm not finished yet!*

But she was most definitely exhausted. She settled back in her seat and let her eyelids drift shut. Emily was a handful, irrepressible, full of four-year-old curiosity and questions and... Oh, she did hope her niece, now her adopted daughter, wasn't making a pest of herself. In one ear she could hear her daughter's high, piping queries and in the other the deeper, grumbly responses of the cowboy in the seat facing them.

"Mama?" Emily jostled her arm. "When are we gonna get there? Can I have a horse?"

"I do not know, and no, you cannot have a horse. Life is dangerous enough as it is."

The cowboy crossed his long, jean-clad legs. "How far are you goin', Miss Seaforth?"

"All the way to Oregon. Smoke River."

"That's about ten more hours," he said from under his hat.

She blinked. "Now, how would you know that, sir?"

He sat up. "Cuz I've traveled this route before. That's where I live."

"Oh?"

He sat up. "I own a ranch near Smoke River. Just sold all my cattle in Abilene and now I'm goin' home. You?"

Emily pressed up against her arm. "Tell him, Mama."

"Why, I am traveling to join someone." She paused and swallowed. "A...friend. I have agreed to be his wife."

"Sight unseen?" He thumbed his hat back off almost black hair.

"Well, yes, actually. When my brother, Anthony, died, Caleb offered to—"

"Caleb? Caleb Arness?"

"Why, yes. Do you know him?"

Gray bit back a groan. Yeah, he knew him. Last time he'd tangled with Caleb Arness, he'd sworn he'd kill the lowlife some day. "Yeah, I know Caleb."

"Ah. Could you tell me a little about him? Please?"

Like hell he would. But her green eyes darkened into an entreaty no man could resist. Not this man, anyway. "What do you want to know?"

She hesitated. "Well… Caleb wrote that he loves children. That he would treat Emily as if she were his own child. Does Mr. Arness have children of his own?"

Gray tried hard not to flinch. Caleb Arness was a liar and a cheat, and if he spent a single minute thinking about anyone other than himself, Gray would cut up his Stetson with his pocketknife and eat it. "Listen, Miss Seaforth. I gotta ask why a woman like you would even consider marrying a man she's never laid eyes on." *A man at the rock bottom of anybody's list of eligible men.*

She cuddled Emily closer to her body. "Whatever do you mean, a woman like me?"

"A woman who—" he sucked in a breath "—is, um, attractive. Okay, pretty." *Really* pretty. Hot damn, she made him crazy.

She blushed the nicest shade of raspberry he'd ever seen, and he bit the inside of his cheek. What could he say to save her from the clutches of Caleb Arness?

* * *

The train chuffed noisily into the station at Smoke River, and Emily began to bounce up and down and peer out the window. "Ooh, look, a horsie! And a funny wagon. Can I ride in it, Mama? Can I?"

Clarissa straightened her hat, then stood up and shook the wrinkles out of her bombazine travel suit. "We'll see, honey. First we must get off the train." They moved past the dozing cowboy, Mr. Harris, and descended from the train. The red-shirted conductor followed, set Clarissa's single suitcase on the platform and disappeared back into the passenger car.

The sun was blinding. She raised her gloved hand to shield her eyes and squinted at the small station house.

"Oughtta get you a sun hat pretty quick," said a masculine voice behind her. Graydon Harris stepped into her field of view.

"Yes, thank you, I will do that."

"Dressmaker in town sells hats," he volunteered. He strode past her and slung the saddlebag he carried over his shoulder into the wagon bed, then climbed up beside the driver.

"Uh, can we give you a lift, Miss Seaforth?"

"Yes!" Emily chirped. "I wanna ride on the horse!"

"No, you don't, Emily," Gray said. "Nobody rides this horse."

"How come?"

"Well…" He jumped down and lifted her suitcase into the wagon. "Because he doesn't have a saddle." He gestured at the seat he'd just vacated. "You ride up here, ma'am. Emily and I'll climb in behind you."

Well! He gave her no chance to refuse, just grasped her around the waist and swung her up into the empty space. She heard the driver chuckle. "Don't do no good to say no, ma'am," he said. "Once Gray makes up his mind, that's pretty much how things are gonna be."

Gracious sakes, what grammar! She sneaked a look at the speaker. Why, he was nothing but a boy! An Indian boy, she gathered from his bronze skin and the strip of red calico tied around his head. He grinned and nodded at her, and she quickly averted her gaze.

Emily squealed as Mr. Harris lifted her up into the wagon bed and climbed in after her. Her daughter's next words made her cringe. "Look, Mama, an Indian! A real live Indian!"

Both Mr. Harris and the driver laughed.

"I apologize for my daughter," she said as the boy picked up the reins.

"No need," he said. "You must be from back East. Everybody out here's already seen what us Indians look like, so it's no surprise to them."

The wagon rattled into the rutted road, and Clarissa clutched the edge of her seat.

"Ooh!" Emily screamed. "We're moving!"

"Sit down, honey." Mr. Harris's voice came from the back. "Don't want you to fall out."

"I wanna go fast!"

Clarissa sighed. Emily always wanted to do everything fast—she talked fast, skipped instead of walking sedately and gobbled her food. Part of Clarissa lived in perpetual amusement; the other part endured perpetual exasperation and worry.

"Miss Seaforth," Mr. Harris called, "that's Sammy Greywolf who's drivin' us."

"H'lo, Sammy," Emily called. "My name's Emily."

"How do you do, Mr. Greywolf," Clarissa added.

"The boy let out a whoop. "Ya hear that, Gray? *Mister* Greywolf."

"Yeah," Mr. Harris said drily. "I hear. Next thing you know you'll be wearin' a black silk top hat."

The boy laughed and flicked the reins. "Where to, ma'am?"

"Oh." Mentally she counted up the precious few coins at the bottom of her reticule.

"I—"

"Take her to the Smoke River Hotel," Mr. Harris said.

"Righto, Gray. Then I'll drive you on over to the livery stable."

The wagon thumped along over what must be the main street and stopped in front of a white-painted three-story hotel. The next thing she knew two strong hands gripped her around the waist and lifted her down onto the board sidewalk.

"You're shakin'," he said quietly. "Anything wrong?"

"N-no. Thank you."

He released her. "Nervous about meetin' up with

Caleb, maybe? Woulda thought he'd be there to meet your train."

"He—he didn't know when we were arriving. Exactly." She couldn't look at him.

"Hey, mister, what about me?" Emily stood in the wagon, arms extended. Mr. Harris swooshed her down so fast she screeched with delight. "Again! Do it again!"

Gray obliged, swinging the girl back into the wagon and then out again, while keeping one eye on Miss Seaforth. Something was wrong. He didn't want to lay eyes on Caleb Arness anytime soon, but she did. He didn't for one minute believe the man hadn't known when they were arriving. So what was going on? Where was he? Probably drunk in some bar, or maybe down at Serena's place.

Well, shoot, it wasn't his problem. He lifted her suitcase out of the wagon and suddenly realized how light it was. "I guess you shipped your trunk on ahead, huh? You want Sammy to deliver it from the station?"

"I shipped no trunk, Mr. Harris."

"You mean you came all the way out West with—" All at once it hit him. She had nothing but what few things were packed in that small suitcase and the clothes on her back. And he'd bet most of the things in the suitcase were Emily's. In fact, he'd bet Miss Seaforth didn't have a bean to her name.

"Wait for me, Sammy." He picked up her suitcase, grabbed Emily's hand and escorted Miss Seaforth up the steps and into the hotel.

"Harold," he said to the skinny desk clerk. "Miss

Seaforth and her daughter need a room," he announced loudly. "And," he murmured, "put it on my bill."

"Yessir, Mr. Harris," the clerk acknowledged under his breath.

"And, Harold, tell Rita that their restaurant meals are included."

He turned to look down at Emily, who was holding on to her mother's skirt, then hunkered down to her level. "Miss Emily? I want you to go next door with your momma and have a dish of ice cream, okay?"

"Are you coming, too, mister?"

"Yeah, in a little while. You got a favorite flavor of ice cream?"

She sent him a grin that made him feel funny in the middle. "Yes! Strawberry."

Miss Seaforth laid a restraining hand on the girl's red curls. "Oh, I don't think—"

"Right." Gray straightened to face her. "Don't think. Your daughter wants some ice cream, and that's all there is to it."

Chapter Two

"Mama, I think ice cream is the deliciousest thing in the whole world! Can I have another dish?"

Clarissa set her spoon beside her teacup. "No, honey. You'll spoil your supper. And it's *may* I have another dish."

"But Mister Cowboy said—"

"Mister Cowboy—I mean Mr. Harris is not your father."

"*Nobody's* my father, not since Papa went away."

She sighed. "Your papa didn't go away, honey. Your papa was lost at sea, remember?"

Emily surveyed her with interest. "What's *lostatsea* mean?"

"It means he is not able to come back, even though he wanted to more than anything in the world." Clarissa swallowed hard over something stuck in her throat. Thank the Lord the restaurant was deserted at this hour of the day. Her nerves were badly frayed. The waitress, Rita she said her name was, said it was too late for lunch and too early for supper, but tea and ice cream would be no problem. The woman wore a crisp blue apron and had a kind face; watching her bustle back and forth made Clarissa feel a little calmer.

The restaurant next door to the hotel was cool and dim, and the red-and-gold carpeting muffled the sound of footsteps. At least the room was not swaying, like the train.

Emily scraped her spoon around and around in her bowl of ice cream. "Can I play with Sammy tomorrow?"

"No, you cannot."

"Then what are we gonna do tomorrow, Mama?"

Clarissa pressed her lips together. She hadn't the faintest idea what she would do tomorrow. She had expected Caleb to meet the train, and now she felt completely at sea, alone in a strange town, a small—very small—Western town, where she knew no one, in a wild, untamed state she had only recently learned *was* a state, with exactly two dollars to her name. What on earth would she do when that was gone?

She drew in a long, slow breath and closed her eyes. She couldn't simply sit and wait for Caleb to realize she was here and come to find her. What if he were away on business? He could be gone for days, even weeks. If he didn't show soon, she must look for some sort of employment, she decided. Even though she had never worked a day in her life, she had Emily to think of. She had to do *something*.

The waitress approached. "More tea, ma'am?"

"Oh, no thank you. Rita, may I ask you a question?"

"Why sure, miss. Fire away."

"Well…um, does this restaurant need a…a dishwasher by any chance?"

The waitress's dark eyebrows went up. "You

don't look like the dish-washin' type to me, ma'am. Besides, we already got a dishwasher, Rosie Greywolf."

"Oh. I see."

Emily perked up. "Izzat Sammy's mama?"

"It is," Rita verified. "Rosie's been washin' dishes here for more years than I can remember."

"What about the mercantile across the street—Ness's, is it? Would they need a clerk?"

"Prob'ly not, miss. Carl Ness has two daughters who help out after school and on weekends."

Clarissa bit her lip. "You see, the problem is that I am running low on funds and— "

"You need a job, right?"

"I—well, yes, I do. Someone was supposed to meet me at the train station, but he failed to show up, and now..."

Rita propped her hands on her ample hips. "Who was it?"

"Caleb Arness."

The waitress's face changed. "Arness, huh?" She studied Clarissa for a full minute. "He a relation of some sort?"

"Well, no. Not yet, anyway. We were to be mar—"

"Aw, honey, I've heard tall tales in my time, but this one takes the cake. Take my advice and clear out of town as fast as you can go."

Clarissa stared at her. "I beg your pardon?"

At that moment Emily let out a cry of delight. "Look, Mama, it's Mister Cowboy!"

Gray spotted them right off. Miss Seaforth was talking to Rita, and Emily was waving her ice-cream spoon at him. He took the empty chair. "Coffee, Rita. And add some brandy, would ya? Been dry for a month."

"Sure, Gray. How was the drive?"

"Long. Miserable. Profitable, but I sure earned every penny."

He turned his attention to Emily. "Had enough ice cream?"

The red curls bounced as she shook her head. "Nope. I'm never, never gonna have enough ice cream. It's the bestest thing in the whole world, next to Christmas."

Rita brought his coffee and he downed two large gulps that made his eyes water.

"Rich enough for you?" Rita asked with a grin.

He nodded, swallowed hard and gave her a thumbs-up. She chuckled all the way back to the kitchen.

"Mama won't let me play with Sammy Wolf," Emily complained.

"Greywolf," Miss Seaforth corrected. "I am sure Mr. Greywolf is busy."

Gray set his cup on the saucer. "I had the desk clerk take your suitcase up to your room, Miss Seaforth."

"Thank you, Mr. Harris."

"Uh, now that you're here, maybe you should give some thought to a few things."

"Oh? What things?"

"Well, for starters, whether you're gonna stay or not."

"Why, of course I am staying. Caleb—"

"Might not show up." Gray downed another swallow of his ninety-proof coffee. "Might be he's, uh, tied up somewhere on, um, business."

"Perhaps. Nevertheless, I am sure he will come soon."

He smothered a snort. She wasn't sure of any damn thing. Clarissa Seaforth was a good bluffer, but the expression in those green eyes gave her away. Uncertainty warred with fear and something else he couldn't pin down. Pride, maybe.

"Listen, Miss Seaforth, like I said, you might start thinkin' what to do if Arness doesn't show up." Actually, if he was in *her* skin, he would be thinking what to do if he *did* show up. Run the other direction, he hoped.

"Emily," she said suddenly. "Are you finished with your ice cream?"

The girl nodded. "Yes, Mama, but—"

"Then we must excuse ourselves and retire to our hotel room. Good afternoon, Mr. Harris."

He watched the slim, graceful woman until she disappeared through the doorway, then chugged down the rest of his coffee just as Rita appeared at his elbow. "Want some more?"

"Want some? Yeah. Gonna have some? No. Gotta ride out to the Bar H while I can still mount a horse."

By morning Clarissa knew she was in real trouble. Her meager funds would soon dwindle, and with a sinking feeling in the pit of her stomach, she acknowledged that the situation called for extraordinary measures. After breakfast she left Emily in the care of the kindly waitress and began canvassing up one side of the dusty street and down the other, looking for employment.

The dressmaker smiled but shook her head. The barbershop, the sheriff's office and the blacksmith had no use for a female. That left the bank and the Golden Partridge saloon, and she soon found that the bank wouldn't hire a woman, either.

Very well. She straightened her spine and stepped off the sidewalk. For the first time in her life she would walk into a saloon.

Inside the Golden Partridge it was dim and smoky, and even at this hour of the morning it smelled of something pungent. Tobacco, she guessed. And spirits. She halted just inside the swinging batwing doors to get her bearings, and in that instant a pall of silence descended. Even the piano player's music dribbled to a stop.

"Excuse me, ma'am," the bartender called out. "Ladies aren't allowed in here."

She clenched her fingers around the reticule holding the last of her money—two dollars. "I...I assumed that to be the case, sir. I was wondering if you...that is, would you have any employment available?"

The bartender's meaty hand swiped back and forth across the expanse of mahogany countertop. "Not for a lady, no."

"For what, then?"

The man paused to size her up. "Well, I dunno. Can you sing?"

Chapter Three

Some hours later, Clarissa marched up and down in front of the big two-story brown house on lower Willow Street for a good ten minutes before she could work up the courage to open the gate. "Go on down to Serena's place," the bartender had instructed. "Ask her for a dress—something not too flashy but—" the man actually blushed! "—real female-lookin'."

She had never been within a mile of such a place! Her knees felt wobbly, but she stuffed down her misgivings, walked up the steps and stood trembling on the wide front porch of Serena's house. Before she could ring the bell, the door swung inward and a tall, gray-haired woman in a lacy black wrapper peered out at her.

"Miss Serena?"

The woman gave a short nod. "Whaddya want, honey? A job?"

"Well, yes, in a way. Tom, the bartender at the Golden Partridge, said I should ask you for an appropriate dress for—"

"Did he, now? Appropriate for what?"

"For singing. He gave me a job singing at the saloon tonight, but…I have nothing to wear. He said my travel dress wouldn't be quite right."

Serena eyed her travel suit. "Got a good eye, does Tom. Well, now, dearie, you just come right on in and we'll see what we can do."

"Thank you kindly, Miss—"

"Just Serena. Well, come on, honey! No need to be shy." She closed the door with a soft click. "Mary?" she called over her shoulder. "Mary, come on down here. Got a dove that ain't soiled yet, and she needs yer help."

A slim girl with very blond ringlets appeared in the parlor. She was clad in something with fluffy pink feathers around the shoulders and a slit up one side. She smelled of something over-sweet, lily-of-the-valley, perhaps.

"Mary, take Miss—what's yer name, dearie?"

"Seaforth. Clarissa Seaforth."

"Tom sent her over from the saloon," Serena explained. "Mary, take Miss Seaforth upstairs and find somethin' with some sass to it. She's gonna sing at the Golden Partridge."

Clarissa followed the girl up the thickly carpeted staircase and into a pleasant bedroom with blue flowered wallpaper and white lace curtains. A narrow bed sat in one corner and a carved walnut armoire stood on the opposite wall.

"Y'all look pretty small to me," Mary remarked. She rummaged through a welter of gowns and finally extracted a handsome crimson velvet creation. "Here. Try this one."

While Clarissa unbuttoned her bodice and

stepped out of her gored skirt, the blonde girl circled around, studying her. Before Clarissa could step into the velvet gown, Mary snatched it back. "Oh, no, that won't be right on you, honey. Try this one instead." She slipped a dark green moiré taffeta creation off its hanger and held it out.

"Oh, I couldn't—"

"Yes, you could, honey. Don't argue."

Mary buttoned the gown up the back and stepped away with an assessing look. Then she folded back one door of the armoire and spun Clarissa around. "Hmm. Here, take a look at yourself in the mirror."

A stranger with huge green eyes in a very pale face stared back at her. "Oh," she breathed. "Surely that isn't me!"

Mary laughed. "Sure is, honey. Green suits you."

"But the neckline is so…so…"

"Low? S'posed to be low, honey. Why do you think Tom sent you to us?"

"Well, he expects me to sing tonight, and he did not care for my travel suit."

Mary frowned. "Where y'all from, honey?"

"Boston."

"Huh! That explains everything. Bet you've never been within a city block of a place like Serena's, have ya? Didn't think so. And y'all aren't fixin' to move in here, are ya?"

"Well, no. I have secured employment as a singer at the Golden—"

"So you said." Mary reached out and tweaked the neck of the green gown lower. "Well, honey, no matter what you sound like, you'll sure look pretty enough."

She would? Clarissa studied her reflected image more closely. Well, maybe she would look dressed-up enough to suit the bartender. It was really a lovely gown, except for the bosom, of course. The green dress was cut way too low in front. She tried hiking it up, but the fabric wouldn't budge.

"Stop that!" Mary pulled her hands away. "Y'all look splendid. Don't fuss with things and spoil it. And take this shawl with you." She folded up Clarissa's bombazine travel suit and thrust it and a green paisley shawl into her hands. "Can't sashay up Main Street exposed like that—Sheriff's liable to arrest you."

Downstairs in the front parlor again, Serena nodded approvingly at the green taffeta dress. "Perfect. You're a real looker, dearie. If Tom don't want you, just come on back to Serena's and I'll put you to work here."

"I am grateful, Miss—Serena. I will pay you for the gown out of my wages."

"No, you won't, my girl. Tom sits high on my list. And besides, he's workin' off a debt of sorts and the cost of the loan of a dress is neither here nor there. He'll pay for the gown." She extended her hand. "Been a pleasure doin' business with you, Miss Seaforth. Wrap up good in that shawl, now, and don't talk to any men."

Clarissa knotted the green shawl tightly around her shoulders and walked as briskly as she could back to the hotel. A cold, hard lump was settling in her stomach.

When she entered the restaurant, where Emily sat chatting with Rita, her daughter flung her arms around her. "Ooh, Mama, you look beautiful! And you're so rustly—like lots of dry corn husks."

It was the first time Clarissa had laughed in the past twenty-four hours. After a quick supper in the dining room—a boiled egg for Clarissa and macaroni and cheese for Emily—she tucked her daughter into bed in their hotel room, gathered up her courage and made her way to the Golden Partridge saloon.

Tom, the bartender, installed her in a back room until her scheduled appearance; she paced around and around the tiny space until her feet ached and finally sat down. At half past nine he rapped on the door.

"You're on, Miss Seaforth. Knock 'em out of their boots!"

Very slowly she rose from the straight-backed chair, walked uncertainly to the door and, with a whispered prayer, twisted the doorknob. When she appeared, the piano player, a round black man, half rose off his stool. "Lordy, Mister Tom, what you plannin' tonight?"

"Meet your accompanist, Miss Seaforth. Baldwin Whittaker."

The pianist swiped off his threadbare cap and blinked up at her. "Ma'am."

She tried to smile. "Good evening, Mr. Whittaker."

He rolled his soft brown eyes at Tom. "You, uh, do much singing before, miss?"

"Well, mostly in church. But I know a number of songs from when I was a girl."

"Hmm. Well, what you gonna sing, Miss Seaforth?"

"'Greensleeves.' Do you know it?"

"Shore do. How 'bout you stand sorta to one side, facing the bar. That way folks can see you and I can pick up on your cues."

Clarissa took her position, steadied her erratic breathing and unknotted the shawl around her shoulders. "Like this?"

The man's mouth dropped open. "Oh, yes, ma'am, just like that! I can hardly wait to see the reaction when the gentlemen clap their eyes on you."

Well, *she* could certainly wait! Every bone in her overexposed body wanted to turn tail and run.

Mr. Whittaker turned to the piano keyboard, played a chord and looked up at her expectantly. Clarissa drew in a breath and opened her lips, but nothing came out. The pianist played the chord again, this time rippling it into an arpeggiated introduction.

Dear Lord, let me not faint dead away before I have sung a single note.

Gray pulled his tired body out of the saddle, tied the gelding up at the hitching rail and stumbled into the saloon. He wasn't too clear about why he was back in town after a restless night and a grueling day digging a well and putting up new fencing at the ranch, but here he was, and he was plenty thirsty.

Tom reached over the bar to shake his hand. "Welcome back, Gray. I was starting to wonder if you'd got religion in Abilene and turned into a teetotaler."

"Not hardly. Just been busy."

Tom snorted. "Yeah? What else is new?" He splashed a shot glass full of red-eye and set the bottle on the bar.

"Nuthin's new except I finally hit wet sand at the bottom of my new well."

Tom leaned toward him. "Got a surprise for you tonight, Gray."

"What is it? Nuthin' much would interest me but a few barrels of fresh water."

"Nah. Something better."

Gray looked up at the stocky man and froze at what he saw reflected in the gold-framed mirror over the bar. A vision in green with long, dark wavy hair tumbling to her shoulders and an expanse of creamy bosom the like of which he hadn't seen for a long time. *Jehoshaphat, that's Clarissa Seaforth! What the hell is she doing half dressed in Tom's saloon?*

The piano rippled out some notes and a voice like smoky silk rose in a familiar melody.

Alas, my love, you do me wrong,
To treat me so discourteously,
For I have loved you so long…

Gray slammed his shot glass down on the bar top and swiveled around to stare at her. She sang the whole verse while dusty cowboys and card-playing ranchers sat goggle-eyed and respectful. Then she started on the second verse, but suddenly the batwing doors banged open and Caleb Arness lurched in.

She didn't recognize him. She just kept singing in that low, silky voice while Caleb stumbled to the bar. "Tom!" he yelled. "Wanna drink."

"Shut up!" someone called from one of the tables. "Can'tcha hear the lady's singing?"

Arness obviously didn't recognize *her*, either. He kept pounding his fist on the polished mahogany surface and yelling for whiskey.

Tom leaned over the bar and said something to him.

"Singer?" Arness shouted. He swiveled around to peer at Clarissa. "A female singer? Why, hell an' damn, that's one helluva pretty—"

Gray's fist stopped the word. It also stopped the song, and an uneasy silence descended.

"Whadja hit me for, ya skunk?" Arness mumbled from the floor where he lay.

"No reason," Gray said quietly. "Just practicin'. Now, either shut up or get out."

Arness lurched toward Clarissa. "Ain't leavin' without kissin' that woman! C'mere, honey."

Gray shot a look at her stricken face and gave her a quick, decisive shake of his head. Her eyes widened. *Who?* she mouthed at him.

Arness, he silently mouthed back.

She went whiter than a pail of milk.

Arness made a grab for her. "Now, come on, honey, be nice. You come on over here and I'll show you a real good time."

Right then Gray knew he had to get her out of there. "Tom," he muttered to the barman. "Keep Arness busy."

Tom rose to the occasion by knocking over a bottle of whiskey, spilling it all across Arness's filthy trousers. While Arness mopped at the damage, Gray strode to Clarissa and bent to speak in her ear.

"Don't scream. I'm gettin' you out of here." He leaned toward the piano player.

"Cover for us, Whitt. Play something loud."

Gray grabbed her around the waist. "Come on." He hustled her into the back room, out the rear door and into the dark alley outside.

He ushered her into the hotel. "Which room?"

She turned fear-dilated eyes on him. "N-number six."

He reached over the counter and snagged the key off its hook.

"Emily will be asleep," she protested.

"Good." He unlocked the door, pushed her inside and marched in behind her.

"Mama!" Emily sat up in the big double bed, rubbing her eyes. "And Mister Cowboy! It is tomorrow already?"

"No, darling. It's still nighttime." Clarissa sank down on the bed and wrapped her arms around her daughter.

Gray laid his hand on her shoulder and she looked up at him. Her eyes looked kinda funny. Dazed-like. "He doesn't know what you look like," he said in a low voice. "But Tom'll tell him your name and that'll let the cat out of the bag for sure."

She nodded.

"I'm going over to the livery to get another horse."

She blinked. "Why?"

"I'm takin' you and Emily out to my ranch."

"But—"

"Pack up," he ordered. "And bolt the door while I'm gone."

Chapter Four

In spite of the voluminous puffy green taffeta skirt, Clarissa managed to mount the animal Gray held for her and watched while he lifted Emily into his saddle, settled her on his lap and folded her tiny fingers around the saddle horn.

"Hang on real tight, Emily."

"Okay." She sent a happy grin up at him, and Clarissa felt a stab of unease. Children were so trusting! And so was she, she reflected. Imagine, letting a man she had met only once kidnap her and take her home with him!

Gray grabbed the reins of her sorrel and kicked his black gelding into a canter. When they reached the edge of town, he moved into a gallop, but he still kept hold of Clarissa's reins. She couldn't bring herself to admit she had been on a horse only once in her life, and that was on her tenth birthday.

In the dark everything looked oppressive—thick stands of towering trees, tangled brush, shadows. There was a sound of rushing water. And no light anywhere. She was used to a measured out grid of orderly streets, gaslights, houses with candles in the windows. Her skin prickled. It was like riding into hell. If she allowed herself to feel anything, it would be a wash of pure terror.

After what seemed like hours, they moved through a wide swinging gate, then trotted up a long lane. Gray still held on to her reins with one hand and kept the other firmly planted around Emily's middle.

Clarissa was exhausted, so winded she could scarcely breathe and her backside was numb. Inside she was still shaking, but knew she was safe now, swept away from a terrible fate. Caleb Arness was a drunkard. And a liar. She was well rid of the man, but her narrow escape had left her unnerved.

But what now? Why, oh why, had she ever left Boston? She didn't know anything about the West. She didn't even know where she was.

Good heavens, Clarissa, pull yourself together. You must be strong for Emily. You have to protect your daughter.

They came up on a gentle rise and up ahead a light winked in the blackness. Oh, thank God, civilization! How long had she been joggled along on the animal beneath her, one hour? Two? It felt like ten years.

Mr. Harris—well, she guessed she should call him Gray, since he had rescued her and Emily from that odious man Caleb Arness. She would be grateful to Graydon Harris to her dying day. How could Caleb have lied to her like that, telling her he was an upstanding citizen of Smoke River, a friend of the sheriff and all the ranchers within fifty miles? A family man who would welcome her and her daughter into his Christian home? The man was nothing but a slovenly drunkard.

The horses slowed to a walk, and now she saw there were two lights—one inside a big white house with a wide verandah across the front and the other swinging from a shadowy man's hand.

"Ramon," Gray called out. "Get Maria!"

The swinging lamp disappeared into a small, dark cabin a few yards to one side of the big house, and in the next minute Gray dismounted, pried Emily's fingers off the saddle horn and lifted her down onto the ground. Then he came toward Clarissa's sorrel.

"Miss Seaforth, I'll help you dismount."

"Where are we?"

"My ranch, the Bar H." He reached up, circled his hands around her waist and lifted her out of the saddle. The instant her feet touched the solid earth her legs collapsed under her and she cried out. Gray caught her under the arms and leaned her up against the horse.

Emily skipped to her side. "Mama, how come you can't walk?"

"I can walk perfectly well," she said as steadily as she could manage. "In...a minute."

"Take your time," Gray murmured. "You don't have to prove it."

It took a full ten minutes before she trusted her limbs to keep her upright, and even then Gray had to half carry her up the porch steps.

"She is ill?" the man called Ramon asked.

"Nah. Just tuckered."

"Maria…she is inside."

Seven steps later Clarissa stood in the doorway of the house and met the startled glance of a short, plump Mexican woman.

"*Ay de mi, Señor* Gray, what have you done?"

"Nothing. Maria, this is Clarissa Seaforth, and—" he glanced left and then right, but no Emily "—her daughter. Clarissa, meet Maria Rocha, my housekeeper and cook."

"Ah, no, I am not cook anymore, remember? Not since I get my new stove in my own kitchen. Just housekeeper."

The man with the lantern swung up on the porch with Emily's hand in his. "I find her outside petting your horse, *señor*." He relinquished her to Clarissa and set the lantern on the mantelpiece of the stone fireplace.

"Ramon's my foreman," Gray explained. "Ramon, this is Miss Seaforth. And Emily."

Ramon bowed. "*Señorita*. I have already meet Emily," he said with a wide smile.

Clarissa untied her shawl and lifted it off her shoulders. Maria's sudden gasp reminded her she was still wearing the green taffeta with the too-low neckline.

The housekeeper marched up to Gray and poked her finger at his chest. "*Señor* Gray, I ask what you do, and you say 'nothing'? Is obvious you do *something*, and now you bring her home!" She shook her head in disapproval.

"Hold on, Maria. It's not what you're thinking."

"Eh? And what I am thinking?"

Clarissa took a shaky step forward. "Mrs. Rocha, Gray rescued me from a very bad man in town."

Maria's black eyebrows folded into a frown. "Is so?"

"Is so," Gray said with a sigh. "Caleb Arness."

The Mexican woman crossed herself. "Very bad man. Very bad." She pointed to the kitchen. "Come. I make coffee."

Gray caught her arm. "Maria, wait. Would you move the things in my bedroom to the room in the attic? Miss Seaforth's gonna be with us for a while."

"Maria," Clarissa said quickly. "Please don't move any of Mr. Harris's things. Emily and I will sleep in the attic."

"But is all dusty up there," Maria protested.

"I can dust."

"And with even cobwebs!"

Clarissa suppressed a shiver. "I can deal with... with a few spiders."

Emily grasped her hand. "I wanna deal with spiders, too! Can I, Mama? Can I?"

The attic room was at the top of a steep staircase, and while Clarissa saw no spiders, a thick layer of dust lay over the chest of drawers and the night table. And the bed! My gracious, when she plopped the suitcase down on top of the quilt, a cloud of dust puffed up into her face.

Maria appeared in the doorway, her arms loaded with bed linens. "*Señorita*, I bring sheets and pillows, with feathers. And—*ay-yi-yi!*—the air up here is make my eyes water!"

"Me, too!" Emily chimed. "It feels real sneezy, doesn't it, Mama?"

"So, the little one is your daughter?" Maria sent a pointed glance at Clarissa's exposed bosom. "But you not married lady?"

"Emily is adopted," Clarissa said quickly. "Actually, she is my brother's child. Her mother died in childbirth."

"Papa not want daughter?"

"He was lost in a shipwreck at sea."

"Ah." Maria tossed the armload of sheets onto a chair and patted Emily's red curls. *"Pobrecita!"*

Clarissa snatched the patchwork quilt off the bed and gave it a good shake. The air filled with dust. Maria spread the clean sheets over the mattress and plumped up the pillows while Emily scrambled into a white lawn nightie and launched herself onto the bed. "Look, Mama, it bounces!"

She stepped out of the green taffeta gown and into her batiste nightrobe. "Maria, what time will Mr.—will Gray be up in the morning?"

"Early," Maria said. "Before the sun. *Señor* Gray likes his breakfast at six."

Six! She was so tired she wanted to sleep until noon.

"You cook food for him?"

All at once Clarissa remembered that the smiling Mexican woman was Gray's *housekeeper*, not his cook. "I—" Good heavens, what should she say? She had no skill whatsoever in the kitchen, or anywhere else. In Boston they had employed servants before… But she couldn't think of that now. "Um, I can try."

With a nod, Maria left a candle on the nightstand and made her way heavily down the stairs. Clarissa tumbled between the sweet-smelling s heets and tentatively ran the fingers of one hand over her derriere. She couldn't feel a thing.

"Mama?"

"Yes, Emily?" she said with a yawn. "What is it?"

"I forgot to say my prayers. Can I say them in bed?"

"Of course." She would say a few hundred herself.

Emily folded her little hands under her chin and closed her eyes. "Forgive us our trash baskets," she whispered, "as we forgive those who put trash in our baskets."

"What? Oh, honey—"

"Shh, Mama, I'm not finished yet. God bless Mama and Mister Cowboy and Ramon and Missus Maria and…and that pretty black horse I petted."

Clarissa mentally added a special blessing for Graydon Harris and for Maria. Then she lay awake, staring up at the thick wooden beams over her head, studying the blue-painted walls and the single grimy window on the opposite wall. Every flat surface was covered in dust. Being "out West" was the farthest thing she could imagine from civilization.

But perhaps there was one bright spot—she hadn't seen a single spider! Still, she didn't know whether to laugh or cry at the fix she found herself in. No money. No job. No husband to give her and Emily a home. And absolutely no idea what to do next.

With a ragged sigh she leaned over and puffed out the candle on the nightstand.

Chapter Five

Gray faced his foreman across the woodstove in the tiny cabin. "You took that woman away from Caleb Arness?" Ramon slapped the side of his head. "*Señor* Gray, have we not trouble enough?"

"Yeah, guess I did take her away. And, yeah, we have plenty of trouble all right. More than before, that's for sure."

"But, *señor*..."

"Yeah, yeah, I know. Arness is bad news." Real bad news. Ever since he'd outbid the rival rancher in the auction when he'd bought the Bar H, Arness had been hounding him to sell and making threats. Not idle threats, either—real ones. Not only were his cattle being rustled, but Gray had also found fences pulled down, water holes fouled and his ranch hands had been threatened.

Ramon plunked his mug of coffee onto the stovetop. "You are, how you say, playing with the devil, you know?"

"Playing with fire, you mean?"

"I mean fire. Yes."

"Heck, Ramon, when it comes to Arness I'm not playin'. I'm fightin' for my life."

"*Si*, that I know. And I am helping, but you don' need no lady to stir up the hornets."

Gray clapped the slim Mexican on the back and headed to the house for breakfast. Hornets he could deal with. He could even deal with Arness when it came down to it, and he guessed it would, sooner or later.

Emily met him in the kitchen, a crust of bread in her hand. "Mama can't walk," she announced.

"Oh, yeah? Well, that happens sometimes after a long horseback ride."

The girl propped her small hands at her waist. "It won't happen to me, ever! I want to ride *your* horse, that shiny black one."

"No, you don't, Emily." Clarissa's voice came from the staircase. In the next instant she stood in the doorway, one hand clutching the edge. "I may be crippled, but I am still your mother."

Gray turned from the stove where he'd set the coffeepot to see a pale imitation of the woman he'd seen last night in a dress that matched her eyes and showed way too much of her chest. "Mornin'," he said. "You sure look different."

"Good morning. I *am* different. I am dead tired and so sore I cannot bear to sit down. And I have a healthy new respect for anyone who can ride a horse for more than ten minutes."

"Can you cook standing up?" he asked.

She looked stricken. "I cannot cook at all, standing or sitting."

"I have a proposition for you, anyway," he said carefully. Immediately he regretted his choice of words, but she took no notice. Probably never heard a remotely suggestive word back in Boston.

"Oh? What might that be?"

"Pretty quick I figure Arness will find out who you are and he'll come after you."

She flinched. "Then I must leave."

"Don't think so. With him sniffing around, you're not safe anywhere in town, and now that he's had a good look at you, he's not gonna give up 'til he corners you."

Her hand twitched. "That p-prospect terrifies me."

"That's real sensible of you, Clarissa. So, here's my—uh, here's one possibility. You and Emily stay out here at the ranch. You need a job and I need a cook." A small voice in the back of his brain began yammering at him. *Are you crazy? Why offer her a job doing something she can't do?* The truth was he wasn't exactly sure, but he knew he had to do something. She was just a baby rabbit with a chicken hawk floating overhead.

"But…but I would be a terrible cook! The only time I entered the kitchen at home was to ask for a fresh pot of tea. However," she said quickly, "I am sure I could learn. Perhaps you have a recipe book? With instructions?"

He couldn't help laughing. She might be hurting, but she wasn't beat yet. The woman had spirit. *Sand* his ranch hands would say.

"Maybe you could learn, like you said. And out here, away from town, you'd be protected. Think about it, why don't you?"

"I am thinking about it. I am thinking about how foolish I was to trust that awful man just because he wrote nice letters that said what I needed to hear, that he would provide a home for Emily."

"Yeah, well, it's too late now. You've got a real problem on your hands, but how about thinkin' about my offer over breakfast? Even if you can't sit down, you've gotta eat. So does Emily."

"Well…"

"How 'bout I pay you a salary, say three dollars a week, to cook for me. In a month or two you could save up enough for a train ticket back to Boston."

"A month!"

"Yeah. Somethin' wrong with that?"

"Could—could we stay in your attic bedroom? I feel safe there."

"Sure." He stood up, lifted the iron skillet off the hook on the wall and pointed to a red-checked apron hanging on a nail by the back door. "Lesson number one, comin' up. Emily, you want to help this old cowboy fry up some bacon?"

"Can I have an apron, too?"

"Yep." He handed her a ruffled Maria-sized yellow garment. "And here's the one for your mama."

Clarissa looped the apron around her neck and tied the ruffled part over the dark blue travel skirt she'd put on that morning. Other than the garish green taffeta dress and her bombazine travel suit, she had only three other garments—a striped calico skirt, a white muslin shirtwaist and her nightrobe. Because she couldn't sit down, she stood by the stove and watched Gray fry bacon and then crack eggs into the pan, then slice bread and toast it in the oven. It didn't look too difficult, but every step she took made her wince.

Emily managed to push three blue-flowered plates across the round wood table and plop a jumble of forks and knives at each place. Gray added a platter of scrambled eggs and bacon and Clarissa steeled herself to perch on one of the straight-backed kitchen chairs. When she emitted a little groan as she sat down, Emily brought a soft cushion from the settee in the parlor to pad the hard surface. Very gingerly Clarissa sank onto her back-side and picked up a fork.

Through the window over the dry sink, she watched the sun come up, turning the sky peach, then gold, and then such an intense blue it looked painted. She prayed it was a good omen. She was frightened right down to her knickers, stranded in a strange, wild place she didn't understand or even like and thinking about agreeing to a job she had not the remotest idea how to undertake. She imagined her brother's laughter. *Cook? Sis, you can't even boil water!*

Gray ate without talking until the platter of eggs was empty, then he poured them both a second cup of coffee and answered Emily's endless stream of questions. "What do horses do at night? Does Missus Maria have a little girl I could play with? How far can you see at night? Do you like red flowers better than yellow ones?"

Finally Clarissa shushed her and asked a question of her own. "Why do you dislike Caleb Arness so much? I know you do, because of the way your face looks every time his name comes up."

Gray set his coffee cup down and leaned back in the chair. "Well, for starters, last night you saw the kind of man he is. Then there's my ranch. I busted my—worked hard for almost twelve years to buy it and build it up. It's the most important thing in my life, and Arness wants it. My land sits between his spread and the river, so he's hurtin' for water."

"Go on," she said quietly.

"Arness has nasty ways of tryin' to drive me off. He's cut fences and poisoned my well so now I'm havin' to dig another one. My hands find dead cattle on the range—poisoned, the sheriff says. And I suspect the rustlers that plagued every mile on my drive to Abilene work for Arness. Cows disappear from my herd here at the Bar H, too. I'm losin' stock and money, and I'm getting stretched pretty thin. If I can't stop it, I'm gonna lose my ranch. And I'll damn well die before I lose this ranch!"

She listened in complete silence, not drinking her coffee, just looking at him, her face grave and her eyes soft with understanding. Made him feel kinda warm inside.

"So," she said after a long silence, "I could help in a small way by being your cook."

Gray stared at her. Yes, it would ease things a

bit—maybe a lot—but mostly he was touched by her recognition of how important the Bar H was to him. Even Emily seemed to grasp what was at stake.

"I'm gonna plant a garden an' grow ice-cream cones," the girl announced. "That would help, wouldn't it, Mister Gray?"

Gray's throat was suddenly so tight he couldn't answer.

Chapter Six

Clarissa opened the front door to find a beaming Maria standing on the porch. "*Señorita*, I bring gift." She held up the headless body of a chicken.

Clarissa recoiled. "Oh, I, um, thank you, but I don't think—"

"Is nice fat hen," the Mexican woman explained. "Make very good dinner."

Clarissa gasped. Dinner! Oh, heavens, she'd forgotten her agreement. If she worked as Gray's cook, then of course she must do just that—cook! And that meant not only breakfast but midday dinner and supper each evening. And not next week or tomorrow, but *now*. Today.

She stared at the bird clutched in Maria's brown hand. "Maria, wh-what do I do with it?"

"Is easy." Maria lifted her hand and folded Clarissa's slim fingers around the scaly yellow legs. "First chop feet off, then take off feathers. To do this, boil water and give bath, then—"

"Chop off…?"

"Feet," Maria reiterated. "Then pull out pinfeathers and clean out insides. You know what are pinfeathers?"

"Maria, might I borrow your cookbook?"

"Que? Never have I used a book of cooking, *señorita. I* have learn everything from my mama—tortillas and frijoles, even flan and pan dulce. The rest—American food—I teach myself.

Clarissa swallowed hard. Could she do that? She must have frowned because the Mexican woman suddenly reached out and patted her hand. "Do not worry, *señorita.* You will learn."

"Th-thank you, Maria. I will try."

Chop off the feet? A shudder went up her spine. She retreated to the kitchen, plopped the bird in the sink, and stared at it. *I haven't the faintest idea how to do this.*

On the back porch she found a small hand ax, laid the chicken on the back step, closed her eyes tight and whacked off the legs. Then, recalling Maria's instructions about the bath, she filled the teakettle and set it on the still-warm stove. Finally she shoved more wood into the firebox. At least from watching Gray she knew how to make a fire and heat water!

When the teakettle sang, she dumped the boiling water over the bird and discovered she could strip off the wet feathers quite easily. But the smell made her gag, and she tried not to breathe. When the naked bird sat looking at her, she thought about Maria's next direction—clean out the insides.

Oh, God, how did one do that? She paced around and around the kitchen, steeling her nerves. Then she grasped a butcher knife and made a tentative incision at the thickest point of the chest, between the two wings. No entrails. Then she poked the tip of the knife between the drumsticks, and voila! She slashed in under the skin and—oh, Lordy—she couldn't bear to look. All kinds of awful, ropey-looking things tumbled out. Hurriedly she looked away and gulped in air, then sucked in a deep breath and steeled herself to pull out all the innards and plop them in a bucket.

She would *never* be able to do this again. Whatever had she been thinking to agree to employment as a cook? Tears rose in her eyes. She had made another impulsive, ill-advised decision, like traveling out West to marry Caleb Arness, and now she was paying the price. She hated the West and everything in it—especially chickens!

She studied the eviscerated chicken on the counter. She'd already done the hard part—hadn't she?—cutting off the legs and stripping off the smelly feathers. And pulling out the—she shuddered again—guts. How much more difficult could it be to shove it in the oven and bake it?

She rinsed the bird out, sprinkled salt and pepper over the skin, and laid it in a deep-sided pan. After an hour, the kitchen began to smell surprisingly good—so good, in fact, that her stomach rumbled. And by eleven o'clock, Emily was alternately dancing about the kitchen and complaining about being hungry.

"Just a few more minutes, Emily. Why don't you set plates on the table, and then we'll have dinner?" In the pantry off the kitchen she found a mason jar of green beans and the remains of a stale loaf of bread in the bread box. Tomorrow she must think about learning how to bake bread, even though she could not imagine herself in the kitchen with floury hands. Still, it could not possibly be worse than cleaning a chicken, could it? She gave an involuntary shudder.

Promptly at noon, Gray tramped through the back kitchen door and sniffed the air. "Mmm, somethin' sure smells good!"

"It's a chicken!" Emily shouted. "All baked 'n' everything. Maria showed me chickens are nice."

Clarissa set the platter holding the roasted bird on the table next to his elbow and handed him a sharp knife. "Would you please carve it?" she pleaded. "This chicken and I are not exactly friends."

"Oh, yeah?" It did look kinda odd, the skin over-brown and stiff as parchment. When he stuck in the knife, he heard a crackling sound. Still, roast chicken was roast chicken, and he was plenty hungry. When he slid the knife in to slice off a drumstick, it was so dry it was like sawing through wood.

He set the knife down and shot a look at Clarissa's tense face. "What happened to it?"

She worried her bottom lip between her teeth in a way that made him uneasy in an unexpected way. "Maria brought it over this morning. I did everything she said, but..." Her voice choked off and she swiped a sheen of tears off her cheek.

Emily stared at her mother with round blue eyes. "Mama, are you crying?"

"Of course not," she said quickly. "It's quite warm in here."

Gray studied her face, then looked down at the platter. "Looks pretty well overdone," he said. "But heck, it's only a chicken, Clarissa. Nothin' to cry about."

"Oh, y-yes it is. You hired me to be your c-cook, and I can't!"

"Can't what?"

"Can't cook."

"At all?"

"No," she sobbed. She looked so heartbroken, he wanted to laugh, but he figured that would just make it worse, so he clamped his jaws together. "Listen, there's worse things than overcooking one chicken."

"Oh?" Her lips were still quivery, which made him feel downright funny inside.

"Yeah. You could be overcooking a chicken in Caleb Arness's kitchen."

She gave a strangled cry and buried her face in her hands. Emily scrambled out of her chair and smoothed her small hand over Clarissa's dark hair. "You could learn, Mama. You learned lots of things before we got on the train, remember? How to iron my dresses and pack up all our stuff in one suitcase. Lots of things."

Gray wanted to hug the little girl. "Listen, I have to ride into town this afternoon. How about I bring you back a cookbook from the mercantile?"

Clarissa's face lit up like Christmas. "Oh, c-could you? You can deduct it from my earnings."

Gray studied the woman across the table. "What did you do before you learned to iron?"

"We— My brother had servants. He was gone at sea for months at a time, so his wife and I always had servants and plenty of—"

"Money," he supplied. "Maria told me about your sister-in-law dying. And then your brother didn't come home, and you lost it all."

"Yes, I lost everything—the house, the bank account, even the furniture. The lawyer said we had nothing left and we had to move."

"Didn't your brother have a will? Some way to provide for you and Emily?"

"Apparently not. At least they could never find one."

He spooned some green beans out of the blue ceramic bowl, but he was fast losing his appetite. How could a man just forget about something as important as providing for his sister and his child?

"That why you agreed to come out to Oregon and marry Arness? You had no money and no home?"

She was quiet for a long minute. "Emily, why don't you go upstairs and bring me my shawl."

When the girl's footsteps faded, Clarissa leaned toward him. "Part of being, well, overprotected all one's life is that it makes one naive. I realize now how foolish I was to accept Mr. Arness's offer of marriage. All I could think about was making a home for Emily."

"Even if it meant marrying someone you'd never

met? Clarissa, seems to me that's more than fool-ish—that's downright stupid."

Her face changed. "But thousands of women travel out West every year as mail-order brides. Surely you are not saying that all of them are—"

"Stupid. Yeah, I am sayin' that. Marryin' any-body, even someone you've known all your life, is—"

Her eyes got big. "Stupid?"

"Yeah. Why tie yourself down to someone whose guts you're gonna hate in a few years?"

She bit her lip. "Did that happen to you?"

At that moment Emily clattered down the stairs. "Here's your shawl, Mama. Are we havin' any dessert?"

Clarissa looked blank. "Oh. Dessert. How about we have, uh, some cookies with our tea later? After I consult a cookbook," she added under her breath.

"Okay. Can I go play with Maria? She has a dolly."

"That's news to me," Gray said when Emily had streaked out the front door. "Well, it's turning out to be a real interesting day, wouldn't you say?"

He rose, gave Clarissa a grin and strode out the back door.

"Señor!" Ramon waylaid him on his way to the barn. "Where you go?"

"Town."

"Why because? We need to fix all that fence that was broke last night."

"Later," Gray said.

Ramon caught his reins. "But, boss, cows will get out."

"Yeah, I know. We'll chase 'em in the morning."

Ramon shook his dark head. "You do things your way, always. Not always best way, *señor*."

Gray chuckled. Ramon was right most of the time, but he'd always done things his own way, and Ramon or no Ramon, Clarissa needed that cookbook. He started to rein away.

"*Señor*, why you not listen to Ramon?"

"Because I like to do things my way."

"I think you are wrong." Ramon doggedly pursued him.

Gray leaned over the saddle horn and stared down at him. His foreman had a point. Over the years of struggle to keep this ranch going, maybe he'd become too convinced he was the only person who knew best. Or maybe he was just stubborn. But he wasn't wrong about riding into town. He hadn't been able to stomach the chicken Clarissa had roasted to within an inch of its life, but he'd liked even less the bereft expression on her face. A woman in tears made his belly hurt.

He spurred Rowdy forward and trotted over the cattle guard and through the Bar H gate.

Chapter Seven

Now, Clarissa reflected some days later, how difficult could it be to bake a cake? Some flour, a little sugar, an egg or two and…what? She could ask Maria, but after her roast chicken disaster she was hesitant to admit to an even greater lack of knowledge about what she'd been hired to do.

She studied the woodstove in the kitchen and let out a deep sigh. She prayed that Emily was right—she could learn to cook, couldn't she? *And she must do it as quickly as possible.*

She flipped over the page of *Mrs. Beeton's Household Hints.* Aha! A recipe for something called Plain Yellow Cake. "Take two good handfuls of flour…" What, exactly, was a handful? Would it be a large hand, like Gray's? Or a small one, like hers? What if Emily wanted to bake a cake with *her* tiny little hands?

She gazed out the window over the kitchen sink into the grove of willow trees behind the house. In the clear spring sunshine the new leaves looked like green glass, but now the light was fading. *Face it, Clarissa, you don't belong out here on a ranch in the West.* She felt inept. Foolish. Out of place in this godforsaken land, and what was even worse, she felt a kinship with no one. At least she didn't feel at odds with the man who had rescued her from Caleb Arness, or with down-to-earth, understanding Maria. But everything else out here was like being on a different planet.

With a groan she tried to focus again on Mrs. Beeton's book. She simply *must* stop feeling sorry for herself. She'd gotten herself into this pickle, and she would have to get herself out of it. Besides, thousands of women were surviving—even thriving—out here in this rough, untamed country. A month ago she'd even thought she might become one of them, but one look at Caleb Arness had told her how wrong she had been. Now she realized how foolish and misguided it would be to be any man's wife, mail-order or not.

Back in Boston she'd been an acknowledged spinster at twenty-four. "On the shelf," everyone said. But even so, she had a life in Boston. She had fit in. There were concerts, afternoon teas, even happy hours spent in the library. On fine days people walked along the streets and in the lush, green parks, stopping for a soda at the candy store or the creamery. She missed it all.

She marveled that Emily was not lamenting the lack of ice-cream sodas. But her daughter seemed to revel in every new and exciting thing she found in the West—horses to pet, Maria's cornhusk dolls to play with, spring wildflowers to pick, even the nightly tall tales Gray spun to lull her to sleep. Even now she could hear his low, gravelly voice coming from the parlor where he sat with her daughter cradled on his lap.

"And then," he continued, "I left home. Well, to tell the truth, I ran away from home."

"Why'd you do that?" Emily queried. "I'd never run away from *my* mama."

A long silence fell. Instead of measuring out flour for the cake she was determined to bake, Clarissa found herself listening intently.

"Well, it's like this, honey," Gray continued. "My ma and my pa didn't like each other much. They yelled and screamed at each other every day for fourteen years, and finally I'd had enough."

"What'd you do?"

Another silence. "Not sure I should tell you, Squirt."

"Yes, you should tell me!" she persisted. "I won't tell anyone, I promise."

Clarissa heard a low chuckle and then his voice continued. "Well, let's see, what did I do? What do you think I did?"

"I bet you found a horse and a lot of money and you ate lots and lots of strawberry ice cream."

"You like strawberry ice cream, huh?"

"Uh-huh. I like it better than anything."

"Better than…scrambled eggs and bacon?"

"Yes!"

"Better than…roast chicken?"

"Way better! Especially when Mama bakes it."

Clarissa's lips tightened.

"Better than…Maria's molasses cookies?"

"Yeah!"

"Guess that settles it, then. Gotta churn some ice cream one of these days."

"Strawberry!" she shouted. "But first you have to finish my story."

Clarissa laughed out loud as she mixed the listed ingredients together. Once Emily set her mind to something, she never gave up.

"Ah. Well, let's see…where were we?"

"Your mama and your papa were screaming and you got a horse."

"Yeah. Well, I lit out. Uh, you know what that means?"

"It means you…bought a big lamp?"

"That's right in one way, Emily. I got myself a job and *then* I bought a lamp. I went to work in a silver mine, way down deep underground."

"Was it dark?"

"Plenty dark. And cold."

Clarissa dropped her mixing spoon. *At only fourteen years of age he went to work in a silver mine?*

"What'dja do?"

"I worked my a—worked really hard. And pretty soon, guess what?"

"You bought some ice cream!"

Gray's rich laughter washed over Clarissa, but his tale was sending chills up her spine. How awful that must have been, working in a mine. What happened then? she wanted to ask. She slid the cake into the oven, still listening intently.

"No, I didn't buy ice cream. I bought something else. Something a lot bigger."

"What was it?"

"I'll tell you tomorrow night, okay?"

"No! Tell me now. Please? *Puleeze?*

Clarissa snapped Mrs. Beeton's cookbook shut. "Emily…" she warned. "Time for bed."

In the next moment her daughter's light footsteps pattered up the stairs, and Gray appeared in the kitchen doorway. "Hope you don't mind me tellin' her these stories."

She looked up. "They are certainly…educational," she said carefully.

"Never thought of it that way, but yeah, I guess it was educational. For me, anyway."

"It would seem you learned a great deal, at a very young age."

When he didn't answer, she shot a look at his face. He had a hard time keeping his unruly dark hair out of his eyes, which, she admitted, were quite nice—an odd gray-blue, like the barrel of the revolver he kept in a holster hanging over the front door. She liked his mouth, too, except when it narrowed in disapproval at something one of the ranch hands did. Mostly his lips were firm and usually curved in a smile, especially around Emily.

But tonight it was his eyes that caught at her—steel hard and unblinking. "I guess I shouldn't be telling her those things," he said slowly.

"You mean about working in a silver mine?" At his startled look, she added, "I was listening as I made the cake."

"No. Other things I guess maybe I shouldn't be telling her, about my ma and pa and why I left home. Bet you never met anybody who ran away from home before."

Something in his voice changed, and all at once she didn't know what to say. He pushed past her toward the back door. "Gotta check the barn before I turn in."

"Gray?"

He stopped and stood unmoving, his back to her. "Yeah?"

"My cake will be done when you get back. I'll cut a piece for you and leave it on the table."

"Yeah. Thanks, Clarissa." He grasped the doorknob, then spoke over his shoulder. "Cut a piece for yourself, too. Maybe heat up the coffee. There's something I want to say to you."

When he disappeared through the doorway she found her mouth had gone dry. He wanted to say something to her? What was it? Was it about Emily? About Ramon spending his valuable time showing her daughter how to plant seeds for a kitchen garden?

All at once she was certain she knew what it was. *He's going to fire me.*

She untied the apron and paced back and forth across the kitchen floor, waiting for the cake to finish baking and the cold coffee to heat up. Where would she go? What would she do?

She couldn't think about it. At last she peeked in the oven, tested the cake with a straw from the broom on the back porch, and lifted out the cake pan using her bunched-up apron as a pot holder.

She *was* learning to cook! But perhaps not well

enough to warrant her weekly three-dollar salary. Perhaps he expected his fried eggs not to be too hard or so runny they slid off his fork and the biscuits to be light and fluffy, like Maria's, not hard enough to bounce, as her first batch had been. She couldn't even *think* about attempting another roast chicken; she had to work up her courage for that.

The more she mulled it over, the more unsettled her stomach grew. She picked up a knife, sawed two squares from the cake and set them on two small plates. Before she could find forks, the back door banged open.

"Coffee smells good," he remarked.

"It's not fresh, I reheated this morning's."

"Still smells good." He dropped into a chair. She poured him a large mug and slid the plate of cake toward him.

"You havin' some, too?"

"Yes."

He took a bite, and Clarissa watched avidly as he chewed and swallowed.

"Tastes kinda...um...flat."

"Flat?" She took a tentative bite. The cake was nicely browned on top, and it had a fine texture. But he was right—it had no flavor at all. What had she done wrong? She grabbed Mrs. Beeton's book and thumbed through the pages until she found the recipe. Flour. Sugar. Eggs. Saleratus. And salt. *Salt!* Good heavens, she'd forgotten to add salt. No wonder it tasted flat!

She snatched Gray's plate away.

"Hold on a minute, it's not that bad, honest!"

"Don't lie to me, Gray. Don't ever, *ever* lie to me."

He blinked and his fork clattered onto the table. "Clarissa, I never lie. I've never lied to anyone in my entire life, not even—" He broke off.

Her breath stopped. "Not even who?"

"Not even my pa when I left home, uh, I mean ran away. I wanted to, though. God, I wanted nothin' more than to tell him the truth, but...well, I couldn't. But I couldn't lie, either. So I didn't say anything at all, I just up and left."

Clarissa stared at him. "You hate my cake, don't you? You just don't want to tell me."

Gray chuckled. "No, I don't hate it. It's true, it's not a very tasty cake, but maybe you can pour something over the top, like a frosting or something. Maybe Mrs. Beeton can suggest something to rescue it."

She began idly riffling through the pages.

Gray sipped his coffee and watched her. "You know, there's lots more important things in life than one flat-tastin' cake."

She said nothing, but he could tell by her face that she wasn't convinced. She'd probably been raised so starchy and proper in her rich brother's house in Boston that she expected everything she put her hand to to be perfect. Well, he had news for her. Nobody's life went like that.

For a brief minute he thought about telling her so, but the wary expression in her eyes made him hesitate. There were other emotions in her face, too—some he could read, like tiredness and disappointment and discouragement; other things were a mystery, especially an odd, hungry look she tried to hide that made his breath catch.

"I'm going for a walk," he announced. He escaped out the back door and again made his way down the path to the barn where he plopped down on a hay bale to think things over. The warm air smelled like straw and horse dung. There was nothing in particular he had to do out here, so after a while he found himself talking to Rowdy.

"Had to get out of the kitchen, fella. Felt kinda closed in, hard to breathe, you know? Don't understand why, exactly, just felt surrounded. Clarissa *feels* things, see. Me, I try *not* to feel things. That's what's kept me safe all these years."

He stood up and nuzzled the gelding's black nose. "We'll talk again soon, boy. Next time I'll bring you an apple."

Chapter Eight

Some days later, Clarissa finished wiping the last of the supper plates and paused for her nightly stocktaking meditation. She had saved a few dollars already. Precious dollars. But she needed many more for the train ticket back to Boston. Emily was adapting, almost effortlessly, to life on the ranch but Clarissa grew more and more dispirited with every passing day. Or rather every passing breakfast, dinner and supper. It was a wonder Gray had not complained. It was an even greater miracle he had not fired her! Maybe that was what he'd wanted to talk to her about that night.

With a sigh, she hung the damp dish towel on the hook by the stove and drifted out the open front door to the porch where everyone had gathered— the ranch hands, Shorty and Nebraska, and even Erasmus, the old man who took care of the horses and swept out the barn. Maria and Ramon sat on the top step, holding hands.

The day had been scorching right up until the sun sank behind the far-off purplish mountains to the north with a last wash of flaming crimson and orange. Out here in the country night fell with a finality she still found unnerving. She gazed out at the unrelieved blackness, then stepped off the porch and looked up at the sky. Back in Boston the stars had never seemed this close, like tiny blobs of silvery dough scattered across the velvet sky.

She remounted the steps, settled herself in the porch swing and breathed in the scent of roses and the honeysuckle vine that twined over the trellis. Nebraska was tuning up his fiddle and soon launched into "Red River Valley." After one verse Erasmus pulled a battered harmonica from his overalls pocket and joined in. It wasn't a symphony orchestra or a chamber ensemble, as she had enjoyed back in Boston, but the music sounded lovely, anyway.

Maria brought out a big pitcher of lemonade and a bowl of ripe strawberries, and Clarissa nibbled and let her thoughts drift. What would her life have been like if Anthony and Roseanne had lived? Emily would have had a real mother and a father, and she herself...well, perhaps she would have walked out with an admirer, maybe even married and had a child of her own. As it was, she'd been too absorbed in caring for Emily to entertain many callers, and outside of an occasional concert or visit to the library, she'd spent all her time learning to be a mother. She wouldn't trade Emily for anything on earth, but sometimes she did wonder about what she had missed in life.

Emily was quiet this evening. Perched on the porch between Gray's long legs she wasn't even clamoring for a story. The music rose and fell, and soon Emily's head began to droop onto Gray's knee. After a while, Ramon stood and beckoned Maria into his arms and they began to dance around and around on the porch.

Emily seemed to wake up at this, and jiggled Gray's knee. "You gonna dance with me?"

"Well, now," he said in a low voice, "I don't know. I'm not real good at dancin'."

The girl jumped to her feet. "I bet I could teach you!" She tugged on his hand. "Come on. You're not scared, are ya, Gray?"

"Scared?" Gray got to his feet and took both the girl's hands in his. "I'm not scared of a four-year-old girl with a thousand questions, no." But he had to admit he was plenty scared about other things, like losing more of his cattle to rustlers or finding more bad water. Or losing his ranch. And he was definitely uneasy about Caleb Arness. He'd expected the man to show up before now, and he couldn't help but wonder why he hadn't. Probably he was in jail. Again. Next time he went into town he'd ask around and stop by the sheriff's office and inquire.

He had to bend down a bit to dance with Emily, but the ecstatic look on her freckled face made the effort worthwhile. He liked making her smile. She had to take two or three steps to every one of his, so their progress around the porch was slow, but Emily didn't seem to care. Her red curls bobbed in time with the fiddle music, and she alternately grinned up at him and grinned at her mother where she rocked in the porch swing. It was kinda fun steering the girl around the floor. Maria smile broadly at him, and Ramon sent him a wink.

When they two-stepped in front of the swing, Emily suddenly dropped his hand and darted forward. "Mama, look at me—we're dancing!" She grabbed Clarissa's skirt. "Come and dance with us!"

"Oh, no, honey, I couldn't do that."

But Emily wasn't about to be put off. She seized Clarissa's skirt with both fists and yanked on it until her mother gave up and got to her feet. Emily entwined one of her hands with Gray's and with the other she glommed onto Clarissa's. Before he knew it, they had all joined hands to form a threesome.

Clarissa sent him a look that made him chuckle—half apology, half amusement, but her warm hand fit nicely in his, and he had to admit he liked that. The three of them began to circle around the porch in time to "Down in the Valley." Emily swooped and giggled with such uninhibited verve that Gray laughed out loud, and then he caught Clarissa's gaze. Suddenly the sounds around him faded until nothing remained but a faint humming in his brain.

What the hell?

In the next instant Emily dropped his hand, gave a happy chirp and twirled off by herself, leaving Gray and Clarissa facing each other.

"Well," Clarissa said with obvious embarrassment, "I suppose we should—"

"Dance," he finished.

Without another word Gray pulled her into his arms and began to move in a slow, steady pattern.

Clarissa blinked. Where on earth had he learned to waltz? Certainly not in a silver mine! Perhaps at some place like Serena's on Willow Street; after all, he was young and virile and…

She missed a step. He held her gently, his hand at her back pressing just close enough that her breasts brushed the front of his chambray shirt. Heavens, could he feel that? The contact made them tingle in a decidedly pleasant way.

Emily settled herself near Ramon and Maria and snuggled her head against the woman's arm. Ramon began singing along with "Clementine," and Maria was sitting with her head on his shoulder. They looked so happy together her throat ached.

Gray danced her to the edge of the porch, then to the far end where the honeysuckle twined up to the rooftop. What an odd sensation, being this close him. She hadn't danced with anyone since she was ten years old, but this was decidedly different. She felt light and floaty inside. Never in her life had she been so intensely aware of another human being, not even when she had first held baby Emily in her arms.

Gray forgot everything but the feel of the woman he held in his arms. Something smelled real sweet, maybe her hair. It was dark and shiny, and she wore it gathered in a loose bun at the nape of her neck. Kinda old-maidish, but she sure didn't seem like one. Clarissa Seaforth might be an overly proper

Boston lady, but in his arms she just felt like a woman—soft and alive.

Surprisingly alive. Surprisingly arousing, if he were honest with himself. He'd never felt such an undercurrent of can't-ignore-it desire. He decided to ignore it anyway and hope it would go away.

But it didn't go away. It just kept building and building like a summer storm. He tried to keep his mind on the fiddle music, the painted boards of the porch under his boots, the look on Ramon's face as he sat beside his wife. That didn't help much. Kinda made him feel hungry and lonely at the same time.

He closed his eyes and tried to think. He didn't have time for a woman—any woman, and especially not a proper lady. He only had time to brand cattle and mend fences and dig wells and keep his ranch together.

All he had to do was pay Clarissa the three dollars she earned each week as his cook and pretty soon she would climb on the eastbound train and be gone. Then he could stop tossing and turning half the night thinking about her sleeping just one floor above him.

The top of Clarissa's head brushed against his chin. Hot damn, her hair was soft! It took a lot to get his mind off his struggling ranch, but the fleeting touch of any part of her could sure do it in a hurry. *Hell and damn, anyway. I don't need this.* He needed to focus on his ranch and forget that Clarissa Seaforth smelled good and felt so good in his arms it made him crazy.

* * *

The next night after supper, while Gray lounged in the parlor with Emily, he was surprised to hear Caleb Arness's voice.

"Harris?" the man bawled. Sounded as though he was just outside on the porch. Quickly he set Emily on her feet.

"Go into the kitchen, Squirt. Tell your mama to take you to the pantry and stay there."

When the girl scampered off, he puffed out the lantern and retrieved his revolver from over the door. "You're trespassing, Arness. Whaddya want?"

"My fiancée, Clarissa Seaforth. Come to take her back to town."

"You're wasting your time, Arness. She's not your fiancée. She works for me."

"Huh! Doin' what?"

"She's my cook."

"An' what else?" Arness boomed. "You got no claim on her. I do."

"No, you don't. Now get off my land."

"Oh, yeah? What if I don't?"

Gray put a bullet through the screen door that kicked up the dust at Arness's feet. "Don't tempt me, Arness."

The stocky man jumped back, then shook his fist at Gray. "You ain't heard the last of this, Harris. That girl belongs to me!"

Arness shuffled off, and a few moments later Gray heard the sound of receding hoofbeats. He shut the front door, locked it and moved into the kitchen. Halfway across the floor to the pantry he stumbled into Clarissa, with a heavy iron skillet gripped in one hand.

"Where's Emily?" he barked.

"In—in the pantry."

"How come you aren't?"

"Well, I—I thought..."

He lifted the skillet out of her hand. "You thought I might need some help, is that it?"

"I th-thought you might want—"

He was trying hard to be angry at her, but the truth was he was touched. Darn fool woman. "Get Emily and go upstairs," he said more brusquely than he intended.

She snapped to attention. "Yes, *sir*, Mister Harris, *sir*. I was only trying to—"

"Get yourself kidnapped or killed," he grumbled. She said nothing, but he could hear her ragged breathing in the dark.

"Sorry, Clarissa. Go on to bed now. You know you're safe here."

"Yes," she murmured. "I know. Thank you."

Chapter Nine

Gray reined Rowdy around to face the tall, skinny ranch hand they all called Shorty. "Shorty, grab that roll of barbwire, will ya?"

"Sure, boss. Done rounded up all those cows that got out yesterday. Any idea what happened?"

"Same as last month. Arness and his crew of rustlers is what happened."

"They cut the fence and try to take cows," Ramon said. "But we see them."

"We run 'em off," Gray's newest hand, Nebraska, chimed in. "And then we took out after the cattle."

"Thanks, fellas," Gray said. The new kid might be wet behind the ears, but he could sure ride. "Glad you work for me and not Arness."

"I'm glad, too, boss. Don't like cheaters or people who steal. Back in Nebraska we string 'em up."

Shorty scratched his head. "Boss, how come Arness keeps doin' us dirt? What's he got against you?"

Gray spit off to one side. "He wants my ranch to fail. Wants me to go under."

"Some reason?" the tall man queried.

"Guess maybe because I beat him out of buyin'

the place for himself when it came up for auction some years ago. Arness wanted it, but I'd saved up more money."

"And now," Ramon interjected, "he wants the *señorita* who lives here."

Nebraska pricked up his big ears. "Might be that women are more important than cows, huh?"

"Way more important," Shorty answered.

"Knock it off!" Gray snapped. "Got fences to mend."

All four riders spurred their mounts and moved off into the meadow. Shaking his head, Nebraska followed with the wagonload of barbwire. Gray rode on ahead. Losing the number of cows he had this past year was making him plenty nervous. On the drive to Abilene, rustlers had made off with close to seventy head; he couldn't afford to lose any more.

That evening the hands were lounging around the bunkhouse after the chores were done when Maria accosted Gray on the front porch.

"*Señor* Gray, Sunday is May first. We go to picnic, no?"

"No." Ranch work was more important than picnics.

Maria peered at him. "The girl, Emily, she would like it."

"Yeah, she probably would, Maria, but we've got calves to brand and—"

Maria propped her hands on her hips.

"*Señor*, is no work on Sunday. Is May Day."

"Yeah, I know. So what? A ranch doesn't care what day it is."

"*Señor*, you think too much about ranch work. Think of Emily! She knows nothing of ranch work. She is a small child only. She deserves to have fun, is true?"

Gray sighed. In the five years he'd owned the Bar H, he'd never won a single argument with Maria. You'd think he'd have learned that by now. He threw up his hands. "Okay, okay. Make that chocolate cake you're so famous for, huh?"

"Oh, *si, Señor* Gray. *Gracias*."

"A picnic!" Emily squealed. "A real picnic with potato salad and everything?"

Gray set his coffee mug down on the supper table. "Yeah, 'and everything.' Would you like that?"

"And ice cream?"

Gray had to laugh. "Maybe."

Clarissa sent him a pensive look. "I don't have a recipe for potato salad."

"*Nobody* has a recipe for potato salad," he said. "You just boil up some eggs and some potatoes and mix 'em up together with some onion and a chopped pickle or two. And some salt," he added. He was relieved when she laughed.

Emily patted his arm. "Are you gonna tell me a story tonight?"

"Maybe. Have you been a good girl today?"

"Not 'xactly, but I want a story, anyway."

"How 'bout if your mama tells you a story to-night?"

"No!" the girl sang. "Mama's stories aren't exciting, like yours."

That caught his interest. "Not exciting?" He caught Clarissa's gaze. "Living in a big city like Boston isn't exciting?"

"Not exciting the way things are out here in Smoke River," Clarissa said. "Life in Boston is more...well, civilized. You know, with libraries and concerts and museums."

"Man, I never thought of libraries and museums as bein' exciting!"

Clarissa's voice rose. "But they are!"

"Can't wait to get back there, huh?"

Clarissa opened her mouth to reply, but Emily cut her off. "*I* can wait! I like it out here lots better."

Gray stuffed down a chuckle. "Clarissa, looks like you've been outvoted."

"About the picnic, yes. About going home to Boston—never. All I need is enough money for a train ticket."

Gray said nothing. It wasn't surprising that she wanted to go back to Boston; what was surprising was his reaction. He didn't want to think about the stab of disappointment that knifed through his chest.

Emily tugged on his sleeve. "Please, Mister Gray, tell me a story about you."

"Listen, Squirt, I'll make you a deal. I'll tell you a story if your mama tells one, too." He glanced up at Clarissa. "Well, how about it?"

"Oh, no, I couldn't do any such thing," she began.

"Why not? Doesn't have to be about libraries or museums, does it?"

"Tell about when you an' Papa were little," Emily begged.

Gray stood up. "And to sweeten the pot," he said, gathering up the supper platter, "I'll wash up the dishes."

Clarissa bit her lip. "Very well." She settled Emily on her lap and took a sip from her coffee mug. "When your papa and I were very young, about your age, we got in trouble one afternoon. Your grandfather took us to the park to play. We took off our shoes and socks and ran over the green grass and let it tickle our toes, and then we found a little hill. Anthony, that's your papa, decided we should lie down and roll all the way to the bottom."

"Ooh, was it fun?"

Clarissa laughed. "It was fun until Anthony rolled over a big rock. It hurt his back, but he laughed, anyway. However, your grandfather didn't think it was the least bit funny, so he tipped me over his knee and paddled me good."

"Did you cry?"

"I tried not to, but I did, a little."

"Did he buy you ice cream when you cried?"

Clarissa gave a quiet sigh. "Honey, neither Anthony nor I ever tasted ice cream until your grandfather was gone."

"How come?"

She hesitated. "Our fath—your grandfather

didn't like ice cream. He said it was frivolous and his money would be better spent elsewhere."

"What's *frivlus* mean, Mama?"

"It means something that is silly. Not important."

"What *did* grandfather like?"

"He liked money." Her voice had gone flat.

At the sink, Gray froze. Money? Didn't he like his son and his daughter? He plunged a plate into the soapy dishpan. Something wasn't right there. It sounded kinda like the way he had been raised, except that his folks were dirt-poor, and they ignored him because they were too busy drinking and fighting. Clarissa's pa just didn't care.

Emily's little arms stole around Clarissa's neck. "What about your mama?"

"My mother…" Her arms tightened around her daughter. "My mother did not survive my birth."

"Like *my* mama?"

"Yes, honey, like your mama." Her voice caught.

Gray grabbed the dishtowel and dried his hands. "Okay, Emily girl," he said quickly, "now it's my turn for a story. You ready?"

"Yes!" She scrambled off Clarissa, who quickly averted her face. "Can I sit on your lap?"

He got comfortable on the settee and lifted Emily onto his lap. "Okay, Squirt, here we go. Once upon a time—"

"I wanna story about *you*," Emily demanded. "About when you ran away."

"I already told you about runnin' away, and about the silver mine, didn't I?"

"Tell me again!"

"No!" came a voice from the kitchen along with a splash of water from the sink.

"Tell about something new."

Gray sat up with a jerk. Oh-ho, Clarissa was listening, was she? Kinda made him swell up inside to think she was interested. "Well, um, when I left the silver mine, guess what I did?"

"You married a pretty lady," Emily announced.

Gray swallowed. "Nope." Fat chance. He'd never wanted to tie himself to a woman, no matter how pretty. Brides turned into wives who nagged and drank and fought with their husbands, like his ma and pa. "Guess again."

"You joined a circus and rode a big elephant?"

"Nuh-uh. Sounds like fun, though."

"You bought a horse," the voice called from the kitchen.

Gray chuckled. Now, how did she guess that? "Yeah, I bought a horse, a big roan mare with a white blaze on her nose. And a saddle. I hired on with a rancher in Montana and drove a herd of cattle to Kansas."

"Didja get rich?"

"Nah. I saved up all my pay. Stuffed it all in a clean sock and bided my time."

"Until when?" Clarissa called.

Gray let a slow smile tug at his lips. Guess he was more entertaining than he thought. "Until I had enough."

"Enough for what?" Emily demanded.

"Enough to buy this ranch."

Emily squirmed. "Did it cost a lot?"

"Every penny I had," Gray said with a sigh.

"How come you wanted to buy it?"

"Because—" He stopped. He'd never said this out loud to anyone and it kinda scared him "—because I'd never owned anything in my whole life, and I just plain wanted it."

"But why, really?" Clarissa asked. By now she stood in the kitchen doorway, wiping a plate.

Gray shot a glance at her, but she wouldn't look at him. "Well, I figure it was because I...uh, I wanted to feel safe."

She looked at him now, and with real interest. "Safe from what?"

He drew in a slow lungful of supper-scented air. Hell, he'd never really thought about it that deep. "Safe from hurtin', I guess. Having a home, a place that's mine. If you own something it can't ever turn on you."

He thought she might laugh, but she didn't. She looked straight into his eyes and didn't even smile. Oh, God, her eyes were green! He'd tried not to notice that so much these past few days, but tonight was different. Maybe it was because he'd bared his soul to her about the ranch and what it meant to him. Made him damn nervous.

Clarissa knew in the pit of her stomach why Gray's ranch was so important to him. It was the same hunger she felt for finding a home for Emily and herself. Every single night with her daughter cuddled next to her in the attic bedroom, she had to acknowledge how misguided her acceptance of Caleb Arness's proposal had been. After Anthony's death and the eventual loss of the home they had grown up in, her longing for a place where she belonged was like a toothache that shot pain through her entire body.

But she would not find it out here in the West. And definitely not here in Smoke River on a ranch she didn't like or understand. She could hardly wait to return to Boston, where she had friends, where she knew how to fit in. She could even find employment. Out here in this hot, dry country she felt like a delicate petunia in the desert. Never before had she so clearly understood the phrase *fish out of water*, but that is exactly what she was.

The only bright spot in her dismal situation was how much Emily had reveled in life out here for the past few weeks. The girl adored Maria and Ramon, who made toys and dolls for her and spent hours teaching her Spanish words. She even adored Gray, who owned this little corner of hell. The ranch hands—tall, gangly Shorty and the young boy they called Nebraska—treated Emily with gentle forbearance, even though she was underfoot most of the time. Emily loved the horses, the garden Maria had helped her plant, even the horse trough, where she watched in fascination when the ranch animals drank and happily sailed willow-bark boats on the surface.

Gray set Emily on her feet, stood up and moved toward Clarissa. "The picnic is tomorrow in the center of town. You'll come, won't you?"

"N-no."

"Like hell you're not. Emily's all excited. You can't disappoint her."

She went white as buttermilk. "Oh, but—I might run into Caleb Arness."

"No, you won't. Shorty says Arness is in jail for bein' drunk and disorderly at the Golden Partridge."

"But—"

"No buts, Clarissa. Arness is out of the way. I checked on it. There'll just be a lot of town folks and ranchers and their families. And lots of children... Emily will like it."

"I—I know."

"You're still afraid of Arness? He won't bother you."

"How do you know?"

Gray surveyed her pale face for a full minute. "Because he's in jail, like I said."

"Are you sure?"

"Heck, yes, I'm sure. The man's always drunk too much. He spends most of his time in jail."

Chapter Ten

In the end, in spite of her trepidation, Clarissa packed up the potato salad she'd made, dressed in her clean white shirtwaist and her blue-striped calico skirt, and borrowed one of Maria's sun hats. All the way into town, riding beside Gray on the wagon bench, she found herself admiring the drifts of spring wildflowers covering the meadows—yellow desert parsley and red Indian paintbrush and fluffy white Queen Anne's lace. Swaths of pink-headed wild buckwheat rippled in the wind and big yellow daisy bushes dotted the fields of new green grass.

This part of the day was quite pleasant, she admitted. The part she dreaded was making conversation with the townspeople. Strangers.

"Do you think Miss Serena will attend?"

"Serena?" Gray shook his head. "Nah. She's got better things to do."

Emily piped up from the wagon bed. "What's better'n a picnic?"

"Makin' money, I guess."

"How can she do that on Sunday?"

Clarissa tipped her head away from him, but Gray saw that her cheeks had turned bright red.

All he could see under her wide-brimmed sun hat was the tip of her nose and a bit of her chin. She didn't say anything for so long he wondered if she'd gone to sleep.

"Mama?" Emily persisted, "how can she make money on a Sunday?"

Gray cleared his throat. "Let's just say Miss Serena works, uh, long hours every day of the week, Sunday included."

"Like you did when you saved your money in a sock?"

He had to work to keep from laughing. "Well, kinda." He guided the wagon into town and straight down the main street until they reached the leafy, green town square. Ramon and Maria were just dismounting at the hitching rail, but the rest of his ranch hands were nowhere to be seen. He'd left Erasmus, the grizzled old stable hand, in charge, with his picnic supper on a plate and Gray's shotgun. The man would probably enjoy the peace and quiet with all of them spending the day in town.

Gray braked, climbed down and reached up for Clarissa. Holy smokestacks, her waist was so tiny he didn't see how she could eat much. And he could sure tell she wasn't all laced up tight in a corset. Sensible woman.

The minute Emily's feet touched the ground she raced away toward Maria. "Bet she can't wait to take off her shoes and wriggle her toes in the grass," Gray remarked.

"Or roll down a hill," Clarissa added. "There aren't any hills, are there?"

He lifted out the wicker picnic basket and grabbed an old quilt to sit on. "No hills," he said. "But you can wriggle your toes in the grass if you want, Clarissa."

"Certainly not!"

"I'll spread out the blanket far enough away from the center of things that you won't hear any of the long-winded speeches the mayor's gonna make."

"For that I am grateful, Gray. Why is it that the minute a man gets elected to an office he has to make speeches?"

"Dunno. Smoke River's judge, Jericho Silver, doesn't, and neither does the new sheriff. Two more close-mouthed men you'll never meet."

Clarissa settled onto the quilt next to the picnic basket, and after a moment Emily and Maria joined her. Gray wandered off for a game of horseshoes with Ramon and Nebraska, leaving Shorty with the women.

"Miss Clarissa sure is pretty," Nebraska murmured to Gray. He let fly with a metal shoe that fell far short of the steel pole embedded in the ground.

"Oughtta keep your mind on the game, son." Gray tossed a perfect ringer.

"You mean to tell me you never noticed?"

"Never," Gray lied.

Ramon's snort of laughter was loud enough to carry back to the picnic blanket. "Is a sin to lie, *señor*!" his foreman chided. He dropped his horseshoe on top of Gray's.

"Loser has to deliver a package to Serena's, a

dress Clarissa is…donating," Gray said to change the subject.

"You mean winner, don'tcha?" Nebraska quipped.

Gray shook his head. "Only if you're young and green and new in town, kid."

"Heck, boss, I *am* young and green." He sent Gray a hopeful look.

"Si," Ramon intoned, spitting on his second horseshow for luck. "But you not new in town."

Gray slanted a look at Clarissa, sitting on the quilt with Maria. Looked like they were having a serious talk about something; Maria was leaning her head close to Clarissa, and Clarissa's face looked like a cloud had settled over it. He'd give a fistful of silver dollars to know what was going on.

Emily sat between the two women, looking bored to death.

Late in the afternoon they devoured all of Clarissa's potato salad, which tasted really good, and most of Maria's fried chicken and Mexican chocolate cake, then lounged on the grass playing mumblety-peg and hide the nickel to keep Emily entertained. Maria leaned back against Ramon's bent knees and they talked quietly in Spanish.

Clarissa gazed off in the distance, thinking about Anthony's death and his child, who now called her Mama. The afternoon was "soft," she decided. The warm air smelled of pine trees and the spring sunshine felt gentle on her face. A moment ago Maria had said that in time she would get used to life out here in the West, but she knew she wouldn't. She began to think about her return to Boston. Funny that it didn't bring the jolt of happiness it usually did.

Shorty and Nebraska started up a poker game, and after a few hands Gray joined in. "Playin' for matches or pennies?"

"Playin' for who's gonna get breakfast duty at the bunkhouse tomorrow morning," Shorty answered. "Ain't gonna be me." He grinned and dealt Gray in.

"Can I play?" Emily asked, her blue eyes sparkling with curiosity.

"Not unless you can count, Squirt."

"Well, I *can* count! Mama taught me."

"Okay, you can play on my side. See this card? That's a jack. There's three more like it somewhere in the deck, and I'll pay you my winnings to keep track of them."

Suddenly Clarissa emerged from her reverie and focused on what was happening right in front of her. "Surely you are not teaching my daughter to play cards?"

"Yeah, I am," Gray said with a sly smile. "How else is she gonna learn?"

"Gray, I am not at all sure I want Emily to learn such a game. Playing cards is not something a proper young girl should do."

"It's proper out here in Oregon, Clarissa. Things are different in the West."

"I do not intend to stay in the West," she said, her voice cool.

Gray shrugged. "Deal me two cards, Shorty."

"Mama," Emily said suddenly. "Who is that man? He keeps staring at us."

"What man? Where?"

"Over there, in those trees. See him?"

No, she didn't see him. All she saw was a tangle of brush and maple trees at the far edge of the park. And then a shadow moved and she went cold all over. Caleb Arness.

Gray sent her a sharp look. "Somethin' wrong?"

She leaned close to him and intoned, "I thought I saw Caleb Arness over behind those trees."

"I don't think so, Clarissa. Like I said, he's in jail."

"Oh." But she couldn't stop staring at the trees. Gray's eyes followed her gaze.

"Do you think he could recognize me?" she whispered.

"No. He was drunk when he saw you at the saloon that one time, remember?"

"Yes, very drunk. Disgustingly drunk."

Clarissa tipped her head down to hide her face. Surely Caleb wouldn't remember her; he hadn't known who she was that night she sang at the saloon. He had known that she would be arriving in Smoke River, but maybe he had been too drunk even to remember that.

After a long minute Gray brought his head close to hers. "It's not Arness, Clarissa, but if you're uncomfortable I'll take you home. Maria and Ramon can watch over Emily."

She nodded, and without another word he spoke to Ramon and went to fetch the wagon. "I'm takin'

Clarissa back to the ranch," he announced when he returned. "Too much potato salad."

The ranch hands grinned but didn't stop their card game. Ramon took over Gray's hand, and Emily was so engrossed she scarcely looked up.

Gray walked Clarissa across the grass to the wagon and lifted her up onto the bench. "You're shaking."

"I know. I'm frightened."

"Some reason, other than Arness?"

"N-no. I just feel safer at the ranch house."

He said nothing as he climbed up beside her and lifted the reins. All the way out to the Bar H, she didn't say a word, and when a roadrunner blundered into the wagon wheel, she didn't even look up.

It bothered him that she was frightened. All of a sudden he wanted to protect her, keep her safe. Aw, hell, he wanted to make her smile at him, like she had an hour ago when he taught her to flip a jackknife into the ground and she beat him at mumblety-peg. The look she'd sent him still made his stomach flip over like a drunken kite.

Chapter Eleven

❧❧❧

The minute the wagon rattled through the Bar H gate and across the cattle guard, Clarissa let out a relieved breath. Life in Oregon was fraught with risks and dangers, especially now that Caleb Arness was lurking about. But she did appreciate Gray's solidly built ranch house with its sturdy beam ceiling and cozy kitchen, the gracious verandah across the front and the tiny bedroom at the top of the attic stairs. She felt safe here. She liked the pink climbing rose that rambled over the porch post, and she was growing fond of kind, down-to-earth Maria. And she appreciated Ramon, who took extra time every day with Emily, answering her incessant questions about cows and horses and dragonflies and saddles and the horse trough where she floated her toy boats.

But now more than ever, Clarissa wanted to return to Boston.

Gray set the brake on the wagon, climbed off the bench and reached up for her, sliding his warm, strong hands about her waist. Effortlessly he lifted her down, but she was surprised that he didn't release her.

"Clarissa, you're still shaking."

"Am I?" She worked to keep her voice steady.

"Yeah. What's going on with you?"

"I don't know—I just can't stop trembling. Maybe it was seeing Caleb Arness at the picnic."

"Forget about Arness. It wasn't him."

He still had not let her go, but for some reason she didn't mind. She sensed his strength, and his hands curving gently around her waist felt comforting. She stared at the top button of his blue chambray shirt, then raised her eyes to the hint of dark hair visible on his upper chest and stared at his bare throat. Finally her gaze went to his mouth.

He was not smiling. He didn't move under her perusal, but his breathing changed.

So did hers. He smelled of wood smoke and sweat and something faintly spicy. And he felt solid. Dependable. Safe. Her stomach did a slow somersault up into her rib cage and her hands came up to rest on his exposed forearms. Well, maybe not so safe, she amended. But nice. Very, very nice.

She could feel his heart thudding under her palm. *Lord help her, when had she moved her hand to touch his chest?* Her eyes lingered on his lips, and after a long moment he bent his head and covered her mouth with his.

She had been kissed only once before, at a New Year's Eve celebration in Boston when she was seventeen, but that was nothing like this swirly, dizzying rush of sensation. Warmth and gentle, insistent pressure opened up into something deep and hot that made her ache. Without thinking she laced her hands together behind his neck.

Without breaking contact, he reached up and disengaged them, then lifted his mouth from hers and stepped back. His breathing was uneven. Hers was… She had no idea. Disoriented, she wondered if she was breathing at all. Her pulse thrummed in her ears.

She opened her lids to find Gray's gray-blue eyes looking at her oddly—half puzzled and half penetrating. "Hot damn," he murmured. "What just happened?"

She gave a shaky laugh. "I d-don't know. Does kissing always feel like that?"

"Never."

"Ever?"

"Never happened to me like that."

"I have only been kissed once before, when I was a girl. It was nothing like this."

Gray looked up at the sky. "Yeah. Kinda scary for me, too."

He didn't touch her again, but he didn't move away. Instead, he stood staring at her with that dumbstruck look.

"You ever drink whiskey?" he inquired, his voice husky.

"Heavens, no. Why do you ask?"

"'Cuz right now I need some."

Inside the kitchen, Gray studied her from across the round wooden table and rotated a glass of whiskey between his palms. Her hair was mussed and one wayward strand had worked loose from the bun at her neck. He wanted to touch it, but he didn't dare. Her mouth looked soft, and her eyes still had that smoky look that punched into his gut. His heartbeat was hammering all over the place like a crazy woodpecker and he had to concentrate on holding on to his glass to keep his hands from trembling.

What the hell was happening?

She'd filled her own glass with water, but she hadn't touched it. Instead, she studied the scarred cedar tabletop while he watched the ruffle on her white shirtwaist flutter with her every heartbeat. Some insistent element of male satisfaction swelled inside him, but he didn't feel aggressive or proud; he felt poleaxed, like he'd been run over by a steer. He wasn't sure he liked it. What the heck had possessed him to lay a hand on her? Even more, he kept wondering why he hadn't wanted to stop.

Well, sure, Clarissa was female as hell; maybe that was why. But there'd been other females before. Nothing had ever felt like this. *Nothing.*

"Gray," she said quietly, "would you...would you consider advancing me the money for my train ticket back to Boston?"

"No." Usually he considered his words before he spoke out, but now he'd blurted the word without thinking.

An arrow of hurt went across her face. "I would pay you back, I promise."

"No," he said again.

She bit her lower lip. "But whyever not? You know how out of place I feel here on your ranch."

He tossed back the rest of his whiskey and tried to corral his thoughts into some semblance of rational order. "Because...because I don't want you to go back to Boston."

If he'd thought for a hundred years, he couldn't have predicted what would come out of his mouth. When did the thought of losing her make him so crazy?

"Gray, you know that I don't belong on a ranch."

He gripped his whiskey glass so tight his knuckles turned white. "Yeah, I know that. But dammit, I still don't want you to go." *Maybe I'd better knock off the sauce... I'm sure not making much sense.*

She stared at him, her mouth all trembly and her eyes like two soft patches of spring ferns. "Gray, I don't fit in here. I don't understand life on a ranch. Much of it I don't even like."

Her words fell on his ears like hammer blows. "Yeah, I know all that." He splashed two more fingers of whiskey into his glass.

Face it, Harris. She doesn't like it out here, so there's no point in getting all fussed up about her. Might be some point in kissing her again, but I wouldn't want to lead her on.

But he couldn't get the thought of kissing her again out of his mind. He drew in a ragged breath and tossed back the rest of his whiskey. Guess he'd better think up some way to keep busy until she got on that train to Boston.

Guess he'd better not let her mean so damn much to him.

* * *

"Mama?"

Clarissa surveyed her daughter, who scrambled from her kneeling position beside the bed onto the quilt. "Yes, Emily? What is it?"

"I like it here! Maria shows me fun things to do, and Ramon lets me pet the horsies, and Gray tells me stories."

"That's nice, honey," she said absently.

"You like Gray's stories, too, don't you? Even though they're not very happy stories, about working down in a dark hole and saving his money in a sock?"

Clarissa bit her lip. Yes, she liked Gray's stories. She liked his low, gravelly voice and the sound of his laughter and…

"I like Maria's stories, too," Emily confided.

Clarissa paused while pulling on her white nightgown. "Oh? What stories does Maria tell?"

"About riding a long, long way across the desert with Ramon. And being hungry."

Heavens, what difficulties people endured to reach this rough, raw country. There must be something about Oregon she was missing. It wasn't anything remotely like Boston; it wasn't even civilized! So why did people struggle so hard to get here? Even more puzzling, why would they fight so hard to *stay* here?

"Emily, do you really, truly, honestly like it out here on this ranch?"

"Yes, Mama, really truly honest. Don't you?"

Clarissa opened her mouth to list all the reasons she felt uncomfortable and out of place here on Gray's ranch, then thought better of it. Emily shouldn't be burdened by her mother's difficulties. "I like *some* things about it, yes."

The girl snuggled under her arm. "What things, Mama? Tell me."

Clarissa pursed her lips and thought hard. "Well...I like the color of the sky when the sun rises, all pink and gold. And then it turns into a beautiful clear blue, as blue as the flowers painted on our china dinner plates." She drew in a long breath and looked up at the gabled ceiling. "And I like the birds singing in the evening. Gray says they are sparrows, but they certainly don't sound like sparrows back in Boston. Out here they seem to go on and on singing until it gets dark."

Emily's small hand crept into hers. "I like the birdies, too. What else, Mama?"

She smoothed her daughter's tumbled red curls. She liked the smell of wood burning in the big stone fireplace in the parlor. And Gray's low laughter at Emily's often inadvertently pointed questions. Last night at supper her daughter had asked, "How come you don't have a wife? Ramon has a wife. Don't you want one?" Clarissa had had to turn away to the stove to hide her burning cheeks.

As she recalled, he hadn't answered the question.

"Tell me some more 'bout what you like," Emily entreated.

"Oh, let me see, what else do I like? Wildflowers—those big meadows full of yellow blooms like tiny little daisies. And those red poppies on the hillside. And the sunflowers! Heavens, they are growing taller than I am! Maria showed me how to shake out last year's ripe seeds and toast them."

She also liked the sound of the ranch hands' laughter drifting from the bunkhouse in the evening. She'd bet they were playing poker, and they were most definitely enjoying themselves. *I wonder if I could learn to play poker? I bet I would be good at it since I'm learning how to hide my feelings.*

Finally Emily's eyelids drooped shut and her breathing evened out. Clarissa tucked the blanket around her and let herself admit the one thing she'd tried and tried not to think about. She liked the way Gray had made her feel when he kissed her, all warm inside, as if sunshine had washed through her body and left tiny sparkles everywhere.

She leaned over and brushed her lips across Emily's temple, settled herself beside her and closed her eyes. There was absolutely no reason to think any more about Gray or his kiss. She would be leaving within the month, and that was that.

Two days later at noon Gray tramped through the back kitchen door and announced, "This afternoon we're gonna make us some ice cream!"

Emily squealed and threw her arms about his legs. "Can it be strawberry? Oh, please?"

Gray ruffled her hair and knelt down to her level. "Strawberry, huh? Well, you know, it takes a heap of strawberries to make strawberry ice cream."

"Let's go pick some right away, okay?"

He chuckled. "Hold on a minute, Squirt. Bet

you can't guess what Nebraska's brought back from town this morning, can you?"

Emily's blue eyes rounded. "Strawberries? Really?"

"Really." He rose and turned to Clarissa. "Got an ice-cream freezer somewhere in the pantry. It's probably dusty inside, so you might want to wash it out. Been a while since I made ice cream."

Clarissa sent him a look he couldn't decipher. Approval, he hoped. But now she'd glued her gaze to the stovetop so he couldn't tell. Damned puzzling woman. He never knew what she was thinking. Ever since that day after the picnic when he'd kissed her, she'd been skittish as a hummingbird. He'd probably scared her to death.

Scared himself, too, but for a different reason. In his entire life he'd never let himself care—really care deep down—about a woman. Nothing in skirts was ever going to matter more to him than his ranch. But it was sure unsettling not being able to get Clarissa out of his mind.

"Emily," Clarissa said, "put out the plates, please. I'm about to dish up our dinner."

Gray sniffed the air appreciatively. "Roast chicken?"

She nodded.

"I thought after the last one you didn't ever want to roast another chicken."

She leveled a look at him. "I didn't. But this morning, Maria brought me another hen. And then I read Mrs. Beeton's cooking instructions."

He raised his eyebrows at her. While Emily

clattered three blue-flowered plates onto the table, Gray studied the woman who disliked everything about living on his ranch, including dead chickens. So, she'd roasted one for their dinner? And, he noted as she pulled something out of the oven, she'd made biscuits. And…was that gravy in the big china bowl? And mashed potatoes? Made his head spin.

Expertly she wielded the carving knife he kept razor sharp and cut off a drumstick for Emily. Then she hesitated. "What part would you like, Gray?"

"Uh…" For some reason he couldn't get himself to say the word *breast* in her presence. Guess he spent too much time thinking about hers under that thin muslin shirtwaist she wore. "I'll have a drumstick."

She dropped it onto his plate without looking at him, then sliced off a thick piece of breast meat for herself and pushed the bowl of mashed potatoes toward him.

All through the meal Emily chattered on about strawberries and the new pony in the barn and making ice cream, while Gray and Clarissa avoided looking at each other. He *wanted* to look at her, but she didn't glance up once except to pour coffee and set another plate of hot biscuits on the table. He felt tongue-tied like a woodpecker with a string tied around its beak.

Finally Emily set her fork down with a click and fixed him with narrowed blue eyes. "How come you're not talkin' about things like you usually do?"

"Um...well, I guess I haven't got anything to say, Squirt."

"That's not true," she challenged. "You *always* talk a lot. Are you sick?"

Gray laughed. "Not so sick I can't churn ice cream! Think you could wash up those strawberries I left out in the pantry?"

She was out of her chair and off like a shot before he realized his mistake. With Emily gone, the silence in the kitchen was louder than a Gatling gun, and there was nowhere to look but up at the ceiling or down at his plate. But, he reflected, it had been like this for two whole days.

He'd had enough. He sucked in a big breath and reached over to capture her hand. "This can't go on, Clarissa."

"What can't?" she said carefully. "I am not aware of anything unusual."

"You and me, tiptoeing around each other, not talkin' and not lookin' at each other."

"Oh." She kept her voice neutral.

"I'm not gonna kiss you again, if that's what's botherin' you."

"Oh." *Hot damn, she sounds disappointed!*

She glanced up and then instantly dropped her gaze. "Why not?"

"Huh?" Dumbstruck, he stared at her bent head. "Well, one reason is you're going back to Boston first chance you get."

"What is the other reason?" she said, staring at her plate.

"The other reason? Guess I thought you didn't like it."

"Oh." Neutral again. But then she said something that slammed hard into his gut. And below.

"I didn't say I didn't like it, Gray. As I recall, I didn't say anything at all."

Before he knew what he was doing, he bolted to his feet, leaned across the table and slid his hand around the back of her neck. Then he tugged her head forward and kissed her. Hard.

By jiminy, it happened again! His heart tumbled end over end and flopped into his belly, and all the blood in his belly went straight to his groin.

"I've washed the strawberries and have found the ice-cream freezer!" Emily sang from the pantry. "It's all dusty."

Gray lifted his head and stuffed his hand into his pants pocket to keep from touching Clarissa. Her face looked like something had washed her cheeks with raspberry juice. Lordy, she looked like he felt—smacked hard in the midsection.

"That's good, Emily," she called. Her voice shook. "Bring the freezer to the sink, all right?"

The girl maneuvered the wooden churn onto the dry counter, then clunked it into the sink while Gray and Clarissa stared at each other.

"Strawberries," he murmured, his voice hoarse. "You taste like strawberries."

Chapter Twelve

That afternoon Clarissa added another item to her surprising list of things she liked at Gray's ranch—rocking back and forth on the porch swing and watching his strong, capable hand turn the crank on the ice-cream freezer. He sat on the top step of the front porch with Emily perched beside him, effortlessly making ice cream out of nothing more than cream, strawberries and the churn-like contraption filled with ice and rock salt.

As he moved the crank around and around, Emily peppered him with questions, which he answered in a voice so low Clarissa had a hard time hearing the words from where she sat. How on earth could her daughter think up so many questions in a single hour? A better question might be how on earth could Gray come up with so many *answers*?

She had a few questions herself, she admitted. Private ones. Embarrassing ones. Not the least of which was the one that had nagged at her all afternoon: *Why did Gray lean across the dinner table and kiss me?*

He sat facing away from her, so she studied his back, watched the play of muscles under his pale gray shirt and the steady motion of his arm turning the wooden freezer handle. The fine dark hair on his wrist and forearm, exposed where he had rolled up his sleeve, held particular fascination. Seeing that felt…well, intimate somehow.

She jerked her gaze away. Across the yard chickens clucked contentedly in Maria's henhouse, and a lazy drift of smoke wafted from her chimney and dissolved into a sky so blue and cloudless it looked like a painting. Birds twittered in the locust tree, and the branches of the two plum trees in the yard were starting to droop with fruit that would ripen come summer. She must read Mrs. Beeton's instructions about canning fruit. Or perhaps not. Maria said she simply cut up the plums and dried the slices in the hot sunlight, which seemed a lot easier. *Mrs. Beeton will forgive me for taking the easy way out.*

She let her gaze drift past Maria and Ramon's tidy cabin to the spacious red-sided barn where Gray kept the horses, along with a new pony, the milk cow, the barn cat that prowled for mice and the nest of baby kittens Emily had not yet discovered. Perhaps she should learn to milk the cow. Gray rose at dawn to do the milking, and each morning Clarissa found a brimming pail of warm, foamy milk just inside the back door. She had learned to let the thick cream rise to the top of the milk pans, and yesterday she had even churned her own butter! Maria had smiled and smiled when she showed her.

Maria was always smiling. Was it because she was happy being married to Ramon? Sixteen years,

Maria had told her proudly. Imagine, living with a man for sixteen years! She could not envision that, unless it were with—

With a man like Gray. At this moment his head was bent, listening to Emily's chatter, but his turning arm never slowed. He cranked the ice-cream freezer and talked with Emily, occasionally laughing at something she said, but she noticed that his arm never stopped moving. The business of making ice cream took precedence over even Emily's conversation.

Clarissa closed her eyes, let her head rest against the back of the swing and listened to the burr of the crank and her daughter's happy laughter. The air was soft, the sound of the freezer crank lulling. The pink rose rambling over Maria's cabin smelled spicy-sweet, and suddenly she remembered the scent of Gray's skin.

"Mama," Emily called out. "How old are you?"

Clarissa didn't open her lids. "I am twenty-four, honey."

"Gray says he's thirty-one. Is that more than twenty-four?"

"Yes, Emily. It's seven years more."

"Emily also wants to know if she can marry me," Gray said with a chuckle.

"Certainly," Clarissa answered. "But you have to promise to make strawberry ice cream every day."

"Deal." His rich laughter rolled over her, sending a shiver up her spine. He stopped cranking and said something to Emily.

"It's ready!" she shouted. "My ice cream is ready!"

Gray rose in one easy motion. "*Your* ice cream, Squirt? Don't I get some? And your mama?"

"Yes! And Maria and Ramon, too," the girl sang.

He moved toward Clarissa. "You want a big bowl or a small one?"

"For me or for Emily?"

"For you. Emily can take care of herself." He stood looking down at her, his eyes twinkling. He had laugh lines in the corners, she noted. While she gazed up at him, his smile gradually faded. "How about it, Clarissa? Big or small?"

"Well…"

"It's not too hard a question. It's a little bit like life." He sent her a challenging look. "You can nibble away at it, or you can take it in big bites."

"Gray," Emily called suddenly, "what do you love better'n ice cream?"

"My ranch," he said slowly. "There's nothing in this world I love more than my ranch."

After supper that night, Gray and Emily volunteered to wash up the dishes and Clarissa stepped out onto the front porch, then decided to go for a short walk to clear her head. All through the meal Gray's eyes had sought and held hers; it made her so nervous she could scarcely eat.

She circled once around the ranch house, then walked all the way around Maria's cabin, where delicious smells drifted from the open window. Then she circled the bunkhouse. She could tell by the raucous laughter that the ranch hands were again playing poker. She moved to the barn. The animals had been fed, so all was quiet. How peaceful it was! She drew in a deep breath and closed her eyes. Tonight she didn't miss Boston so acutely; it was never this quiet in the city.

A twig snapped nearby. She turned toward the sound and all at once something soft and dark dropped over her head and a sickly sweet-smelling cloth pressed against her nose and mouth. She fought to breathe.

The last thing she remembered was a rough voice in her ear. "Got you now, pretty lady. What I want is gonna be mine!"

Emily threw herself at Gray where he stood at the kitchen sink drying the supper dishes. "Mama didn't come back," she wept.

"What?" He almost dropped the platter he was wiping. "Where did she go?"

"Outside."

"Outside? Outside where?" He was already untying the apron around his waist.

"On the porch."

"Stay here," he ordered. He grabbed the kerosene lamp and burst through the front door.

She wasn't on the porch. Maybe she'd gone for a stroll, but where? Quickly he inspected the bunkhouse, then banged on the heavy wood door of Maria's cabin. Maybe she was visiting his housekeeper?

Ramon answered and shook his head. Gray sent

a white-faced Maria to stay with Emily, and his foreman lit a lantern and joined him. At Gray's shout, the bunkhouse emptied.

"Nebraska, search the barn! Shorty, Erasmus, look down by the river."

He and Ramon moved around the barn in ever-widening circles until Ramon gave a yell.

"*Señor,* look!" His foreman bent over a scuffed-up patch of ground. "Small footprints…and big ones! And horse tracks."

Gray went down on one knee and lifted the lantern to study them. The horse had a broken shoe. None of his animals ever wore broken shoes. A cold fist punched into his chest, and with a shout he ran for the barn and saddled Rowdy.

Ramon caught at his bridle. *"Que pasa?"*

"Arness took her. Nebraska, Shorty," he yelled. "Saddle up! Ramon, get my revolver."

Chapter Thirteen

Clarissa opened her eyes and tried to move, but found her wrists were tied down. Where was she? She peered around the dim interior of what looked like a rough cabin. Cobwebs hung in the corner near the cot she was bound to, and in the flickering light she saw a hulking male form sprawled on a wooden chair near the only window.

Her blood turned to ice water. God help her, it was Caleb Arness! She lay perfectly still, hoping he wouldn't notice she was awake.

An hour passed. At least she thought it was an hour; actually, it seemed like days. Suddenly she heard hoofbeats, and Arness stiffened.

"Smart man," he grated. "Sure didn't take him long to figure it out." He doused the kerosene lamp and banged through the cabin door.

"Arness!" It was Gray's voice. She strained to hear.

"I've got somethin' you want," Arness yelled. "When you give me the deed to the Bar H, you can have her back."

Clarissa held her breath. The Bar H meant everything to Gray. He'd worked hard all his life to buy it and hold on to it. He could never give it up for her sake. Besides, he knew how eager she was to leave and return to Boston. Despite the fact that he had kissed her and awakened feelings she had never dreamed of, she knew nothing meant more to Gray than his ranch. He'd worked long years to build up his thousand acres. He'd known Clarissa for only a few short weeks.

"I hear you, Arness," Gray shouted. "Not sure we can bargain over this."

"That so? You sayin' you don't want her?"

"You figure it out," Gray shouted.

Clarissa tried to shut her mind off. *Gray didn't want her?* Of course. She remembered all too clearly the day he'd said he never wanted a wife. Why should she be surprised? Still, a hard ball of pain lodged in her chest. It wasn't that she wanted to marry Gray—not exactly, anyway. But it would have been nice if *she* could have made the decision.

She clamped her jaws tight. She must think about escaping Arness on her own. She had to get back to Emily. *But surely Gray would want to help?* And he knew she could not possibly stomach staying with this awful man.

You simple-minded goose, he is stalling for time!

Arness paced back and forth on the dusty cabin floor, alternately watching out the single window and swearing. "If he don't want her, what's he waiting for?" he muttered. "Harris? You hear me? Bring me the deed to your ranch and you can have her."

A long silence stretched, and then Gray's voice rose. "I hear you. Keep your shirt on."

"I'll give you two hours. Ride out of here and come back with the deed."

She heard hoofbeats recede into silence and knew that Gray and, she supposed, whoever was with him—Ramon? Shorty?—were riding away. But he would not just give up and leave her here for Arness, would he? She had to think.

She pulled hard against the ropes that tied her wrists to the cot. Her skin burned where the bonds chafed, but she pulled, anyway.

Arness chuckled in satisfaction and tipped back in his chair, watching out the window.

Good. One of her wrists had stretched the rope binding enough that she could almost squeeze her hand through. One more pull and—

"You lyin' quiet over there?" he asked suddenly. "He don't want you, but looks like I'm gonna get his ranch, anyway." He paused. "You thirsty?"

Thirsty! Her throat was parched, but she didn't think it was water Arness had in mind. Still, maybe it would keep him busy.

"Yes, I am thirsty."

He tramped to the door and retrieved a bottle of something from over the door frame. "Ain't nothin' like good whiskey."

She gave another desperate tug and managed to squeeze one hand free. Arness lumbered toward her, the bottle in one hand, and she noticed that his holstered gun hung at his side. She caught her breath.

He uncorked the whiskey bottle and just as he bent over her she snaked out her hand and grabbed the revolver.

Chapter Fourteen

Gray left Ramon and the others stationed around Arness's cabin and headed for the Bar H as fast as Rowdy could gallop. He could never, ever, remember riding this hard. He clattered over the Bar H cattle guard and up to the ranch house, dismounted and pounded into the parlor and up the stairs, past a frozen Maria and a white-faced Emily. His safe stood next to his desk in his bedroom.

Then he was back out into the yard and was in the saddle before the startled horse could stop wheezing. He spurred Rowdy across the cattle guard and out into the night, the deed to the Bar H safe in his shirt pocket. Funny that he hadn't given a second thought to relinquishing his ranch. Funny that he hadn't realized until three days ago what Clarissa Seaforth meant to him.

Yeah, but she wants to go back to Boston.

So what if she did, at least she'd be free from Arness. He wasn't about to let Arness have her. He didn't want *anyone* to have her unless it was himself. He'd ask her to stay—*beg* her to stay. Damn, loving someone sure tied a man in knots! But if that's what she really wanted...oh, hell, he couldn't think about it anymore.

As he neared the woods near Arness's line shack, Ramon and Shorty fell in behind him. They picked up Nebraska just before they reached the clearing where the cabin stood. Gray reined up.

"We'll walk in. When I get a few feet from the porch I'll call Arness out." He dismounted and started forward. He hadn't gone a dozen yards before a shot rang out, and he went cold all over. *If that lowlife has hurt her...* He raced for the cabin.

"Clarissa?"

"Gray! In here!"

She was half sitting on a cot, a revolver dangling from one hand. He reached her and tossed the gun aside, folding her into his arms. Good God, she smelled of whiskey!

Arness's body sprawled awkwardly across the floor. He didn't move.

"Is—? Is he d-dead?" she whispered.

"Think so, yeah."

"I sh-shot him, Gray."

"Yeah, looks like you did." His heart was banging away so hard he could scarcely talk.

"Are you all right?"

"I think so. I—I want to go home."

He cut her other hand free and gathered her up in his arms. Ramon pulled Arness's body out of his way, and Gray carried Clarissa to his horse, lifted her into the saddle and mounted behind her.

"Better send Nebraska for the sheriff," he called to his men. Then he reined away and headed for the Bar H. He had sent his foreman on ahead to explain things to Maria and ask her to take Emily to their cabin for the night.

When they rode through the Bar H gate, Clarissa began to cry. "I n-never thought I would be so g-glad to see this place," she sobbed. "But, oh my, it l-looks so beautiful!"

He lifted her down and pulled her trembling body close. "I sent Emily home with Maria," he whispered against her hair. "Thought you might want to pull yourself together before you see her."

She nodded and clung to him. He rubbed her back, then guided her up the porch steps and into the house. Maria had left a fire crackling in the fireplace, and he could smell coffee in the kitchen. He walked Clarissa over to the warmth.

"You want some coffee?"

"No."

"Whiskey?"

"Heavens, no! I took a swallow of the stuff at the cabin just to c-calm my nerves. I never want to taste it again."

He laughed wryly. "Well, I sure in blazes need some! This has been one helluva night."

Clarissa sank onto the settee before the fire while Gray rattled around in the kitchen. He returned with two tumblers, one of water and one half full of whiskey. He sat down beside her and let out a long breath. "Lord God, deliver me from another night like this one."

"I'm not sorry I shot Arness," she said quietly. She shuddered. "I have never been so frightened in my life."

"Pretty spunky of you to shoot him, Clarissa. But you know that means you can't go back to Boston right away. You'll have to stick around until the sheriff talks to you."

She gave him a long stare, her green eyes looking so deep into his he wondered if she could be reading his thoughts. "It was wrong of Caleb Arness to try to blackmail you into giving up your ranch," she said. "It was stupid of him to use me as the bargaining chip."

"It wasn't so stupid, Clarissa."

"It didn't work, did it?" she said in a shaky voice.

"No, it didn't. But it almost did."

He set the glass of whiskey on the hearth and turned to her. "Clarissa, I would have given up the ranch in a heartbeat to get you back. I had the deed to the ranch in my shirt pocket."

She stared at him. "But—"

"Don't argue." He slid his arm around her shoulder and leaned over to kiss her. "You're worth ten ranches."

The instant his mouth touched hers she moved into his embrace. "You sure you want to go back to Boston?" he whispered against her lips.

"Gray," she murmured. "Oh, Gray, you know I don't belong out here."

He was quiet for a long minute. Then he smoothed the hair off her face and gave her a little shake. "You know what the old-timers out here in the West say, don't you?"

Clarissa studied his face. "No. What do they say?"

"That you have to bloom where you're planted."
He kissed her again. "Am I changing your mind?"

"You know I still can't cook very well," she
whispered. But she could do other things; she could
learn. And, oh, God, for Gray she *wanted* to bloom
out here in the West.

He drew away and took her face between his
hands. "Clarissa, it might seem funny, but I don't
give a rat's, uh… I don't care if you can't boil
water."

"You're gonna get married?" Emily flung herself
into Clarissa's arms. "Really and truly?"

Clarissa laughed and bent to hug her daughter.
"Really and truly."

"Oh, Mama! Then we can stay here and everything? And Gray will be my papa?"

Gray laughed. "Would you like that, Squirt?"

"Oh, yes! Yes, *yes*!"

The wedding of Clarissa Seaforth and Graydon
Harris was more like a fiesta than a solemn ceremony. Clarissa wore a pale pink dimity dress and
carried a bouquet of the roses that threatened to
smother Maria and Ramon's small cabin. Emily
sprinkled rose petals all over the lawn where the
ranch hands and some of the townspeople had gathered, then demurely took her place between Gray
and her mother, one hand clasped in each of theirs.

Reverend Pollock rode out from town to perform
the ceremony and stayed for cake and strawberry

ice cream. Nebraska played his violin, and the ranch hands and the assembled town folks danced and sang until the moon rose. Ramon brought out his guitar and sang Mexican love songs until the toasts of lemonade and whiskey subsided and Maria took Emily home to sleep at the cabin.

At last Gray put his arms around Clarissa and the two of them moved over the lawn in a dreamy two-step. "I'm not payin' much attention to my feet," he whispered.

"It's not important," she murmured. "I'm not paying much attention to anything except you."

He tightened his arms about her. "Think you'll grow to like bein' a ranch wife?"

She smiled up into his face. "I will probably never grow to love plucking chickens," she said quietly. "But that's not important, either."

He stopped dead. "Yeah? What *is* important, Clarissa?"

She stood on tiptoe to brush her lips against his cheek. "*You* are important, Gray. Emily is important because I love her, and you are important because I love you, too. All three of us are important, don't you see? And, after all, life here in Smoke River, with you, has all sorts of advantages."

When he finished kissing her right there in front of everyone, the assembled guests burst into cheers and applause. After more kisses and well-wishing, Gray and Clarissa waved goodbye to their guests from the front porch of the big white ranch house and disappeared inside.

Upstairs in the bedroom, Gray opened the window wide so they could hear the music, and kissed Clarissa thoroughly. Then he began to undo the row of tiny pearl buttons on her pink dimity wedding dress.

It didn't take long.

* * * * *

HIS SPRINGTIME BRIDE

Kathryn Albright

Dear Reader,

I love stories about prodigal sons—or daughters—
who finally decide to fight for their happily-ever-after
despite seemingly insurmountable obstacles. Gabe and
Riley have secrets from their pasts that threaten to ruin
any hope of being together, but they also have grit…
and determination.

I hope you enjoy Gabe and Riley's story.

Kathryn Albright

This story is dedicated to my dear friend Aletha—
sister of my heart,
fellow pilgrim and keeper of dreams.

Chapter One

Southern California
1879

Gabe Coulter stopped walking and stared at the shingled roof of the old homestead through the pines. He let out a slow breath, feeling the tension that had coiled deep inside him start to loosen. The cabin still stood. For five hundred miles he had tried to squelch the worry that the ranch house—his home—would be gone when he arrived—burned down by hate mongers, invaded by squatters, any number of things. He'd been away too long—four years too long—without word of the place.

A man in prison didn't have much say in property rights.

He was so close now he could smell the scent of moist earth from the water in the creek and hear the wind rustling the leaves of the oak trees on his property. The afternoon sun beat down on his back and shoulders. He forgot how tired his feet were and how empty his stomach. From here he could see the road leading up to the gate and the stretch of meadow behind the house that sloped toward the stream. Infused with renewed energy at the sight, he walked on.

Excitement pressed against his rib cage and simmered with the first breath of hope he had felt in years. First he would check to see if the water pump worked. Then he would probably have four years' worth of cobwebs and mice to chase from the small cabin. His land—the one place on earth he felt as though he belonged. He would fix it up and live here until the end of his days, doing what he did best...ranching.

Thoughts of his father and mother overwhelmed him and he realized that the first thing he would do would not be at the well—it would be to check to see that his mother had been buried next to his pa. The anger he once felt for her no longer simmered inside. Prison or time or maturity had intervened. Yet mixed with that was the frustration that now he'd never be able to talk with her to learn the truth.

His first inkling that something wasn't as it should be came when he spied a small herd of cows hugging the shade of the large spreading oak down near the water. Who would be running cattle on his property? From here it looked as if they were branded, but they were too far away to make out which brand.

As he approached the house, a paper tacked to the door fluttered in the warm breeze. He stepped up on the small porch, his foot sliding into the worn indentations made from years of his father's boots pounding the wooden planks, and snatched the paper down.

"'SOLD. April 4th, 1876. Mr. Frank Rawlins owner. No Trespassing.'" Gabe read the words aloud. He took a deep breath and tried to bank the full-bodied rage that sprang up inside.

Rawlins. He should have known.

He slammed his fist against the door. This was his place! His land! Worked and earned by his own sweat and the sweat of his parents. It rightfully belonged to him!

Rawlins was the one man on this earth he should steer clear of. The one man he hated for the things he'd done to his father, his mother and himself. Guess hurting Gabe's family over the years wasn't enough. Now he had taken his land.

His hands shook as he stared at the notice and tried to sort through his options. Just because he'd killed one man and served time for it, didn't mean he had a compunction to kill whenever he got riled. Life was precious. No one knew that more than him. And besides, Frank Rawlins was Riley's father. No matter what, he wouldn't be hurting her. But he wasn't going to just let the man walk in and take his land. Rawlins had enough as it was.

He looked out to the large oak tree in the pasture and inhaled long and deep, and then exhaled, forcing himself to calm down. He resisted the urge to rip the notice to shreds, and instead folded it and stuffed it in his hip pocket. Sign or no sign, he was going over there to see about his mother's grave. Then it would be time to have a talk with Mr. Frank Rawlins.

* * *

Twilight was encroaching by the time Gabe strode under the wooden arch that marked the entrance to the Golden R Ranch. The actual ranch house sat two miles back within the Rawlins spread, down a twisting dirt lane lined with manzanita and scrub oaks and a few pines that scented the air as he passed by. When he arrived, a cowboy heading across the expanse of yard from the bunkhouse to the main house spied him and stopped. He stood there, bowlegged and relaxed as though he owned the place. "If you have come looking for a job, we are done hiring for the season."

Gabe would work for anybody else in the valley but Rawlins. "That's not why I'm here."

"A bit late to be calling then."

"Name is Coulter. I want to talk to Frank Rawlins."

"Johnson. Foreman." His gaze narrowed and he scratched his scruffy dirt-colored beard. "Coulter? From around these parts?"

Gabe lifted his chin in acknowledgment.

"Most Injuns never make it to prison if they kill a white man. And if they do—they don't make it out."

Gabe stiffened. He'd heard the same thing before from guards at the prison—their tone much uglier. It wasn't the only time his father's blood had saved him, but it was the most important time. In a world where both whites and Indians looked upon him with suspicion, he had quickly learned to trust no one. He had fought it when he was young, trying to fit in, but it did no good. Now all he wanted was to be left in peace. Obviously, Johnson had heard of him and didn't care about that.

"Then it's a good thing I'm half white. Tell him I'm here," Gabe said. By his tone, he made it clear he wasn't asking.

The foreman eyed him for a moment longer and then clomped up the steps and, after a sharp rap on the door, let himself into the house.

Three minutes later, Johnson ushered him inside.

Gabe had been in the house a few times when he was young. His folks had been invited to a ten-year wedding anniversary party for Rawlins and his wife. That's when he'd first met Riley. He had been quiet and she had been all gangly tomboy arms and legs and talked up a storm. He remembered swinging on the rope swing that hung from the old oak in the side yard with her and a few other children. He had never seen blond hair before that, and each time he tried to touch her braids, she would whip them around just out of his reach to tease him. She laughed and the other kids laughed right along with her, which made him mad—mostly at his own awkwardness.

Had Riley ever come back to visit her father? Once she had loved the ranch and vowed never to leave, despite her mother's schemes to position her for a rich husband back east. By now she probably had that rich husband along with a baby or two. With effort, he pushed his memories of Riley to the back of his mind. Thoughts of her would only complicate the confrontation ahead with Rawlins.

He squared his shoulders and followed John-son. The foreman stopped in the hallway before the study and indicated Gabe was to enter. "No such thing as a half Injun," he said, his eyes cold as Gabe passed by. "Bad blood taints the good."

Rawlins sat behind a massive cherry-wood desk, his expression inscrutable. He had to be in his early fifties now, with silver-streaked hair and black hawkish brows over striking blue eyes. A small amount of paunch around his middle where there hadn't been any before spoke to his more seden-tary days of late. As Gabe stepped farther into the study, Rawlins walked slowly around from behind his desk and hiked one hip onto the corner to sit. "So you are out."

Gabe wasn't here for small talk. "I was down to *my* land today. Saw the sign. Looked new."

Rawlins nodded...watching him carefully. "The sheriff in Nuevo mentioned your release. I thought you might head this way. I also thought you should be clear about the situation here."

"You mean the part about not owning my own land?"

In the doorway, Johnson straightened, alert to the underlying tension in the room. He rested his hand lightly on his gun handle.

"Taxes hadn't been paid in three years," Rawlins said. "I paid them."

"Stole the place, you mean. And you know why I couldn't get them paid."

He nodded again. "Your incarceration was men-tioned in the newspaper. I had my eye on that property a long time, Coulter. Has a nice little stream running through it down from the mountain this time of year."

"I noticed your cattle were enjoying it."

"Hasn't been grazed in years. There is a nice thick carpet."

Of course it hadn't been grazed. After his father's death by the cougar, Gabe's mother had had to slowly sell off the stock to make ends meet. Few would do business with a Kumeyaay woman and her kid. He blew out a breath, unused to having to ask for anything and not liking that he was going to now. He'd best keep calm. "What will it take to get it back?"

Rawlins tilted his head. "Who says I'm interested in selling?"

"I do."

An amused glint entered the man's gaze. "I admire your gumption, but that won't matter in a court of law."

"Having been my father's best friend at one time and considering what a decent man you are, I hoped we might be able to work something out." Both he and Rawlins knew Gabe didn't consider him decent about anything.

"Is that a threat?"

Threatening anybody would land Gabe right back in jail. He wasn't so stupid as to not realize that. He looked down at his scruffy boots and took a deep breath. The man's relationship with his father was his only trump card. "Look. I know my dad beat you to that parcel of land way back when

you were both starting out, and it has always stuck
in your craw. I also know about the water rights
during the big drought. Pa would have never withheld water…but his word wasn't good enough for
you. You had to hire a lawyer that ran us into the
dirt with legal fees. Now you've gone and swiped
that land out from under me while I was locked up."

It didn't faze Rawlins. "Gerald Coulter would
expect his son to stay out of jail in the first place.
Somebody had to pay the taxes while you were
gone. If it wasn't me, then it would have been somebody else. And like I said—I've had my eye on
that property."

Gabe felt the old rage start to bubble up inside
him. His hands curled into fists. "You had your
eyes and your hands on a lot more than that." The
urge to strike the man nearly overwhelmed him.
But he'd learned a few humbling lessons in prison.
Punching Rawlins wouldn't help his cause and right
now it was the land he wanted. With considerable
effort he swallowed what pride he had and told
himself he'd deal with Rawlins's history with his
ma later. It wouldn't help to bring it up now.

"I want that land back. It belongs in my family.
My folks are buried there."

Rawlins gave him a hard look. "Yes, they are."

A sinking sensation tumbled in his gut. "*You*
buried Ma?"

"Somebody had to."

It should have been him, and it tore him up inside that he hadn't been with her when she needed
him at the last. He wouldn't let Rawlins know that.

It nearly choked him to say it, but he was grateful for that bit of respect Rawlins had shown his mother. "Thank you. I'll pay you for the land. Pay off the taxes and then some."

"You have the money?"

"No. But I'll bet I am still the best horse trainer in the territory. I'll find work and pay you for it."

"That will take you years."

"Doesn't matter."

Rawlins stood, walked behind his desk and stared at a framed picture sitting there. A troubled expression crossed his face. "Perhaps it is time…" He flipped the picture face down. "Your father was the best horse trainer I've ever known. Did he teach you?"

Surprised, Gabe met his eyes. "Yes."

The man studied him. "Room and board only?"

Was the man actually considering taking him on? He hadn't come here to ask for a job. He figured he'd hire out to any other rancher in the valley, but not Rawlins. As he waited, the oddest sensation stretched his chest—like a screw backing out and slowly loosening its tight grip on two pieces of wood.

"I'll give you a try. Johnson will introduce you to the other men." Rawlins nodded to his foreman and then strode from the room.

It was decided so fast that Gabe was left dazed. He would be working for the largest and richest ranch in the area. He would have a roof over his head and food in his stomach, but could he tolerate it, knowing what he knew about Rawlins? Rawlins took what he wanted. Always. First he took Gabe's mother in a vulnerable moment—after his father's death. Then he took Riley away from him and sent her back east. And now Rawlins had the land and he hadn't said a word about giving it up.

What the heck was Gabe doing? Was he being as gullible—as weak—as his own mother?

He refused to consider that. He wouldn't let Rawlins play him as he'd played her. He was smarter than that.

Whatever had loosened momentarily in his chest tightened back up. No one would get the better of him—especially not Rawlins. He would bide his time and somehow get his ranch back and then be done with Rawlins in his life for good.

Chapter Two

Two months later

Six horses pummeled the road with their hooves, the dirt clods and dust flying high into the warm spring air as they pulled the Wells Fargo coach the last leg of Riley Rawlins's journey. She stared through the window at the passing parade of oak trees, granite boulders and grasslands that butted up against the foothills, surprised that after fourteen years of exile she recognized any of the countryside at all. Farther on loomed the mountains of the Cuyamaca range jutting up against a clear azure sky.

Once this place had been as familiar as the back of her hand. Memories of her life here rose up and threatened to choke her. Determinedly, she blocked them out. The past had to stay in the past. This was to be a new start for her and her son.

Yet her stomach knotted with anxiety at what lay ahead. She glanced at her son who sat across from her on the opposite seat. Brody was taller than her now, with moody gray-green eyes and a bronze complexion that reminded her daily of his beginnings. He sat in sullen silence, gazing out the window, unhappy at being pulled away from all that was familiar—his friends and her mother's side of the family back in Philadelphia.

She'd been only two years older than he when she had boarded the train to leave her father's ranch and travel east. Unknown to her on that trip, she carried a stowaway. When she arrived at her grandparents' home in Pennsylvania and had missed her monthly a second time, she began to suspect there was more to her upset stomach. Brody was coming full circle back to his beginnings although he didn't know it.

During the first few days of their journey on the Kansas Pacific, Riley had seen a spark of excitement in her son's eyes as he badgered the engineer about the mechanics of the train. He was enthralled from the initial whistle blast to the grinding of gears that forced the massive beast into motion. He had thrilled at the escalating speed that had them racing like a bullet over the prairie. Watching him, hope had grown in Riley that she was making the right choice in dragging him away from all he knew.

Brody needed a man's guidance…a healthy dose of discipline and responsibility meted out with wisdom, and she was counting on her father to supply it. With her long hours away from home at the watch factory, she simply couldn't keep track of him well enough. He was out of control. Belligerent, angry and withdrawn, he'd begun avoiding chores and avoiding the home she'd made for them both. The deciding moment had been when a police officer returned him to the house late one night and said he'd been caught with a member of the city's west-side gang. Fear for him—for his future—had swept over her as she finally faced that she was not just losing control of him, but losing him completely. That realization had finally broken through the stubbornness that had kept her from returning to the ranch and to her father. Brody was more important than any hurt feelings she might harbor… or any pride.

Although he had wanted to sit outside with the driver on the stagecoach, she had insisted he ride inside with her, unsure at the time if it was to bolster him or to bolster her for the impending meeting with her father. She grasped her hands together to still them in her lap, her palms clammy. How would her father be toward her? How would he react to seeing Brody for the first time? Would he accept him as a Rawlins, or would he ignore him as the grandson born on the other side of the blanket? The next hour would tell. That is…if he met them at the Nuevo station at all.

At least she wouldn't have to deal with Gabe Coulter. Brody's father knew nothing of his son— not even that he existed. The last she'd heard, he was in a prison far to the north. Fear of running into him had kept her from returning to the area for years. Learning that he was locked away had cinched her decision that it was at long last time to come home.

Brody had the same volatile temper she remembered in Gabe. Her son reminded her of winter…

and of a house all boarded up to keep the heat in, but that heat just kept building and building. If something wasn't opened…a chimney flue, a window, a door…sooner or later the house would burst with the pressure. Brody was closed up so tight that he wasn't seeing the beautiful spring flowers along the roadside or noticing that their scent floated delicately on the breeze. He didn't appreciate that this was a new beginning, a new start for the both of them. All he saw, staring out the window, was what he had left behind.

She sighed. It was spring…a time for hope…a time for renewal. All he had to do was open his eyes.

The coach rounded a rocky bend in the road and the village of Nuevo came into view. If she remembered correctly, the station and pen with fresh horses stood on the south side of the dusty town. From his seat overhead the driver called out announcing the place. The stagecoach slowed and finally pulled to a stop in front of the change station.

The dirt yard was empty; however, a buckboard sat off under the shade of a juniper tree. Perhaps that was her ride. The caw of a Steller's jay broke the silence of the afternoon. A lean, broad-shouldered man stepped through the station door and out into the sunlight. She recognized him and froze. Scuffed boots, brown canvas pants, a cotton shirt with rolled-up sleeves, a green bandanna at his neck and the darkest brown eyes Riley had ever seen under a tan felt hat. Gabe Coulter.

Her breath whooshed from her like a deflating balloon. What was he doing here? When had he been released from prison? She stared at him, captivated and at the same time annoyed that after all these years he had grown more handsome. His collar-length black hair framed a face chiseled and sharp with angles, his nose straight as always, his jaw firm and square. The only thing not hard on the man was his lips...and they looked exactly as she remembered...enticing and kissable.

Abruptly, she pulled away from the window, hoping that he would walk away and never know she was there. Her heart raced. He still packed quite a presence. She swallowed, angry with herself for feeling anything at all. No amount of time was sufficient to make her forget what he'd done. She would never forgive him.

The driver placed the box step and swung open the door. "All out! Nuevo!"

She didn't move.

"Aren't we going, Ma?" Brody watched her.

She took a steadying breath. Perhaps it was silly to be nervous about running into Gabe after all this time. Hadn't she just been telling herself to leave the past in the past? This was a test of her resolve. That's all. Nothing more.

She tugged down on the hem of her shirtwaist and then straightened her straw bonnet. Ready. She stepped through the doorway and onto the box the driver had set for disembarking passengers. The bright sunlight blinded her. She wobbled slightly, her legs unused to activity and stiff after riding for four hours.

A strong hand grasped her upper arm, steadying her. The grip hardened to steel. "Riley? Riley Rawlins?"

His voice was richer, deeper, than she remembered, and he sounded astonished. Careful to keep all of her colliding thoughts contained and squashed deep inside, she looked up and met his eyes. "Hello, Gabe," she said with cool reserve.

Then she stepped down to the ground and promptly stumbled.

He grabbed hold with his other hand and steadied her. Both grips were tight bands on her upper arms. He stared at her with unveiled shock in his eyes. "*You* are the company that Rawlins is expecting?"

She stiffened. "I am."

He let go immediately. "Then I guess I'm here to fetch you."

Her pulse raced. Her entire body felt on edge, as though half of her wanted to bolt one way and the other half run another. "You are working for my father now?"

"Started not too long ago."

With their exchange of letters, her father had known for over a month that she was coming home and yet he had hired Gabe? It didn't seem possible. Years ago when he discovered they were involved in something more than friendship, Father had been dead set against them being near each other. He also knew how upset she'd been when Gabe had deserted her. Was this his own brand of retribution he was forcing on her?

She squared her shoulders, resigned that this "new beginning" had taken a decided turn for the worst. "Very well." It wasn't the most gracious of responses, but at the moment it mirrored how she felt.

His eyes narrowed as he took a closer look at her.

It was as if he was reaching back through the years and trying to read what had happened to her since then...and perhaps wishing she would return to where she had come from. Heat mounted on her cheeks under his scrutiny.

"Ma."

She startled at her son's voice behind her and turned to him. "Brody, this is Mister Coulter...a ranch hand of your grandfather's."

Gabe's brow raised at the last, just the slightest bit, but he turned and watched Brody disembark. If Brody's size...nearly five feet six inches...surprised him, not a muscle moved on his handsome face. When her son lifted his sullen gaze, all Gabe did was thrust out his hand.

Her son hesitated but then grasped Gabe's hand in a firm shake.

"Brody," Gabe said, as if testing his name and committing it to memory. His shake slowed and he glanced at Riley with a question lighting his eyes. Then he let go. "I'll get your bags transferred to the wagon."

"I can do it," Brody said, his voice challenging. He scrambled to the top of the coach and tossed down their traveling cases with enough force Riley worried they might break open. It didn't seem to faze Gabe as he caught them. What was her son trying to prove? When he had climbed back down and Gabe had left them to carry two of the cases to the wagon, she took Brody aside. "What was that all about?"

"I don't like the way he looked at us—at you."

It wasn't the first time her son had acted protective of her, but it had been a long time since he had even cared—more than a year.

"I hope you are a bit friendlier upon meeting your grandfather." She also hoped her father was a bit friendlier than Gabe had been. Then squaring her shoulders, she braced herself for the long ride to the ranch and followed her son to the buckboard.

Gabe's entire body was shaking on the inside when he settled the luggage in the wagon bed. Riley was back—and with a son! Just the thought of her with another man made Gabe knot up inside, stupidly jealous of something that had happened years ago. He hadn't expected her to stay unhitched. She was too beautiful to stay single for long. He darted a look at her as she walked toward the wagon. Still slender, still with that long, wavy, honey-colored hair—although it was up in a knot under her hat. He'd never forgotten her eyes—gray-green with long dark lashes. They'd haunted him for as long as he could remember.

He helped her onto the wagon seat, irritated that his hands tingled when he let loose of her. Brody gave him a penetrating look before climbing up beside her. It wasn't hard to decipher the stare. Gabe had felt possessive often enough with his own mother whenever Rawlins had come slinking around. The boy didn't have a thing to worry about. As much as he had once loved Riley, he had learned his lesson there. He was just the hired help in her family's opinion and nowhere near good enough for her.

"I need to pick up a few things before we leave town," she said in the slightly husky voice he remembered. "If you don't mind, I'd like to stop at the dry-goods store."

She sounded hesitant...more than he would expect from a Rawlins. And she didn't look right at him.

He walked around to the other side of the buckboard, took his seat, flicked the reins and turned the wagon around, heading the two horses to the main road. He pulled up in front of the store and wrapped the reins around the brake lever, and then he stood, ready to jump down and help her descend.

"No. Please," she said quickly. "I can manage. I will only be a minute."

He sat back down, wondering if maybe she knew of his recent prison address and didn't want his help because of that. It would be one more strike against him in her eyes. He leaned back on the wagon seat while she climbed down on her own. Her son did not assist her, but jumped to the ground and sauntered into the store ahead of her like he owned the place.

He couldn't get over the fact that it was Riley he'd been instructed to collect at the station. Rawlins wouldn't know that Johnson had ordered him. The man would probably be hot as Hades if he found out. Last time Rawlins had caught Gabe with Riley, he had pushed a shotgun in his face and said he wasn't good enough for his daughter. He could only hope Rawlins never found out about this. After eight weeks, Gabe was slowly starting to fit in with the rest of the ranch hands. He didn't want to mess it up. It felt good to be working again.

This being his first time here since his release from prison, Gabe surveyed the dusty town while Riley shopped. Although the trees had grown, the place looked much the same as when he'd left— a handful of wooden buildings built for purpose rather than beauty. A few were whitewashed. He figured that would ward off the heat from the strong sun once summer arrived, but now the spring rains made the oaks that shaded the town look green and inviting—as inviting as a town could be so long as you weren't a convict or an Indian.

Riley swished past the doorway holding something draped over her arm. She sure had matured into a striking woman. The blue dress she wore brought to mind the feel of her small waist when he had helped her into the wagon. She might be older, but she wasn't much bigger than a mite and that hadn't changed.

"Here now!" a man bellowed. "I see what you're doing. You get on outta here!"

Gabe straightened in the seat and listened.

Brody stormed out. An angry expression twisted his face and his hands were clenched. He took hold of the wagon and hauled himself up, climbing into the back with the travel cases.

Gabe's first thought was for Riley. Was she all right?

He jumped down and strode to the doorway. Riley stood at the counter paying for her items. Her cheeks were stained a deep pink. She and the shopkeeper appeared to be the only ones in the store. Gabe headed inside to help with her packages.

The stout owner, a man in his forties with gray streaks in his wavy dark hair, moved sideways a step and reached out to let one hand settle on a rifle propped in the corner. "No Injuns allowed. Especially murderin' ones."

So word had hightailed it through town about him. "I don't want trouble. I work at the Golden R and I'm just here to help Miss Rawlins with her packages," he said cautiously. He had no idea whether she was a miss or a missus, but now wasn't the time to ask.

On hearing the name Rawlins, the shopkeeper looked closer at Riley.

Gabe took that moment to heft the box under one arm. "All set?"

She nodded, a bit flustered, and headed for the wagon.

Gabe set his jaw and followed her. He had earned his freedom. The owner had a right to do business with whoever he wanted, but Gabe had done his time. He would make sure to use the small store in Santa Ysabel from now on rather than come back here. He sure didn't want any of his trouble rubbing off on Riley…or Mr. Rawlins for that matter. He'd come to realize no one else in the valley would have hired an ex-convict and although he didn't like being grateful to Frank Rawlins considering their past history, he was beholden to him for the job.

He deposited the box in the back of the wagon. Brody sat there with his arm draped over his luggage. The boy darted a look at him that said to leave him alone. Gabe wondered what had happened in the store but figured it was better to keep quiet. It wasn't any of his business. He helped Riley onto the wooden seat, then walked around the flatbed and climbed up. He glanced sideways at her. She sat prim and proper, her gloved hands in her lap, looking straight ahead, her cheeks still aflame from whatever had happened in the store.

He snapped the reins and turned the horses toward the road that led out of town. "Sorry about that back there," he muttered. He wasn't apologizing for the storekeeper's attitude or his own past… just that Riley had to be buffeted by any of it.

They rode in silence until the town was nothing but a speck the size of a flea behind them. About the time he began to relax, the wagon jostled over an uneven patch and his leg rubbed against hers—rough denim against heavy cotton. Tingles scattered from his hip down to his knee. He moved over a mite at the same time that she tucked her skirt beneath her thigh and scooted away from him. It wasn't long, however, before the jostling of the wagon had them touching again. He tried to keep himself from thinking on it. Riley adjusted the folds of her dark blue dress, first one way and then another, several times. He began to think that maybe she was as uncomfortable at being thrown together as he was.

"This is my first trip back since…" She pressed her lips together. "Never mind. It's not important. Has the ranch changed much?"

"Some." He didn't miss the quick corralling of her thoughts. The sound of her voice brought back a multitude of memories he didn't need to be thinking about now. She looked a bit wilted, what with all the traveling she had been doing. Wearing that fancy dress, she sure didn't look like the Riley he remembered—especially with the bonnet. The Riley he knew had worn a Stetson. And if he remembered correctly, after she'd outgrown pinafores, she had stubbornly held out for split skirts instead of dresses so she could ride astride. That had caused some friction between her and her mother. He snorted softly to himself…*friction* was too pleasant a word for the tension he felt coming from her direction at the moment. She sure wasn't acting anything like the Riley he remembered.

The buckboard jostled—a quick violent jerk as the wheel rolled into and then out of an unavoidable rut in the road. Taken unaware, Riley suddenly gripped his thigh for support. "Oh, my!" she gasped, and then immediately let go.

He yanked at his neckerchief, loosening it up some. Day was getting hot.

"What do you do at the ranch?" Brody asked.

So the boy could talk. Had to be an improvement over the dagger looks he'd been firing. "Everything. Cutting, roping, branding, riding fence."

"You ride a fence?" Brody repeated sarcastically.

Didn't the boy know anything about ranching? "Ride along the fence line to make sure no wire or posts are down. If they are, I fix them. Can't have cattle getting through."

"Think Grandfather will make me do that?"

Gabe couldn't speak for Rawlins and he wouldn't try.

"Not at first," Riley answered. "First you'll have to learn to ride. And before that you'll need to learn something about the horses. He won't want you near them otherwise."

That stopped Gabe. Riley's son not knowing how to ride? "How old are you, Brody?" At the question, Riley stiffened beside him.

"Just turned fourteen."

Gabe counted back mentally. The numbers worked. He glanced at Riley, but she kept her eyes on the road, and her pert, upturned nose pointed straight ahead calm as you please. He couldn't imagine that she would keep it from him if he had a son. They might not have parted on the best of terms, but she would have gotten word to him somehow. Wouldn't she?

The only other possibility was that Riley married a man the first year she went back east to that finishing school. That thought left a rancid taste in his mouth. To think that she had gone right ahead and found somebody new that quick made him angrier than a Mexican bull.

So where was her husband now? She always was a princess. Always had gotten her way with her father up until he found the two of them together and the whole world blew up in Gabe's face.

"Mr. Coulter, would you teach me to ride?"

Spending time with Brody—or with any of the Rawlins—didn't sound wise at all. "I answer to Mr. Rawlins."

Rebuffed, Brody immediately clamped his mouth shut and pulled back, sitting stiff and drawn into himself.

Gabe could feel the tension and figured he'd had a hand in at least part of it. Guess it wouldn't hurt to say something to the boy. "For a woman, your mother was the best rider I ever saw. She even won a couple of awards. She will make a fine teacher."

Brody looked at his mother. "She never told me."

Gabe took a deep breath and let it out, keeping his eyes on the road. "There's a few things she never told me either." And he'd be asking her about them the minute he got her alone. He clicked his tongue at the horse and flicked the reins, urging a faster pace. The sooner he got these two to the ranch, the sooner he could breathe free again.

The sound of Gabe's voice stirred memories that taunted Riley. She had once loved the deep baritone, the spare words, even the silent stares he'd once directed her way. But no more. She sat on pins and needles, listening to his conversation with her son, worried that Gabe would ask an embarrassing question of her. He had to be wondering about

a lot of things right now—not all of them compli-
mentary to her.

But she had her reasons! He was the one who
had wronged her. He had used her for his own private revenge. She would never forget that and never
forgive him. The passage of time didn't matter. It
was the same today as it had been fourteen years
ago—he didn't deserve to know the truth about
Brody. And if the shopkeeper was right? Then Gabe
had been sent to prison because he killed someone!
If that was true, she didn't want Brody anywhere
near him and his volatile temper!

It was with relief that they turned down the lane
to the ranch and he finally stopped the buckboard
before the ranch house.

The place had changed from the way she remembered it and yet much was still the same. The
two-story, rambling house had a new coat of pale
yellow paint with the trim now a darker gold. The
half circle of pine trees edging the yard at the back
of the house were taller with thicker trunks. The
oldest tree on the property, the oak at the side of
the house, still held the swing she'd used as a child.
Seeing that, her throat clogged with memories.

She drew in a shaky breath. "I'm home." She
could feel it deep inside. She splayed her hand over
her heart in an attempt to quiet the rush of feelings.
She had blocked this place from her mind for years
because the yearning only made her hurt inside.
Now the memories bombarded her. She had loved
living here. This just had to be the new beginning
she needed for herself and her son.

She closed her eyes and breathed in the smells and sounds surrounding her—the pines rustling, the sage in the air, the flowers in the field, even the cattle lowing in the meadow. The stiff, dusty hair on their hides would be warm from the sun beating down on them this time of day. She could imagine the flies bothering them and the lazy swish of their tails as they chewed their cud.

At the dip and creak of the seat, she opened her eyes. Gabe walked around the buckboard and waited to assist her. She studied his face, just as he did hers. Not a whisper of a whisker studded his square, hard chin. Under thick black brows, tiny lines fanned out from the corners of his eyes. He had once meant so much to her. She had loved him unreservedly. Being this close...feeling his strong hands on her waist...it was unnerving. Did he have a family? Someone who cooked for him, mended his clothes? Did he have other children? What was his life like apart from working for her father, and after all this time...was it any of her business and did she really want to know?

She held on to his shoulders, feeling the hardness of his muscles ripple against her palms as he helped her down. "Thank you," she murmured and stepped back from him.

He pressed his mouth into a determined line, and then turned to remove her luggage from the wagon. Carrying it to the porch, he left it alongside the ones Brody had deposited and then tipped the brim of his hat to her. "I'll get back to work now."

He seemed anxious to leave.

Before he could, the front door banged open and her father strode out, the sound of his boots loud and deliberate on the expansive wooden porch. He paused when he noticed Gabe. "Take the bags upstairs, Coulter," he barked.

"Sir." Gabe passed behind her and followed orders, disappearing into the house.

Without sparing him a second glance, her father turned to her. He didn't say anything at first. Just stood there looking her over like a field marshal surveying his troops.

Suddenly she felt ten years old again and not sure if she was to get a scolding. Frank Rawlins had always made her knees tremble just a bit, he'd been so big and so powerful. But he'd never raised a hand to her. And he had taught her to ride and to judge good cattle stock. She had confided in him in a way she had never been able to with her mother—especially when Gabe left. He was protecting her even as he put her and her mother on the train headed east—even though she knew his own heart was breaking. She loved him for that.

Now the rich, dark brown hair he had once had was streaked with silver. His skin was weathered and ruddy, and his crystal-blue eyes now sported deep lines at the outer corners. His nose was the same...a curved beak.

"You change your mind about that snake pit of a big city?" he asked sharply.

Taken aback at his brusqueness, she responded in kind. "I'm here, aren't I?"

He didn't move to hug her, didn't move at all.

She swallowed her disappointment and darted a glance at her son. Would Brody understand it was just her father's way to be direct and uncompromising? But then his eyes softened, surprising her. "What took you so long?" he finally said.

"Perhaps I'm as stubborn as you."

He huffed at that and then surprised her by shaking his head. "Dagnabit, we've both been stubborn fools. Don't ever let it happen again, daught—"

Before he could finish, she rushed to him and hugged him. "I've missed you so!"

His arms wrapped around her in a quick hug, ready to back away immediately. But when she wouldn't let go, he relaxed and hugged her back. "Well," he said gruffly. "Well."

After a moment, he set her from him and turned to look Brody over from his flat cap to his brogans. "So this is my grandson. Nearly grown."

"Yes, sir. Brody, sir."

They eyed each other, sizing each other up.

"I put you upstairs in the room next to your mother's. You'll figure out which one it is. Go on up now."

Brody shot a dark look at his grandfather and then stormed into the house at the same time that Gabe stepped back outside. "I'll get back to my work now."

"Wait." Her father turned to Gabe. "Who told you to pick Riley up at the station?"

"Johnson."

Her father's lips tightened. "He mention who you were collecting?"

"No, sir."

"All right. Go on about your business."

Gabe took one more look at her, tucked his hat back on his head and strode away.

Riley watched him until he disappeared inside the stable.

"Not much in your letter to go on," her father said, his gaze pinning her. "What's this all about?"

She had informed him that she was coming; she hadn't asked. And she hadn't mentioned her recent troubles with Brody. "Is it too much to simply want to come visit you?" she hedged.

"Been waiting a long time for you to come to your senses. I was beginning to think I might have to head east to fetch you."

She didn't believe him for a minute. He hated the city. How he ever had enough in common with her mother to marry her was a question Riley had asked herself a number of times. He would have never come east. No...she was the one that had left the ranch—it was up to her to come home. But one of the reasons she'd finally returned was because she thought Gabe Coulter had left the area. "What is Gabe doing here?"

"He needed work."

She put her hands on her hips. "Why can't he work somewhere else?"

"He just got out of prison. No one is going to take him on. Not around here."

Having Gabe around would be difficult for her. There had to be another solution. "So he's staying?"

Her father studied her, his right brow quirking up ever so slightly. "Coulter is a hard worker. Knows ranching. I was hard on him at first, thought he wouldn't fit in with the men, thought that he would cause trouble, but he is doing a good job. Either he is trying mighty hard to change or he already has. He needed a chance, and I owe him that much."

"Owe him?" She didn't understand. "Even after what he did to me?"

"You both had a hand in that."

She took a step back, rebuffed. "You don't mince words, do you?"

He blew out a breath. "Riley, I knew you wouldn't like him being here. I have my reasons for taking him on. Give it a few days. We'll talk again when you are settled in more."

He was serious about Gabe remaining on! "Father, he has a prison record."

"Maybe you should ask him about that before you go judging him."

"Do you know the details?"

"Appears it was over a woman."

A lead weight dropped in her stomach. A woman! "Perfect," she said derisively. "I don't want him anywhere near Brody. My son is difficult enough to manage."

"So you never wrote to Coulter? Never told him?" He watched her closely. "That had to be one interesting wagon ride."

"He didn't deserve to know anything. He left me. Remember?"

"I remember," he said in his deep, gruff voice.

"That was a long time ago. Might want to leave it in the past. Start new."

She glared at him, her temper getting the better of her. "Start new, you say. That's what I had hoped for in coming here, but now you've thrown Mr. Coulter into the mix and I don't see how I can!"

He huffed and even looked slightly amused when he headed toward the door. "Good to have you home, daughter. It's been too tame around here these past few years."

Riley stared at his back as he walked up to the porch and through the front door. Things certainly hadn't been tame for her, and if today was any indication, things were only going to get wilder.

She looked over her shoulder at the open stable door. Gabe had moved farther inside and out of sight. This was to be a new start, a new beginning for her and her son but it seemed old wounds were already opening and threatening to swallow her hope. She hadn't missed the challenge in her father's voice. It sounded as if he wanted her to bury the hatchet and let go of what had happened in the past. How could she possibly do that? Every time she saw Brody, she was reminded that Gabe had used her. She would never get close enough to him to let it happen again.

Chapter Three

That evening while the four other ranch hands played poker at the long table, Gabe stood on the stoop of the bunk house and stared at the ranch house. His thoughts were in turmoil. Why hadn't Rawlins let him go when he learned Riley was coming home? It didn't make any sense. As he watched, a shadow passed by the window. Riley. Was she here for a visit? Or to stay? He'd sure like to know. Before long the lanterns were put out and they all turned in. Finally he did, too.

The next day a steady rain kept everyone inside. Gabe mucked out the horse stalls and repaired the brake lever on the buckboard. He'd noticed yesterday that it barely held. While he worked, he stole glances at the big house, wondering what was going on inside. The chance he'd hoped for…catching Riley alone to talk to her…never occurred.

The following day dawned bright and sunny, the earth washed clean from the rain. At the crowing of the rooster, Gabe sat up and stretched. He rose and dressed quickly and then pulled on his boots. He would work the stallion today, along with the two geldings Rawlins wanted broken. His shoulder was still sore from the last time he'd come off a horse. Seemed the foreman's idea of initiation consisted of leaving the toughest work assignments for him. It was nothing Gabe hadn't experienced before—in prison and when he was younger and going from ranch to ranch. It was never fun, but Johnson seemed to have an extra burr under his saddle concerning Gabe.

He walked out to the well and pumped the handle until water flowed freely, then he washed his face and neck and slicked back his hair. Once he was done, he joined the others for breakfast in the long kitchen area of the bunkhouse. Rosaria ladled out biscuits with gravy and eggs. After chasing the meal down with a cup of coffee, Gabe bridled the stallion and led him to the corral to put him through his paces.

The sun rose higher, warming his shoulders and back. He started working the stallion, making him back up, then rush forward and stop abruptly. He was a beautiful horse. Big, strong and sleek. Smart, too. Gabe barely had to think where he wanted the horse to move and the stallion sensed the direction. With only a slight change of weight he maneuvered the animal through a series of footwork. He would hate to see the animal go. Rawlins had mentioned a man was coming to see about buying the stallion sometime this week.

Before long he sensed someone watching him and realized Brody was leaning on the corral fence. Gabe nodded to him briefly just to let the boy know he'd noticed him. After a good workout for the horse, Gabe walked it back to the stable and rubbed him down. Brody followed and watched, leaning over the door of the stall. He wore dark green pants with suspenders and a cream-colored cotton shirt. He wore the same cap that he'd had on before. The boy needed a wider brim. Hadn't Riley at least purchased a decent hat for him in the dry-goods store?

Gabe bridled the gelding he was to break to the saddle. A large, bay mustang—fourteen hands worth. He had been working with the horse for the past week, letting the animal adjust to his handling and trying to instill a sense of trust. He led the horse out to the corral and then stood in the middle with a long lead line, putting the gelding through its paces, round and round the perimeter of the corral one way and then the other until the horse was warmed up and attentive.

Brody climbed up and sat on the corral railing.

Gabe threw a blanket onto the gelding's back. The horse handled that just fine, so after a while he grabbed the saddle from the stable and slowly lowered it to the horse's back. The gelding shied a little, prancing away from him. As Gabe moved to soothe him, he saw a flash of yellow on the porch. Riley stood at the top of the steps wearing a yellow dress, her arms crossed over her chest, watching.

Gabe cinched up the saddle, walked the horse around the corral twice, just letting him get used to the feel of the new weight on its back. Then he stopped to recheck the cinch strap and adjust the length of the stirrups to suit him. Slowly, methodically he worked, speaking in a low, quiet tone. The gelding shifted its weight and snorted nervously, craning its neck to see what Gabe was up to. Gabe stuck his boot in the stirrup and eased himself up, settling into the saddle. He spoke in low tones, encouraging, praising the horse.

It helped for all of thirty seconds.

The horse decided enough was enough and reared. Gabe had been expecting it and held on tight—one hand grasping the reins and the other holding on to a hank of mane while the gelding bucked. Coming down on all four legs at once, the horse kicked out with both its back legs. It repeated the motions once more, this time jarring him violently enough to get his way. "Damn!" Gabe flew through the air over the mustang's head and then slammed against the base of a corral post.

Riley had stepped outside, intent on fetching her son, but now her attention was riveted on Gabe's still form. Her breath had caught in her throat as she witnessed his flight and abrupt landing. He wasn't moving! He wasn't getting up! She gripped the porch railing, hesitant and unsure. Was he dazed and taking a moment to get his senses whipped back into order, or was he badly hurt?

She glanced about the yard. Where were the other ranch hands? Why had they left him to do this alone? It was dangerous work for heaven's sake! The bay snorted and pranced, coming dangerously close to Gabe's still form.

That spurred her. She ran down the path from the porch and across the yard to the corral. Slipping between the rails, she yelled and waved her hands, startling the mustang. With a snort, it backed away to the far side of the pen.

"Ma!" Brody sat up straighter and appeared ready to jump down from his perch.

"Check on Mr. Coulter!" She couldn't have Brody in the corral aggravating the horse further. The mustang might do something unpredictable. She glanced over her shoulder at Gabe's crumpled form.

He moved slightly, enough that she saw his chest expand with a breath. Slowly he straightened his twisted body and then braced his hand against the ground to push himself up.

She breathed a sigh of relief and her heart slowed to a more normal rate. When she heard a creaking sound to her left, she snapped her head around to see Mr. Johnson duck between the rails in the corral and move to catch the horse.

"I'll take over Miss Rawlins. You move on out of here. I'm sure your daddy doesn't want you getting that pretty yellow dress dirty."

He'd obviously been watching. "Where were you?"

Johnson looked amused. "Didn't see a need to step in."

"He could have been hurt by that…that beast!"

"By Lucky? He wouldn't have hurt him."

His entirely too casual attitude irritated her. "You don't know that!"

He narrowed his gaze on her. "He's just a half breed. What do you care?"

"He's a person!"

"I'm fine, Miss Rawlins," Gabe said, dusting himself off. He grabbed his hat from the ground and slapped it against his thigh a time or two to dislodge the chunks of dried mud. Then he took one more deep breath and walked over to take the reins from Johnson.

The foreman snorted and handed them over.

Gabe concentrated on calming the gelding, and by his words, she realized he was readying himself and the horse. He would ride it again. She hadn't been around men much...only her son. Were they always so caught up in acting tough and independent? She let out an exasperated huff and slipped through the corral railing.

"Riley!" her father called out from the porch. "Rosaria has breakfast ready."

"Brody..."

He didn't budge. "Maybe I want to stay here and see what happens."

Riley fisted her hands on her hips. She didn't need a challenge from him now. Her pulse still hadn't slowed all the way to normal. "I can tell you what is going to happen—the same thing over and over until the horse realizes it cannot win. That's what is going to happen."

Brody stuck up his chin. "Well, I want to see it."

"No." She knew Gabe and Johnson watched. "I want you to eat with your grandfather and me."

Her son shot her a belligerent glare, but with grinding slowness climbed down from the fence.

Riley followed him up the path to the house where her father waited.

Once inside she filled her plate at the small buffet in the dining room. She wasn't hungry—she was frustrated. Her son had purposefully challenged her in front of everybody.

It was quiet while the three of them ate. Very quiet.

She remembered watching the ranch hands break a horse when she was growing up. She had felt sorry for the horse, who had no choice in the matter. As a child, she didn't understand why the breaking had to be done. Her father had said it was a silly, romantic attitude for someone whose livelihood came from a ranch and she had better get over it.

Watching Gabe, those thoughts evaporated in the wake of realizing she was watching a master horseman. He exhibited patience and expertise. When the horse threw him, her heart nearly stopped. It took him so long to move that her chest hurt from holding her breath. It still hurt! The horse had nearly trampled him!

And then to have him witness her issues with her son…

She glanced across the table at Brody sitting there, sullen and angry. Starting the day together at the breakfast table had been a Rawlins tradition for as long as she could remember, and it looked as though her father wanted to instigate it again with her return, but even this might be a trial if Brody didn't change his attitude.

During his meal of eggs, toast and jelly, her father kept eyeing Brody. Finally he pushed back from the table. "What are you wearing?"

Brody looked down at his cotton shirt and pants and then shrugged. "Clothes."

"I expect you to remove your hat while inside the house as a matter of respect."

Brody's eyes narrowed angrily, but he slid the offending cap off his head.

"I thought you picked up a decent hat for the boy," he said to Riley.

"I ain't no cowboy."

Her father frowned. "You are a Rawlins, aren't you? No grandson of mine is going to walk around the ranch dressed like a street urchin."

"This is what boys wear in Philadelphia," Riley said. "And, yes, he does have a new hat in his room."

"Grandmother bought this for me," Brody said, adding a defiant lift of his chin.

"Well, stow it in your room. It won't do you any good here. Wear the one your mother bought for you."

Brody slunk down in his chair.

She hated to harp further, but she had to say something about that morning. "There is one more thing. I don't want you hanging around Mr. Coulter."

"I wasn't bothering him."

"I have my reasons."

"How am I supposed to learn about horses if I can't watch and ask questions?"

Her father raised his brows and then his gaze crossed over to Riley.

So Gabe had impressed Brody just by doing his job. And truth was she had been impressed, too. There was such gentleness as he managed the horse…in his voice, in his touch, in his gaze. And at the same time there was strength as he struggled to keep his seat and control the horse. She hadn't been able to look away, for it was a thing of beauty— man against beast—the muscles in both bulging and rippling as they each tried to master the other.

But Gabe had killed a man.

"Brody, just do as I ask." She was worn down from the tension she felt in the room. "When you are finished eating, I will take you to school. See that you are ready."

He let out a groan and jumped from his seat, dashing to his room.

She rested her head in her hands. She was so tired of this!

"He is giving you quite a run." Her father's tone held judgment.

"He is constantly testing me."

"You were like him at that age—always pushing the boundaries I set."

She frowned. "So you're saying Brody simply has the Rawlins need to control everything along with a heavy dose of stubbornness? I think I figured that part out."

His eyes twinkled. "He has something of his father battling inside him, too. As I recall Coulter was worse, especially the year his father died. Gabe had to be fourteen or fifteen."

How had she forgotten about that? "He would disappear into the woods for days searching for that cougar only to return empty-handed and angry and wanting to pick fights."

"It's not an easy age for anybody, but you and Brody will get through it."

"I hope so." She felt more reassured having talked it out with her father. Had she spoken to her mother, her mother would have only blamed Brody's inadequacies on his blood. It made her wonder why she had been so set on trying to make things work for herself and Brody in Philadelphia. "In all the time I was gone, why didn't you try to contact me?"

Her father drummed his fingers on the pine table as though he were considering an answer.

"I can understand at first," she said. "You were trying to protect me. Coming back here…there would have been too many places, times I had shared with Gabe that I wouldn't want to face. But later—after Brody was four or five. I never heard from you."

He concentrated on his hand rather than looking at her. "Your mother waited a long time to take you for a visit with her side of the family. I thought you'd both be gone for a visit and then come back, but then you wrote about the baby coming and wanting to stay there where you had all her family supporting you. That sounded smart to me. I didn't know anything about babies. Later, I sent money so that you could all come home. Your mother replied that the three of you were settled and happy and wouldn't be coming back—ever." He looked into her eyes. "I couldn't see the point in forcing you. Your happiness...that was important to me."

"When I didn't hear from you, except for the money you sent every Christmas, I thought you hated me or were embarrassed about Brody."

His Adam's apple bobbed in his throat. "No."

"Oh, Father," she said on a sigh. They had both wanted to see each other, but both had been too stubborn to say anything. Now it was too late. Much too late, to have those years back. "I'm glad you finally told me."

The school sat at the crossroads on the outskirts of Santa Ysabel, a good three miles from the ranch. It was the same schoolhouse that she had gone to as a child. Brody was not happy about entering a new school at his age, but he needed to complete his education all the way to the eighth grade. He had one more year ahead of him. Besides, this would be a way for him to meet his neighbors. After enrolling him, Riley drove the buckboard back to the ranch alone.

When she stopped the rig in the yard, Gabe emerged from the stable door. He wore the same cream-colored shirt he'd worn that first day at the stage station, his sleeves rolled up to his elbows. Suspenders held up his brown pants. His thick wavy hair was wet and combed back. When he saw that it was her, he tucked the rag in his back pocket and walked to the buckboard, took the reins from her hands and wrapped them around the brake lever.

She stood at the edge of the wagon. "Where are the other men?"

"Moving a bull." He reached for her waist at the same time she reached for his shoulders. Even though she was prepared, a gasp emerged at the sudden sweep when he lifted her to the ground. He really did not appreciate his own strength. It left her slightly stunned each time. With the movement, his musky scent wafted over her. It was disconcerting to realize that despite the years, she remembered his scent...and found it stirring.

His hands lingered long enough that she had to pull away herself. "I'll need the rig again this afternoon to go after Brody."

"I'll have it ready." He walked alongside the horse, smoothing his hand over the gelding's flank until he took hold of the bridle.

A simple thing—yet reassuring to the horse, she imagined. "Are you...all right?"

He turned back to her with a question in his eyes.

"I mean to say...after your fall this morning."

"A little stiff. Nothing I haven't dealt with before." He searched her face, before turning away and leading the horse and rig to the stable door.

"Well, that's good," she said, following him and trying to cover up for asking such a personal question. "You just started working here. I'd hate for you to get injured right off." Her words came out stilted and awkward.

He paused in the doorway. "Are you just going to stand there? You owe me an explanation."

She followed him into the stable, completely flummoxed. "I owe you?" She didn't even try to keep the astonishment from her voice.

He removed the tracings from the horse and wiped down the bit with a rag.

The air was still and hot inside the building, and the sweet scent of fresh straw and hay enveloped her. "I owe you?" she repeated, tugging off her leather driving gloves. She slapped them down on a three-legged stool nearby. "You have that wrong, Mr. Coulter."

He raised his brows. "It has been a few years, but we do know each other...well. You could call me Gabe when we are alone."

No...oh, no... Rekindling that kind of familiarity with him would not be wise. She had loved him once...and he had used her to get back at her father. She had learned her lesson. Never would she be that gullible again. She raised her chin. "Just what are you doing working here? If I remember correctly you hated my father!"

Gabe looked up from his task. "He happens to hold the deed to my ranch. I'm working it off. Figure it will take about five years. After that you will both be free and clear of me for good."

She blinked. Their lives had been entangled for years because of Brody and she doubted they would ever be totally free of each other. "Your ranch? How did that happen?"

"He paid the back taxes while I was in prison."

Her father had omitted that small point when she had asked him about Gabe's presence on the ranch. What else had been carefully omitted? "You never cared about your property before. You said it tied you down. You always wanted to escape."

He dropped his rag onto the bench. "That was a long time ago. People change. I changed."

"In prison?"

"Before that. Prison made it clearer." He closed the gap between them until he stood right in front of her. "My turn. What took you so long to come back, Riley?"

His brown eyes drew her in and his deep voice could easily mesmerize her if she wasn't careful. "It's…complicated."

"I've got time."

She inhaled long and deep. She didn't want to tell him that it was because of him, because he'd hurt her in turning his back on her when she needed him. "I suppose stubbornness more than anything. I liked Philadelphia and wanted to raise Brody there. I wanted to be near my mother and she didn't want to come back."

"I remember her," he said, his tone slightly hostile. "You loved this place. I never thought you'd leave for good."

She pressed her lips together. He had always been able to see through to her true thoughts.

"It was nearly for good," she whispered. She

didn't want to talk about herself. The topic could too easily come to questions about Brody, which she wasn't prepared to answer. "What about you? How did you end up in jail?"

He didn't seem upset with her question. Slowly he turned away and hung the tack up on the wall hook. "I killed a man."

Even though she knew it, to have him say it so bluntly, so matter-of-factly, shocked her. "You always did have a temper." It was the wrong thing to say.

His lids shuttered down. He started looping up a rope, winding it methodically between his thumb and elbow.

"I shouldn't have said that. It's just…that's how I remember you—always with a chip on your shoulder, ready for another fight." When he still didn't speak she added, "There must be more to it."

A muscle worked in his jaw. "It was an accident." He looped the coil over a stall post and turned to face her. "I was working at a ranch south of here. The owner got familiar with his kitchen help—a young girl he had hired for a party. After most of the guests had gone home, he cornered her in the pantry. I happened to be passing through the kitchen and stopped him—forcefully. During the fight he pulled his gun. It went off. In the end I was the one still standing and he was dead."

"You shouldn't have been accused of murder."

"I wasn't. It was manslaughter, but I was considered dangerous."

"Y-you are not dangerous."

The glint in his brown eyes darkened…nearly as black as his lashes. "I can be," he said, his voice low and sure and steady.

She swallowed.

His gaze fell to her lips and then slowly raised again to her eyes.

Her mouth went dry. Did he think to kiss her? Her knees went weak with the thought. She doubted that she could move if he acted on that impulse.

Slowly he dragged a calloused finger down her cheek. It left a trail of fire in its wake. "I'm all grown up. I can be dangerous."

Her heart fluttered in her breast. "Gabe…" Was he playing with her? She thought to bolt—a silly aspiration considering she could barely breathe.

A movement near the door made her jump away from him. Johnson stood there, a suspicious smirk on his face. He sauntered farther into the stable and looked from one to the other. "What's going on here?"

"Nothing, Mr. Johnson," she said quickly. Her heart clattered inside her chest. What had just happened?

"Is Coulter bothering you?"

"No." Her cheeks heated anyway.

His gaze slid to Gabe. "That right?"

"Would you believe what I said?" Gabe asked, a challenge coating his voice.

Johnson snorted but didn't answer. "That fence needs mending on the west corner. The bull made a mess of it. As soon as you are done cleaning things in here, see to it." Johnson's order hung in the air, a direct test of his authority over Gabe.

Riley held her breath, wanting to escape from the tension in the stable and, even more, the sensations that Gabe had aroused. Gabe was upset at Johnson's interference although he hid it well. She didn't want Mr. Johnson imagining there was anything going on between the two of them. "Mr. Coulter, thank you for your help."

His eyes narrowed. They both knew he hadn't helped her with anything.

After a moment, Gabe turned away, took up a pitchfork and began clearing out the soiled straw in the next stall.

Johnson opened the door wide for her and the outside air swept through the building. She walked out, letting that breeze cool off her heated skin. Behind her, the door closed with a decided jolt.

Chapter Four

Gabe sat down at the long bunkhouse table and grabbed a tortilla from the plate in front of him then ladled a scoop of scrambled eggs mixed with onions, peppers and salsa onto it for breakfast.

It had been two days since he had cornered Riley in the stable. What had he been thinking to touch her like that? Even now, just the thought of her had heat shooting up his arm and to other parts of his body. She'd caught him off guard when she asked about his fall off the horse. How long had it been since someone was concerned about him? Worried about him? Just like that, the barriers he'd erected around his heart had fallen, and feelings he'd thought dead rose to the surface. Rawlins would fire him for sure if he found out Gabe still had feelings for his daughter—even as muddled as they were. If that happened, he'd lose any hope of getting his property back.

Johnson had called her Miss that day. He'd noticed the way Johnson looked at her when he thought no one was around. Didn't care for it. Whatever Riley's story, she could have easily returned to the ranch with a made-up last name, saying her husband had died or left her. She didn't. He respected her for that. She always had preferred honesty over lies.

So where had Brody come from?

After the men finished their breakfast and left the table, Johnson approached. "Senor Padilla is coming today. Rawlins expects you to show off that stallion."

Gabe had hoped to get away from the ranch for a few days. Rounding up the young spring calves with the rest of the ranch hands sounded a lot easier than dodging Riley. He felt smothered...working and living so close to the woman he couldn't forget. He had only been half teasing when he'd told her he was dangerous. A hard ride, a night or two under the stars, would help ease the tension building inside. "Any one of the men can show that horse."

"Rawlins must think you get along poorly with the others. Besides, rounding up calves requires skill."

Gabe grit his teeth.

"Looks like you are going to miss all the fun," Johnson said with a smirk. "But then maybe it is more fun for you here with Miss Rawlins."

"I'm here for a paycheck. That's all."

"Better not forget she's the boss's daughter then." With that, Johnson strode out of the bunkhouse and toward the stable.

Gabe swallowed and rose from the table. Johnson's digs were getting deeper and more frequent. He could ignore them when they focused on him, but his temper flared every time Riley's name came up.

He headed to the stable to curry the big stallion and ready him for showing. The other ranch hands were there, saddling their horses and preparing to head out for the roundup. They bantered back and forth until they finally mounted and rode out in a noisy group.

The sudden quiet in the barn made him restless, and he led the stallion out to the corral to finish the job. The morning sun felt warm on his shoulders. A light breeze blew through the oaks that shaded the house and carried the scent of flowers from the fields beyond the ranch. Blue sky surrounded him and as he worked the thoughts troubling him eased.

The front door of the ranch house opened and Rawlins stepped out. He glanced at Gabe, looked down the road and then reentered the house. Guess he was anxious to get the situation with Padilla finalized. Or…he was keeping an eye on Gabe as Johnson had mentioned.

Gabe saddled the horse and mounted. He started working the stallion, loosening him up for his showing.

Raised voices erupted from inside the house. Suddenly Brody slammed out, leaving the door wide-open. He dashed down the lane, in a flat-out run.

Riley rushed out onto the porch after him and stopped, an exasperated expression on her face when she saw that he was already too far away for her to catch. She was dressed to go riding today—maybe hoping to teach her son a thing or two about horses. She wore a moss-green split skirt with a cream-colored shirtwaist and had her blond hair in a thick loose braid down her back.

What was going on wasn't any of his business, but he kept an eye on Brody. The kid was fast and showed no signs of tiring or slowing. He disappeared from sight around the bend, not winded in the slightest.

Riley turned back to the house, her shoulders slumping in defeat. That…he didn't like. Before entering the house, she stopped and leaned one hand on the door frame. Her shoulders heaved as though she were taking huge controlling breaths. What the heck was going on?

Had Rawlins said something that upset Brody?

About that time, Senor Padilla and two of his cowboys came into view on the lane, riding their horses toward the ranch. Gabe dismounted and strode up to the house. When Riley noticed him approaching she quickly scooted inside.

He knocked on the open door but didn't enter. "Rawlins?" he called. "Senor Padilla is coming up the lane."

"See to the stallion. I'll be out." The gruff voice came from the study.

Gabe turned to do as he was asked and spotted Riley standing behind the door. Silvery trails streaked down her cheeks from watery light green eyes. The urge to reach out and hold her…try to comfort her…came over him, but then he remembered Johnson's words. She was the boss's daughter. And there was too much muddy water between them.

She sniffed and straightened her shoulders.

"Would you please point out a gentle horse for me to ride? I can saddle it."

"I'll go after Brody, if you want."

She shook her head. "You need to be here for my father. I'll take care of my son."

"He just needs to work through whatever is bothering him." Although Gabe didn't know what had upset Brody, he spoke from experience. He had run miles after his father had died from that cougar attack. It was the only thing that had made him too exhausted to think or feel when the pain would overtake him.

She met his gaze, her own filled with anxiety. "Anything could happen to him. He doesn't know the country. He could get lost."

He wanted to ask…was burning to ask if Brody was his son…but now didn't seem like the right time. Not with Padilla tying up his horse at the corral. Not with Rawlins striding from his study. He looked into her pretty eyes, her dark lashes were spiked and wet from her tears. He didn't like the idea of her going alone. "Farthest stall. A pinto. Gracie."

"Thank you." She rushed outside toward the stable while Gabe followed, striding to the corral.

He was putting the stallion through its paces for Senor Padilla, when Riley rode off. Rawlins noticed her departure and his jaw tightened with disapproval…or possibly worry. Why didn't the man do something? Instead of excusing himself to go after her, Rawlins started to negotiate with Padilla.

Gabe frowned. Riley didn't have a gun with

her. Nothing to protect her. He brought the stallion to a stop.

Rawlins continued his bartering.

Gabe had had enough. He jumped down and tossed the reins to one of Padilla's men. Rawlins stopped talking and narrowed his gaze on Gabe. Too bad. Gabe wasn't about to ask permission to go after Riley and Brody, but he was going to go.

He ran into the stable and saddled the palomino. The horse was larger than the rest and therefore a bit slow at cutting out calves, but perfect for any other riding. He urged the horse into a gallop and raced down the lane after Riley. At the main route he checked for tracks in the dirt, spotted them and headed toward the high ridge.

By now Riley could have caught up with her son. His dashing after the two of them might be a rash, unnecessary waste of time. But if that were the case, they would have turned back and he would see them coming down the road. Gabe was half-angry at himself for caring about either one of them. But the fact was…he did. Why was it that girl… that *woman*…could be gone for fourteen years, be back only four days, and already he wanted to protect her as if she'd never left.

Even when she was little it had been that way. She had always tried to prove that she was as fast, as smart and as tough as the other kids. Often it ended with her in a pickle. This—his going after her again—only proved what he'd always suspected. He had never gotten over her. She'd captured his heart all those years ago and no woman had ever taken her place. Years ago he'd had the audacity to hope he might win her only to be brutally reminded of his shortcomings by her father. Now—an ex-convict—he no longer hoped. He knew that he didn't deserve her.

Three miles farther and something white flashed in the distance. A little closer and he realized it was the pinto tied to a bush at the side of the road. There was no sign of Riley or Brody.

"Riley?" he called.

"Up here!"

Her voice came from a cluster of boulders halfway up the steep hillside. The leaves and branches of a large spreading oak dappled sunlight over the area leaving half in shade while the rest baked in bright light. He didn't see her or any sign of the boy.

He dismounted, tied the palomino next to the mare and started climbing. He skirted a large manzanita bush and continued up the grade, grabbing small clumps of grass for balance on the way up. He stopped at the base of the first large boulder, which was taller than him, noticed evidence of crushed grass and brush, and followed the markings around to the higher side of the hill where he spotted Riley.

In her haste to chase after her son her new hat had fallen to her back, held there by the leather chin cord. A few golden strands of hair, loose from her long braid, now whipped across her face. Her skin was slightly pink from the heat and exertion of her climb. She let out a relieved sigh when she saw him…which made him feel stronger inside just like it had all those years ago. She pointed to the boulders. "He's in there. I...can't climb it."

He turned and studied the boulders, looking for a toehold. "Come on out, Brody."

"Go away!"

"You won't like it if I come in there after you."

"What's it to you? You're just a hired hand."

Gabe had never talked much to kids but he remembered something of being that age. "You are worrying your ma."

"She always worries."

He turned at that and raised a brow at Riley. "Well, I don't like it."

"Think I care about that?"

While Brody talked, Gabe circled around and found a high pocket in one boulder and hauled himself up. From the top, he saw that the stones were shaped in such a way as to create a fort. An open area of dirt in the center made a perfect lair for just about any type of animal. Brody stood to the far side, watching him.

Gabe jumped to the ground.

The boy crouched, ready to fight.

"What's this all about?"

"I ain't going back to school. I don't like those kids."

"It's always tough at first, especially for the new kid. It'll get easier."

"I don't need schoolin'. I'm old enough to learn at the ranch."

"Guess you are mite big for her to force. Your ma just wants you to be smarter than her. Smarter than your grandad. Likely you'll be running the ranch one day and you will need to know things."

Brody's belligerent expression didn't change.

Gabe surveyed the enclosure. Not a bad hiding place. Good thing Riley had spotted him heading for it or they might never have found the boy.

"About this time of day, the rocks are nice and warm and rattlers like to sun themselves. I don't suppose you checked the area or have a plan if you happen upon one."

At that Brody glanced nervously about. "You are just trying to scare me."

Gabe would have grinned but for the fact he was telling the truth. The boy needed to learn a few things about life in the country before running off. "Trying to smarten you up. Now, whatever is going on at school, I do know the time comes to face things. I had to in prison. Seems like learning to now, for you, would make a whole lot more sense." Gabe heard the words, recognized them for ones his father had handed down to him when he was young...except for the part about prison. He hoped Brody did a better job of listening to them than he had.

"So they were right. The kids at school said you just got out of prison."

"Yep." He didn't like the fact that people were talking about him in Santa Ysabel. Seemed he might never live down his past and there was nothing he could do about it.

He focused on Brody. His prison record should

make the boy leery of him. Didn't seem to be the case. "You ready to go back now?"

Brody lifted his chin. "Try and make me."

So much for reasoning with him.

Brody crouched again, ready to fight, his dark brows drawn together in concentration as he circled, angry as a hornet.

The kid was too scrawny to have much of a punch in him, but Gabe would oblige if that's what it took to get him back to the ranch with Riley. Might even be good for him to release some of that pent-up frustration he seemed to be carrying around. Gabe stepped closer.

"I ain't scared of you." Brody lunged and threw his fist—a wild swing of the arm, too far from his body to have any power behind the punch. His knuckles glanced off Gabe's shoulder with the same thud of an acorn falling from the sky.

Gabe stifled a laugh, which Brody heard anyway and which spurred him on even more. He came back with a stronger punch to Gabe's chest. This one was solid.

Something about the boy—the defiance on his face and in his stance when he had started to fight—tugged at Gabe's conscience. He knew the moves Brody would make before he made them. Was it just coincidence? Just who was Brody's father? With each passing moment, he had the sneaking suspicion that he already knew.

In prison, Gabe's large size made other's wary of fighting him. Apparently Brody was so upset he wasn't even registering that reality. Although

Gabe seldom had to defend himself, he had done it enough to learn a few things about intimidation. He smiled slowly. "My turn now."

Brody's eyes widened at that and he took a few steps back. Gabe figured he would just haul the boy over his shoulder and walk down the hill with him. That should be humiliating enough. He took one step...

"Uh...Gabe?" Riley called softly.

The distinct sound of a rattler shaking its rings made him freeze.

Chapter Five

"Don't move, Riley. Not a muscle."

Gabe's smooth words registered somewhere inside. She could barely breathe. Her muscles tensed and yet her legs trembled. She didn't see the snake, but it was near...in the tall grasses? Under the shade of the boulder? Where? She wanted to burst away but that might make the snake strike and she knew she was not quick enough to escape its fangs.

She chanced a look up. Gabe stood atop the largest boulder and searched the ground for the snake. Brody had climbed up beside him.

"Ma!" Brody breathed out with fear mounting in his voice. He started forward...

"Don't. Move." Gabe thrust out his arm to stop her son and slowly slid his knife from his belt, his entire body tense. "It's in the grass right behind you," he said, his voice low and quiet.

Suddenly the knife whistled through the air.

It hit, and the snake revealed itself in a violent jerk. Riley broke away and dashed toward Gabe, her only thought was to get to safety.

With catlike grace, Gabe jumped to the ground and pulled her against him. "It's okay. You're okay." But his arm shook even as he tightened it around her. He held on as she doubled over and gasped for air.

She straightened and stared at the snake. It writhed in its final death throes. The knife's sharp point had sunken deep into the snake's hide just behind its head. Finally it quit moving.

Brody jumped from the boulder and rushed to her. "Ma! You coulda been killed!"

She blinked. Her heart still pounded. "I'm all right. I'm all right."

Brody stared at Gabe with something akin to hero worship.

Gabe let go of her and strode over to the snake. Carefully, he raised the snake's carcass, allowing it to dangle to its full length. It had to be at least four feet long.

"It's a beaut. Let's see if Rosaria will cook it up."

At that, Brody bent over and tossed up his breakfast in a small clump of weeds.

It was a small price to pay for having their lives saved. She was amazed Gabe's aim was so accurate. And she was grateful.

Gabe laid the carcass across a flat rock and carefully cut off the head. "Even after a rattler is dead you want to stay clear of the head," he explained to Brody. "The poison is in glands in the head and that can still bite you." He sliced the snake from neck to tail and quickly gutted it. Then he wiped his knife on the grass and sheathed it. "What if we hadn't come after you? That snake blended right into the grass. I wouldn't have noticed it except that it moved to coil. Looks like your ma had good reason to worry."

Brody swallowed hard. "Yes, sir."

Riley's mouth went dry. Gabe was acting like… talking like…a father. And her son was listening. She backed up, looking from one to the other.

"We are going to walk out of here slowly and carefully now," Gabe said, his voice tense and commanding. "Understand? That one snake means there are likely more." When he tilted his head, indicating Brody was to get going, her son started down the hillside.

She followed, hesitating only a second when she felt Gabe's grip on her upper arm as they maneuvered down the steep slope. Despite her cotton sleeve, under his touch her skin tingled. Knowing he would not let her fall, she was surer in her steps. When they reached the horses, he let go immediately. He pulled a burlap sack from his saddlebag, dropped the snake carcass inside and cinched it. The palomino pranced sideways, nervous at the scent of snake. Gabe quieted her with a calming hand before tying the bag to his saddle.

Her heartbeat finally back in a regular rhythm, Riley knew she had to say something. "Thank you, Mr. Coulter."

His lips pressed together the moment she used his surname. He gave a hard nod, then helped her mount her horse.

She had slipped up a time or two—enough that he probably knew she thought of him as Gabe even if she wouldn't call him by his Christian name. It was her way of keeping her distance—protecting herself—but she could hardly tell him that.

He untied the palomino and mounted, and then held out his arm for Brody to latch on to. Without hesitation her son scrambled up to sit behind him.

On the way back to the ranch Gabe rode ahead of her. Riley stared at his broad shoulders and the proud way he held himself on his horse and tried to meld the man before her into the memory of the youth she had once loved.

What would their lives have been like if her parents had allowed Gabe to court her instead of whisking her off to Philadelphia once they learned of their relationship? She would never know, and she supposed it was foolish to wonder now, but inside her, things were changing. The more he was around, the more she wanted to be with him. Before he'd been hot-blooded, and moody and, oh, so passionate. She closed her eyes, suddenly on fire at the image of his strong arms caressing her.

He had matured so much since then. He was just as strong, but now he was tempered in a way she couldn't explain. Did the old Gabe still lurk below the surface? Perhaps. Maybe that was the danger he spoke of. All she knew was that when he was around she felt safe. And that made her at once content, but also nervous. She mustn't allow herself to be swayed by him again. She knew, with a certain sense of fate, she would never recover from a second betrayal.

When they arrived at the lane leading to the ranch, Gabe pulled back on his reins and stopped the palomino in the shade of the tall pine at the corner. He helped Brody slide to the ground. "Your ma will be along directly. I want your word you won't run off again. And I expect you to keep it."

"All right," Brody promised, but he glanced at her, a question in his eyes.

She nodded. "I'll be there soon." Apparently Gabe had something to say, and after all he'd done, he had earned that much from her.

Brody started down the lane at a brisk jog. When he was far enough away that he wouldn't be able to hear them, Gabe spoke. "Up there on the hillside— that could have cost you your life."

"It is over now. And I'm safe. All thanks to you." Her words didn't have the reassuring effect she'd hoped for. Gabe still seemed agitated.

"I shouldn't have egged Brody on like that—encouraged him to fight. I thought he needed to blow off steam. All it did was put you in harm's way. When I think of what could have happened..." His jaw tightened. "Instead of walking down the hillside I could have lost you again."

Lost me again? Just what did that mean?

"Did he do this back east? Run off?"

She wanted to deny any problems she'd had with Brody. Paint a rosy picture of their relationship. Anything less would be admitting she couldn't take care of her son. But after all that Gabe had done for her today, she couldn't. "Sometimes. If he didn't want to do chores...or was angry. I'm sure all boys run off a time or two in their lives." *You did*, she felt like saying, but didn't. "I can handle my son. He's...adjusting. He'll get through this."

Gabe's silence revealed a lot more than if he had answered her.

She blew out a breath. "All right. There have been...difficulties of late. That is why I came home. So that my father could help with him." The mare she rode seemed as restless as Gabe. From the saddle, Riley repositioned the reins and turned her mare around.

Gabe reached out as she passed and grabbed the bridle. "Where was Brody's father when you were having this trouble back east?"

Her entire body tensed. "He wasn't around."

He narrowed his gaze on her. "The timing is right—fourteen years. And he moves like me—even acts like I once did. In my boots, what would you think about all that?"

She didn't answer. He had put two and two together just fine without any help from her.

"The alternative is that the moment you left me, you jumped right into someone else's arms. I didn't think you were that kind of girl." His tone held a touch of meanness. "Were you, Riley? Were you that kind of girl?"

Shocked, she slapped his cheek. Hard. "How dare you say such a thing! How dare you cheapen what happened between us." Her mare pranced sideways and tossed her head. "Let go of the bridle!"

"Not until this is settled." His dark eyes hardened to obsidian. Without releasing his grip on her horse, he dismounted. "Get down."

Her heart raced, and along with it her breath came in deep angry draws, but she didn't dismount.

"I deserve to hear it from you." His gaze raked over her, leaving a swath of blistering humiliation in its wake. "Why did you never send word that I have a son?"

Her heart told her one thing—that he had every right to be assured he was Brody's father and she should have gotten the message to him long ago—but she couldn't forgive him for deserting her. He had left her on her own to answer to her father's anger and her mother's criticizing. *Gabe used you!* Mother had cried. *He only wanted revenge and the easiest way to get it was to ruin my innocent daughter!* The memory froze her response.

In that moment of silence his jaw tightened further. "You really are a Rawlins. I'm not good enough, is that it?"

She couldn't bear the condemnation in his eyes...his beautiful, moody, brown eyes. "That's not it at all!"

Gabe's teeth clamped together and he let go of the bridle, suddenly setting the horse and her free. "Think I've had enough of you Rawlinses. Just go. Get out of here." He slapped the mare soundly on her rump which, with a jerk, sent her galloping down the lane toward the ranch. It was all Riley could do just to hang on.

He had completely misinterpreted her silence.

He was wrong! All wrong! The words screamed inside. All except for the fact that Brody was his son.

In the yard, she dismounted and left her horse in the corral. Anxious to be alone, she raced to her room. She couldn't face him again—not now. She'd yell or pummel him or, worse, cry. She had to get hold of her emotions before confronting him. What right did he have to question her actions after what he had done?

But he was right. She was a Rawlins—and a Rawlins did not resort to histrionics. Ever.

She paced the room, unable to calm down. What would he do now? Would he tell Brody? Would he try to take her son away? She had believed that coming back home would fix everything. But this wasn't the new beginning that she had imagined at all! Things were only getting worse. Everything was falling apart.

Gabe could barely breathe. Brody was his son. His flesh and blood.

It was written all over Riley's face and in her actions. He had wanted the truth, but he hadn't meant to be cruel. He rubbed the sting from his cheek. Guess he got what he deserved.

He had a son! He blew out a long breath.

Why hadn't she told him when she first knew? He would have made a life for them. He didn't have much back then...mostly guts and foolishness when he thought about it, but... He sank down on the boulder that marked the end of the lane. Who was he kidding? He'd had nothing back then. Certainly not enough to take on a wife and baby.

He thought back to the last time he'd seen her. They'd only made love once, and without hesitation he was sure it was love on both their parts. He'd been furious after seeing Rawlins leave his cabin and then his ma so distraught. He'd wanted to charge after the man right then but was scared of the rage inside and that he couldn't control it. He knew Riley waited for him at the waterfall…and so he'd gone to meet her. She had talked him down from his anger only to have one act of passion exchanged for another. Her sweet, tender kisses had absorbed his pain and his first attempt at loving her had been a release of pent-up need and desire. It was afterward that he had told her he loved her.

But now Riley had become like her father.

He wasn't worthy. He was half Kumeyaay, he didn't own any land and he didn't have property, not even a horse, to his name. But the fact remained— he had a son! Reality quickly tempered his elation. He had a son who thought of him as the hired help and an ex-convict. A son who didn't know squat about him or how to ranch or how to be a man. A son who should have known his father all along.

Like barbed wire in a bundle, it was all a tangled mess.

Slowly Gabe rose to his feet. He walked over and grabbed the palomino's reins. It wouldn't all be figured out in one day. He had some thinking to do and the bunkhouse was not the place to do it. He needed to get away for a spell.

As he reined his horse away from the lane to the ranch the thoughts clamored inside of him, tying him up in knots of frustration and something more that he hadn't experienced in a long time...hope.

"Brody! Where are you?" Riley called out, finally emerging from her room. He didn't answer her. She found him lying on his bed, a sullen look on his face, tossing a work glove up at the ceiling and trying his hardest to ignore life.

"Why did you bring me here, Ma? I don't fit in. Out here everything is different."

She sat down on the end of the bed. "It will take you more than four days to adjust. Tell me what happened at school."

"One of the kids started in on me—saying I was living with a killer, saying I might be next. I didn't think it was true so I lit into the kid. The teacher broke us up...said the stupid boy was right. That Mr. Coulter had been in prison." He scowled.

She lowered her shoulders, relaxing. "I couldn't very well say it right in front of him. Brody... Mr. Coulter grew up on a small ranch with his folks not too far from here. Time changes a person. I haven't been sure about him. That's why I told you to keep your distance."

Her son snorted. "Well, he just saved your life. That counts for something."

"It does. And I'm glad he was there. Besides snakes there are cougars and coyotes and even bears here. Usually they will leave you alone, but not always. If you go away from the house I want you to have someone with you who can shoot a gun. Eventually, you'll learn how to handle one yourself."

Brody's demeanor perked up at that.

She patted his boot and rose to her feet. "I'm going to have a talk with your grandfather." Glancing once more at her son, she then headed down the stairs in search of her father.

She found him on the front porch. "I see Senor Padilla is gone. Did he buy the stallion?"

"Yes." He took a draw on his cigar and blew out the smoke. "Coulter find you?"

She nodded.

"Figured that's what he was doing taking off like that."

"He saved my life. I was nearly bitten by a rattler."

Her father looked startled at that. "What happened?"

She explained about Brody's tussle with Gabe, the rattler and then Gabe's deadly aim with his knife.

"I better keep him on then," he mused. "Seems Coulter is proving himself more and more every day."

"Proving himself? What do you mean?"

"I hired him, thinkin' he'd fail. I didn't expect him to stick it out mor'n a week or two. But that evening when he challenged me about his family's land, there was something different about him—a strength that hadn't been there before. He was proud, demanding answers, yet there was humility, too. As much as he considered me a rival for that land, he thanked me for burying his mother. That took character...and a bit of gumption." He rubbed his whiskered jaw. "Maybe it is time to set a few things straight."

"Things? What things?"

He looked at her as if contemplating telling her more, but then shook his head. "Has he figured Brody out yet?"

"You are changing the subject, Father."

His bushy gray brows drew together but he didn't reply.

Dismayed, she answered him grudgingly. "I didn't say anything but...yes. I think he is pretty sure now."

"And Brody?"

"He still doesn't know. I don't know if Gabe is going to say anything to him." She hugged herself, rubbing her upper arms. "I have wanted to return here for so long. I thought this would be a fresh start for Brody—a fresh start for me. I sure didn't expect Gabe. Now I don't know what will happen."

Frank leaned on the porch railing with both hands and gazed over his ranch. "Your reason in coming here, and Coulter's, too, is to figure out your place—your future. For him, it's to earn back his property. Not all change is bad." He took another draw on his cigar and then flung the stub to the dirt. Walking down the steps he then ground it out with his boot before looking up at her on the porch. "You both might just belong here more than you know."

She watched him stride to the bunkhouse, his last words echoing inside her, giving her a sense of home. After prison Gabe was struggling to regain his place in this world as much as she was. Could she fault him for that? Of course not. But what did it mean for the two of them now?

"I suppose I had better find him and talk to him," she murmured and looked toward the corral. Her horse stood there pawing the ground, still saddled. Gabe had never returned to take care of the mare.

Chapter Six

From the porch, Gabe stared at the land that once was his. He had to figure out what, if anything, he was going to do with the fact that he had a son… and that Brody was a Rawlins. The other hands were rounding up cattle in the back country and none of them would be coming by to check this part of Rawlins's property. He could hole up awhile and think through a few things. Heck…he had that rattler he could eat, water from the well and all around him an abundance of dandelion greens. He was fit for more than a week if need be.

He stepped inside the house. Memories came rushing back at him…his father sitting by the fireplace, oiling his rifle, his mother making tortillas on the open hearth. He'd like Brody to know about his folks. There was a lot he'd like to tell him… teach him. Things a man should teach his son. Things his father taught him.

He headed out to the meadow where his parents' gravestones stood side by side. Sitting down cross-legged in the grass, he stared at the stones and fisted his hands beneath his chin. What would he do now?

He wanted to continue working for Rawlins. He

was learning a lot about managing a ranch even though Rawlins might not suspect it. But to see Riley every day and to keep on acting as though she didn't affect him…how could he do that? The need to be near her was a gaping hole in his chest that grew larger every minute. There was no future in it, no hope, especially when he would never be good enough in her eyes to…

To what? Be Brody's father? Be…someone special to her again?

If he stepped in…told the boy he was his father… Brody might hate him. An ex-convict for a father? Telling him might only make things worse. The kids at school had been rough enough just knowing that Gabe worked at the ranch. What would they be like if they found out he was Brody's father? It would be tough on the boy. He might even get kicked out of school because he had Indian blood in his veins. That's what had happened to him at the ripe age of twelve. If Riley wanted Brody in school, Gabe had to keep his mouth shut.

The pounding of hooves on the hard earth broke the stillness of high noon. He glanced toward the sound.

Riley.

He rose to his feet and crossed his arms over his chest as she reined her mare before the house. She had always been a natural at riding, with a fluid, graceful seat as though she was born for the saddle. She caught sight of him and jumped down, then tied the reins to the gate. Her steps slowed as she neared, moving from the bright sunlight into the shade of the oak.

"I thought you might be here."

He nodded. Trying to keep in mind that to her, he wasn't good enough. That he'd never measure up. But…she had come after him. She was here now.

"Are you coming back?" her voice was husky with worry.

He looked down, aware of the concern in her pretty green eyes. It came to him then, that he had to know there was more to go back for. Not just the land, not just a job. He had to know that *she* wanted him back. Enough to put everything right. *Everything.*

"Would it make a difference to you?"

She hesitated slightly. "You should come back… work off the debt to this land. After all, it really is your land."

"I know where I stand with the land. I'm talking about where I stand with you."

"Then…yes. Of course. You did just save my life. It would be good to have you return."

She sure didn't want to admit much. Guess the feelings between them were only one-sided—from him. That made things easier…and harder at the same time. He huffed out a breath. "Be sure, Riley. Because if I come back, I'm coming back as Brody's father."

The color drained from her face. "No. That's not possible. Do you realize how that will look with me living there and you working there? The gossip? The…stares? I can't do that to my son. Things have been difficult enough for him as it is."

"For him! I've been cheated out of years with my son! *My son!* How do you think that makes me feel?"

She raised her chin. "I'm surprised you care at all. Especially when you used me and then deserted me."

"What? What are you saying? I didn't desert you."

"You left me. After we were…together…I had to face my father and my mother. I defended what I thought was our abiding deep love. Silly me."

He should have suspected that Rawlins would never tell her. No wonder she'd been on guard with him since she returned. "You don't know what happened. Two of your father's men took me to the border and held me there. When they finally released me, you were well on your way east."

The shock and confusion in her eyes confirmed it. She'd never known.

"He said it was a lesson to cool me off. That I wasn't good enough for you and never would be."

"I never thought that! Not once. But when you didn't come for me…"

He heard the hurt in her voice and hung his head, avoiding her gaze. "Guess he got to me. I thought maybe he was right. I wasn't good enough."

She pressed her hand to her forehead. "Oh, Gabe…I didn't know!"

"I see that now."

"When you didn't come back to the waterfall

the next night…or the next one…I began to question things. That afternoon you said that you hated my father. I thought…what happened between us… was your vengeance."

That she had been thinking like that all these years left him cold inside. "You've got things all twisted in knots. Just so we're clear…Brody was made with love, not revenge. That night we made love."

She swayed slightly. "Oh…oh!"

He took hold of her arm to steady her.

Her eyes misted as she looked up at him. "I wanted so badly to believe that. But my father… my mother…"

"Guess they had both of us questioning things." Reluctantly, he let go of her.

"What a mess." She walked away a few steps and then turned to face him. "I didn't know I was with child until after I arrived in Philadelphia. When I didn't hear from you, I came to believe you had used me. It was easier that way to…to justify things." She blinked back tears, her long black lashes spiked and wet. "That is why I didn't return, and that is why you never learned that you had a son."

"So you admit it straight-out. Brody is mine."

"Yes," she said softly.

He'd known inside, but he had needed to hear it from her. For a moment he couldn't say a thing and just let the certainty that he was Brody's father spread through him and settle into his bones.

She met his gaze, her voice resolute. "And I

never thought you weren't good enough. That is your fears talking. Not me."

He whipped off his hat and raked a hand through his hair. "Riley... If only I'd known...I would have helped."

She turned away from him. "You weren't in any position to help. You and your mother were barely making it after that fever took most of your cattle."

"I would have married you."

"We were kids. And knowing now about my father's interference, I understand how things happened. I...I'm not angry about it anymore." She turned to face him. "At least...not with you."

"You still don't believe I cared."

She pressed her lips together. "Not enough. You didn't come after me."

No, he'd been like a crazed man—angry at Rawlins for dragging him away, angry at Riley for leaving him and angry at his mother for whatever had happened with Rawlins in the first place. Then, on top of that, he'd been unsure he was right for Riley. He'd let Rawlins's words get to him. "I can't change the past. I wish I could."

Finally her tears spilled over.

More than anything, he wanted to pull her to him and hold her—to comfort her as she had once comforted him so long ago. He didn't. There was something more important, and he wanted to see her face when he said it—

"I'll marry you now."

Her mouth dropped open. "But...you barely know me anymore!"

"I know you, Riley. And I haven't been able to get you off my mind since you came back. I nearly lost you up there on that hillside. That cleared things up in a heartbeat."

She stood there absorbing his words, appearing half in shock, her face clouded with uncertainty.

Desire for her had tugged at him relentlessly since her return. He studied her upturned nose, her stormy green eyes. Between them, they'd never done anything slowly or sensibly. It had always been one wild ride. He slipped his hand behind her neck. He waited, knowing she could sense what would come next. She could pull away, but she only stared at him with a look of inevitability... and wanting.

He slammed his mouth against hers.

She trembled and her lips softened under his— and parted. She slid her hands up his back. Just like that, the need for her gripped him and would not let go. He deepened the kiss, his heart pounding in his chest.

In her throat her pulse throbbed, there where his palm touched her skin. She wanted him, too—as a woman wanted a man. He sensed it as she pressed herself against him, as her breath shuddered in her breast.

His body responded rapidly. At least it hadn't forgotten how after being locked away for all those years. He had to get control of himself, but the softness of her lips, her skin, her warmth...he didn't want to stop. If only she would give in to him. He'd carry her to the cabin. He'd force himself to go slowly...be gentle...

Riley pushed against his chest.

And his hopes came crashing to a halt. Reluctantly, he pulled away from her.

"Gabe...I..." she said in a stunned voice. Her chest heaved with the breath she dragged in. She put her hands to her flushed cheeks. "Gabe... Oh..." She took another step back.

He was breathing hard, too. He turned away from her in an effort to calm himself.

"I'm sorry," she said, her words halting. "I...I didn't expect..."

He wasn't sorry...not for the kiss. Only sorry she seemed upset now. Finally in control, he faced her. "Make no mistake. I wanted you then and I want you now."

"I need...time."

"You've had fourteen years."

Her small jaw tightened. "There is more going on here than just you and me. There's Brody...and my father."

"Your father..." he repeated slowly. Rawlins would still probably object to them being together—even more so now that Gabe had been in prison. What man would want his daughter marrying an ex-convict? And Gabe had to keep working if he was ever going to buy his land back, ever going to make any kind of a home for her and Brody. That sudden realization brought him up short. "Guess your father still holds all the cards," he said, the words sitting like acid on his tongue. "But a boy should know who his father is."

"I know that. It's just…I'm not ready."

"There will never be a perfect time," he said, sensing that he was losing her. "We could do it together."

She shook her head and backed away. With each step she took, her face closed off a little more. "I'm sorry, but I need more time. Come back to work if you want, Gabe, but understand…the only way you are welcome on the Golden R is as Gabe Coulter, the ranch hand."

Something cold congealed in his gut. He'd lost. Even with the truth between them now, she didn't want him. "That's what you want?"

"Yes."

He blew out the breath he'd been holding. "Then I'm not welcome at all." He turned and walked across the yard and into the house.

Riley stared after Gabe until he closed the door. What had just happened? Was that some kind of backhanded proposal she'd just been a part of? One minute he was saying he would marry her and kissing her blind, and the next minute he was walking away! Just what had happened? All she had wanted was time…a little more time! Didn't he understand that she was doing the best she could for Brody?

She took hold of the saddle, ready to mount and then stopped. Or…was she the one who didn't understand?

A boy should know who his own father is. Gabe was right. What right did she have to keep it a secret from Brody? Or keep Gabe from his son for one more minute?

She collapsed against the sun-warmed leather. She didn't want to leave things like this. She believed Gabe now…about loving her back then. And, oh, how she had loved him. Could they get back to that point? Was it even possible after all the lies and misunderstandings?

She squeezed shut her eyes. What was the right thing to do?

Time. She needed time, just as she'd told him. She climbed into the saddle, took one last look at Gabe's small homestead and reined her horse away and down the lane.

When she arrived at the ranch she left her horse in the corral and marched straight into the house and found her father. He was eating a solitary lunch at the dining table.

"I just got back from seeing Gabe." Her nerves were on edge with all that she'd learned.

He put his fork down. "So it's Gabe now."

She paced back and forth in front of him, unable to settle down. "All those years ago why did you tell me he left when in fact it was you who dragged him off?"

"You both were too young. You needed to grow up."

"What about later? After you learned of Brody? Why have you let me believe all these years that he deserted me? Do you know how much that hurt?"

He frowned. "Nothing can change that now."

"I still want to know why!"

He wiped his mouth with his napkin and set it on the table. "Once my men released him, Coulter didn't come back. Even his own mother didn't know where to contact him. A year later I learned he was working on a ranch down south—a hundred miles away—and sending money home. I left word for him to come see me, but he never did. Can't say as I blame him. He had his pride. After that I lost track of him until I read in the newspaper that he killed that ranch owner. At that point, I didn't see how telling the truth would help anyone." He placed his big, gnarled hand over hers on the table. "I regret some of what happened. That's one reason I felt compelled to hire Coulter and keep him on even when I knew you were on your way here. I know it isn't easy for you. As for me...I don't want to lose you again. This is a lonely old house without you and Brody."

She would not let him sway her. How much had he stolen from Gabe...from her? She pulled her hand from his. "What happened with Gabe's mother?"

"Ramona?"

"Gabe thinks you...and his mother... He saw you coming from the cabin." She couldn't say it more directly than that.

He frowned. "Now wait a minute. I checked on Ramona from time to time to make sure she didn't need anything. Neighbors do that. I respected her. And I respected Gerald's memory. It was Coulter's job, but he was hardly around." He peered at her. "Apparently he was spending time with you."

She glanced away, embarrassed.

His shoulders slumped. "I'll have a talk with him...if he returns."

Chapter Seven

Gabe didn't come back to the ranch the next day—
or the next. Brody was sure she'd said something,
done something to upset him. She tried to keep herself busy, teaching Brody how to saddle a horse,
how to mount and dismount, and all the while her
heart was slowly breaking all over again.

She had wronged Gabe…she realized that now.
And she still loved him. Her life would be only a
shadow of a life without him in it. If only she could
trust that Brody would be better for knowing that
Gabe was his father. If only she could let down her
guard and give in to what her heart wanted. Had
she ruined everything by asking for a bit of time to
think things through? Would he ever forgive her?

The evening of the third day, the ranch hands
returned with a bevy of young calves. The entire
place was in an uproar as the men prodded and
maneuvered the cattle into a holding paddock behind the stable. Rosaria complained about the dust
and the stink of man and beast while she hurried
to feed them all.

Riley distanced herself from the commotion.
She didn't care about the ranch…not when Gabe
wasn't a part of it. Looking over the dust rising

from the cattle pen as the sun set, she made up her mind. She would ride out to Gabe's ranch and talk to him—try to convince him to come back—as soon as it was light.

On rising the next morning, Riley heard shouts and mooing. In the hall, Brody let out a whoop and then pounded on her door. "Coulter's back!"

Jumping from her bed, she pushed aside the curtains and looked out the window. Gabe rode a black horse through the herd, cutting the young calves out and roping them. He would pull them to another, smaller holding pen where they would anxiously call for their mothers. He had rolled his shirtsleeves, and his face carried a sheen of sweat as he jumped from his mount to untangle his rope from the legs of a calf.

She slipped her arms into her cotton robe, her heart a thousand times lighter than when she'd gone to bed the night before, and opened the bedroom door to her son.

Brody rushed to the window and peered out. "Look at him ride! I gotta learn to ride like that." Then he turned and raced from the room, leaving the door wide-open in his wake.

It warmed her heart to see him so excited after the past few days. She walked to the window. Gabe had his back to her. He removed his tan Stetson, raked his fingers through his thick black hair and resettled his hat. His broad shoulders bunched as he gathered his rope. He stopped, half-done, and twisted on his saddle, looking up at the open window. Their eyes met.

An invisible current pulled at her. And she knew with a certainty he still wanted her and was waiting—waiting for her to decide—waiting for her to come to him. She moved away from the window and began breathing again, the breath shuddering out of her. Heaven help her...she wanted him, too. In her life, in Brody's life, in all ways. She just didn't know how to make it happen.

Quickly she dressed, intent on what she would say to him. She descended the stairs and heard voices coming from the study. She recognized Gabe's. Her father quieted when he saw her at the door. "What is going on?" she asked the both of them.

"Just clearing the air about a few things," her father said. "Coulter is heading back out now."

She needed more than that for reassurance. "So you are staying?" she asked Gabe.

He slipped on his Stetson. "Yes, Miss Rawlins. For now."

For now?

She followed after him. "Wait! What do you mean...for now?"

He stopped in the kitchen, waiting for her. "Just what I said," he replied, his voice low and serious, his brown gaze piercing her. "I did some thinking the past few days. I've done enough running over the years. I've got reason to stay here." He swept the back of his fingers down her cheek, leaving a trail of sizzling heat, and then lightly brushed his thumb over her bottom lip, leaving no doubt what one of his reasons for staying would be. "So I will...and

I'll play by your rules… For now." He turned and walked out the door.

Dazed, she simply stood there and watched his easy saunter to the stable. He might as well have kissed her as touched her cheek. The effect would have been the same—tingles all over her body. Years ago his first kiss had been sweet and tentative. The one the other day, and the way he had looked at her just now, said he was all grown up and wanted what a man would want. *For now*, he'd said. Which meant he wouldn't wait forever.

A noise behind her made her turn. Her father stood in the doorway that led to the dining area. How long had he been there?

"I explained about his mother and me. I think he believes me. It's too bad Ramona passed on before he could ask her about it."

"Did he happen to say why he came back?"

Her father tilted his head slightly, studying her.

Warmth spread over her cheeks. She could no longer hide her feelings about Gabe, and her father wasn't dense. He must know by now that she felt more than just a passing concern.

"He didn't mention anything in particular. 'Course he does want to pay off the taxes on his land. Likely that's the most of it." He shoved his hands in his leather work gloves and headed outside toward the corral.

The day was long and hot and the air full of dust that the cattle stirred up. Riley helped Rosaria make lemonade and sandwiches for the men. It seemed she would make one trip out to the pens and by the time she returned to the kitchen, it was time to make more.

She kept an eye on Brody, who sat on the fence, watching the activity all around him. After a while, instructed by her father, he jumped down and started herding the calves one at a time into the chute, supplying a constant stream of bawling calves to Gabe. At first unsure and a bit hesitant, it wasn't long before her son was as dirty as the rest of the cowhands. He seemed to enjoy the hard work much more than he'd ever enjoyed school.

By evening they were all worn out and tired. No one talked much during supper. After helping Rosaria clean the kitchen up, she found her father snoozing in the large parlor chair. She tiptoed upstairs to her son's room and peeked in. Brody lay sprawled out, facedown on his bed, asleep in his clothes.

She should be exhausted, but instead a vague restlessness gripped her. With the busyness of the day, she had not spoken with Gabe privately. Over and over her thoughts recalled the look in Gabe's eyes that morning.

The moon was full when she crept down the stairs and out to the stable. Glad that no one else was around, she quickly saddled the small mare. Once astride, she rode up the deer trail into the wooded area behind the house and followed the creek that divided Gabe's family land from the Rawlinses' spread. She now knew her destination—the waterfall.

Up near the ridge a six-foot waterfall spilled

into a pool on what had once been Gabe's land. It had been a favorite place when Riley was young. A rope hanging over the water from the branch of an oak made it a fun place to cool off. She could use that about now. Gabe had kissed her there for the first time in her life—a tentative, searching, sweet kiss—a first kiss for the both of them.

The next time they met at the pool had been much different—a passionate seeking of two souls. They had made love—she was sure of that now—and started a baby.

The sound of water trickling over the boulders indicated she was close to the secluded pool. She dismounted and tied her horse to the branch of a pine and then stepped onto a huge flat boulder that overlooked the water. The reflection of the full moon rippled in the gentle current and there, waist-deep in the cold spring water, stood Gabe.

Had he come for the same reason she had? Hot and restless?

She couldn't keep from staring—at his wet, blue-black hair, at the muscular curve of his shoulders and chest, and at the beads of water that clung to his smooth skin. Once she had stroked those curves. At the memory, tension curled inside. Deeper, a warmth spread rapidly through her.

She sat down on the boulder, dangling her feet. Gabe started toward her. Without saying a word, he removed one boot and stocking and cupped the cool water over her foot. The touch of his warm hands along with the icy water on her skin sent shivers coursing through her—and goose bumps. He removed her second boot and stocking and did the same with more water. He didn't release her foot, instead trailing his fingers around her ankle, and then slowly moving his hands up her calf, under the hem of her split skirt, to her knee.

She forgot to breathe.

He moved closer to stand between her knees, stroking each hand slowly up the outer aspect of both of her ankles, to her calves, and to her knees. Then he circled his fingers over the tops of her legs and to the inside trailing his hands back down to her feet.

She started breathing again. Parts of her tingled that had no business tingling. "Gabe…"

"Shh…"

When he pursed his lips like that, all she could think about was kissing them. "Gabe…" She leaned closer. His warm breath tickled her ear and a shiver swept through her.

His eyes darkened and suddenly he was kissing her—tender, warm and breathtaking. He cradled her head and his kiss became more insistent. She parted her lips and he took her with his tongue. He stirred feelings in her that had been long dormant. Hot, and at the same time cold, she leaned nearer, craving his touch. It had been so long since she'd been moved like this. She knew instinctively that he was the reason. She had never wanted anyone but him. She looped her hands behind his neck, her arms languid and heavy as she stared into the depths of his brown eyes. "You were right when you said you could be dangerous, Gabe Coulter.

After all these years, you still have power over me. It's so dangerous to play at this."

The corner of his mouth quirked up slightly. "It's not play to me. I am very, very serious."

He captured her with a look that made her swallow hard. He wanted more—was asking for more. Once she crossed that line, there would be no turning back and things would only get murkier. "Please, Gabe…"

He leaned in and kissed beneath her ear on one side and then the other. "Please what?"

"We should talk."

He hesitated for a brief moment and then kissed the base of her throat, his breath warm and exciting on her neck. "Right now talking is the furthest thing from my mind."

She shuddered as a delicious sensation coursed through her and lifted her chin to allow him further access. A sigh escaped from her when he pressed even closer, his chest up against her as he nuzzled her neck. His breath was ragged and uneven now. She felt the same—wanting to consummate their newfound desire…but she couldn't. She just couldn't. Not until words were spoken…not until vows were said. At that thought, she let out a strangled cry. Smoothing her palms over his shoulders, she forcefully pushed him away. "No, Gabe. Allowing this to continue will only make things worse. I want you for always…not just one night."

He pulled back. He opened his mouth to speak but no words came out.

She swallowed. She had as much as said she would marry him…that she wanted to marry him!

He sank into the pool, letting the water cover his head. He surfaced and with several powerful strokes he swam to the far side and stepped from the water. His nude body glistened in the moonlight for just an instant before he gathered his bundle of clothes from a bush and sprinted into the cover of the woods.

Her skin was on fire. She scooped up a handful of cool water and patted it on her face. Then she pulled on her stockings and boots. Before any time had passed, she heard the rustling of leaves and then footsteps behind her.

"More easy now?"

She nodded, still not trusting her voice after what she had just seen.

"Good. At least one of us is." He took her hand and helped her to her feet. "Are you sure? About what you just said? Or did you say it to stop things?"

"Maybe a little of both."

His shoulders lowered in resignation.

"Gabe…I can't deny that I still care. I do. But… how can it work? What are we to do?" she said on a sigh. As she uttered the words, she realized something had changed inside her. She had said *we*.

He must have sensed it, too. "I love you, Riley. That will never change. You and I…we've always been stronger together than apart. I wish you could trust that."

The tenderness in his eyes, in his words, overwhelmed her.

He took hold of both her hands. "You were right about taking some time. Guess we both needed that. I've had a few days to think things over. I wish I'd been there for you...and for my son. It couldn't have been easy to raise him on your own. We can't go back and fix things, but I don't want to let one more minute go by without you in my life."

She hadn't expected it to affect her when he called Brody his son. It did. It sounded wonderful. The fact that he still wanted her after all this time...still cared for her...began to seep inside. The way he looked at her, the hope in his eyes made her feel special and beautiful and stronger. "Oh, Gabe. I want that, too, but..."

"You're scared," he said, his voice flat.

"Aren't you? A little?"

"No."

"Where will we live?" With the question, she realized that she had made up her mind...and she had chosen *him*.

A slow steady smile grew until it lit up his face. "We'll figure it out. Trust me."

"I do."

After seeing Riley back to the ranch house, Gabe took the mare to the stables and unsaddled her. His hopes had been riding high during the walk, but now they were tempered with reality. He didn't expect Rawlins to give his blessing. Likely, Rawlins would do what he could to stop the entire thing. Gabe being a hired hand was one thing—over the past months they'd come to have a tentative respect for each other—but marrying his only daughter was something else entirely.

Which meant they had to leave.

He had to find a job elsewhere. Maybe even move into town. That thought made him die just a little on the inside. He'd do it so that Brody could finish his schooling. But Nuevo was too close. There'd be stares…and gossip. He'd have to figure out something else. Maybe they should travel north…get completely away from the area. He'd seen plenty of nice-looking towns over the years.

Suddenly the enormity of what he was giving up—the dream of getting back his family's ranch—washed over him. Yet in all of the worries, there was one thing more important than all the rest—despite his past, despite his prison record, Riley wanted to make a life with him.

He couldn't let her down.

It was time to face Rawlins.

Chapter Eight

"Boots on, Coulter."

Gabe opened his eyes. Towering over him, one on each side of his bed, stood Johnson and another man with a star badge. A sheriff. An iron cuff clasped onto his wrist and the sheriff turned the key. Gabe's heart raced from zero to a hundred in the space of a second.

Johnson hauled him up from his straw pallet to his feet.

"What's this all about?" Gabe fumbled—one-handed—with his boots.

The minute they were on, Johnson yanked Gabe's free arm around to his back and secured it with the other iron cuff. His shirt still hung open, unbuttoned, but there was nothing he could do about it. "You're going back to jail. Can't change a rooster's feathers. I told Rawlins you weren't to be trusted."

With the ruckus, the others in the bunkhouse started to rouse.

"I have a right to know what I'm being arrested for."

"Oh, I think you know good and well. Johnson says you were gone half the night," the sheriff said.

"Somebody get Frank Rawlins. Let him know I'm taking Coulter in."

With a tilt of his head, Johnson motioned to a ranch hand. Then the foreman shoved Gabe ahead of him into the yard with enough force to land Gabe on his knees. He heard the door of the ranch house open and he scrambled to his feet.

Whatever was going on, there was no way he was going back to prison. Spending any more time inside that concrete fortress would kill him just as surely as a bullet would. A bullet would be faster...

For an instant Gabe contemplated trying to run. His muscles bunched, his pulse quickened... But then he saw Riley and Brody rushing out of the house behind Rawlins. Guess he wouldn't run... not yet anyway. He didn't want to be flattened with a bullet in front of Riley and his son.

Rawlins strode down the walk. Had he learned about last night? Was this his way to separate them again? Just put Gabe back in prison with a trumped-up charge? Gabe's gut rebelled at the thought. Rawlins wasn't the same man who had ordered men to drag him away. He'd changed over the years. They all had.

"What's going on?" Rawlins demanded. "Sheriff?"

"Patrick Odom won a sizable amount at the poker table last night and then was murdered. When I discovered his body behind the saloon, the money wasn't on him. Tracks led back here."

"I didn't do it," Gabe said. "I wasn't anywhere near town."

"Well, you are the logical place to start," said the sheriff, drawing his gun. "You killed a man before. It's not a long jump to think you would do it again."

"We had a full day of branding cattle yesterday," Rawlins said. "My ranch hands were dog tired last night."

"Apparently not all of them. Doesn't account for the tracks I found."

Rawlins rubbed his whiskered jaw and shook his head. "This is serious business."

Beside him, Johnson gripped Gabe's upper arm and squeezed hard. "About time he recognized you for what you are," he said under his breath.

Gabe knew the reality. He was an easy mark. The sheriff would stop looking for any other suspects as soon as he locked the cell door. Riley had to be having second thoughts about marrying him now. She would realize he was too much of a risk to bring into her life and into Brody's. Heck, in her boots *he* wouldn't marry himself with his odds.

"Can you account for your time after your duties were finished yesterday?" the sheriff asked.

Gabe avoided looking at Riley. He wasn't about to drag her into this. Saying anything about being with her would ruin what was left of her reputation. He met the sheriff's gaze. "I wasn't in town. That's all I will say."

"Coulter's telling the truth."

Gabe snapped his attention to Rawlins. He was vouching for him? The man who had caused him nothing but grief?

"And you know this for a fact?" the sheriff asked. "You saw him here on the premises last night?"

Rawlins stared the sheriff down for a moment and then finally admitted, "No."

"Much as I respect your standing up for your ranch hand, believing a man doesn't carry much weight. He needs an alibi." The sheriff let his gaze touch on every ranch hand there. "Anybody else notice anything last night? Otherwise I'm taking Coulter in for questioning."

Gabe darted a look at Riley. She stood next to Brody, a few paces back from the tight group of men. She stepped closer. A shaft of fear sliced through him. She couldn't be thinking to say something! He shook his head in a small tight movement.

She stopped, the anxious look on her face replaced with confusion. He shook his head again. He wouldn't have her putting herself out there for him. This was his problem. His fight.

She glanced at Brody and in that moment he realized she didn't care about the rest of the men. It was her son's reaction that she worried about. For a fleeting moment Gabe thought back to when he believed his mother was seeing Rawlins. He set his mouth. He didn't want Brody thinking those kinds of thoughts about Riley.

She opened her mouth to speak.

"Let's get this over with, Sheriff," he said, curtailing her words.

"All right then. Mr. Rawlins, if you could spare a mount..." the sheriff said as Johnson jerked Gabe toward the stable. A ranch hand ran ahead of them, appearing a moment later with the gelding. Between the two of them, they got Gabe up into the saddle.

He should have known something like this would happen—especially the way Johnson had been acting toward him. He'd never be free again—not really—not with his past. Why hadn't he realized that? Even if by some lucky coincidence the sheriff found the real killer, he would always be looking over his shoulder, expecting a noose. He chanced one more look at Riley, knowing it might be his last. The fear on her face tortured him. He straightened and looked away. He'd gone from soaring hope to hopeless in a matter of hours. *Just get me out of here.*

The sheriff mounted his own horse. Taking the lead rope to the gelding, he started down the lane. Behind him, Gabe heard the men start talking— some laughing, some defending. And he heard something more...

"No. Please. You can't take him."

He looked over his shoulder and saw Riley running toward them. "No, Riley! Don't!"

She hugged his leg, and he felt his heart bottom out in his chest. She would ruin herself...

"He didn't do it," she called out to the sheriff. "You have to believe him!"

Surprised, the sheriff halted his mount and turned to her. "Miss Rawlins?"

"It wasn't him."

"I need more proof than that. How do you know it wasn't him?"

"Because he was with me."

The quiet of the morning was broken only by the cawing of a Steller's jay as it soared overhead and landed in a tall pine. Gabe swallowed. It was out now and there was no taking it back. He darted a look at his son. Brody stared at his mother with a look of shock and horror on his face. Guess that answered Gabe's question—the boy knew about what went on between a man and a woman. Last night had been innocent enough...but the flush resting on Riley's cheeks right now would lead to all kinds of speculation among the men.

The sheriff dismounted. "Then the tracks are yours? Are you saying that you went into town?"

She shook her head. "No. I saddled the pinto and rode east."

"East?" he said derisively.

"To the pool where I met Mr. Coulter. If you check, you'll find the mare's tracks lead there."

"You bet I'll check that out. That still doesn't explain the tracks coming from town. Until I'm sure, I'll keep Coulter with me." He took hold of his saddle to mount again.

Despair filled Gabe. It didn't matter what Riley said...he was going to jail. The man was set on it.

"But..." Riley said slowly, as though she were just remembering something. "When I saddled Gracie last night, another horse was missing from the stable—the bay mustang."

The men turned their attention to Johnson. That was his horse.

"Now wait just a minute. I didn't kill anybody,"

Johnson said, backing up. "Sure. I went into town, had a few drinks… But I didn't kill anybody."

"Interesting that you didn't tell us about that right off." The sheriff reached up behind Gabe and removed his handcuffs. "You are coming with me, Johnson."

Gabe quickly dismounted, rubbed his wrists and breathed a sigh of relief. It happened so suddenly. All of his hopes, his dreams, had nearly been ripped from him and now… What would happen now? He finished buttoning his shirt and darted a look at Riley. She stood beside him, looking as unsure as he felt. How much had she given up in helping him? How much did she regret it now? He took hold of her hand and felt her grasp him tightly.

Brody gave each of them a disgusted look and dashed into the house.

Johnson mounted the horse—Gabe noticed the sheriff had cuffed him with his hands in front— and they started down the lane.

"You men get to work. There are still calves left to brand," Rawlins ordered before turning back to Gabe. "Coulter, I'll speak with you in my study. You, too, Riley." He headed for the porch, clearly expecting them to follow.

Gabe still couldn't quite believe Rawlins had stood with him. He had a feeling that one instance of camaraderie was now over after what Riley had done. He turned to her, worried about her now. "You didn't have to do that. I would have figured something out." He was half angry she'd said something and half relieved. He wasn't in this alone—and that felt mighty good.

"I did. I couldn't lose you again," she said, her voice tremulous.

It was the same thing he'd said when the rattler threatened her. He cupped her face. Gave her a quick reassuring kiss.

"What now?"

"Now, I guess we best hear what your father has to say." Gabe wasn't looking forward to a verbal flogging. Likely he wouldn't have a roof over his head come nightfall.

Together, they walked inside and down the hall to the study.

"Take a seat," Rawlins said from behind his desk. "You, too, Riley."

Gabe ignored the command and was pleased when Riley remained standing right beside him. He squared his shoulders.

"What happened at that pool, whether it amounts to anything or not, won't be confined to the ranch after today. You can bet Johnson will talk it up in town," Rawlins said with a frown. "Something must be done."

"That something is… I'm marryin' your daughter. It's time we were a family…something we should have been all along."

Rawlins raised a brow. "I've just gotten my daughter and grandson back. You think I'm going to let you take them away?"

Riley swallowed. "I don't want to leave here,

Father, but I do want to marry him. And—" she squeezed Gabe's hand "—I'm old enough now."

Instead of reacting with anger as Gabe had expected, Rawlins leaned back in his chair and focused on him. "So...you were willing to let the sheriff take you away to protect what's left of my daughter's reputation."

He remained quiet.

"And she was willing to give up that reputation...for you." Rawlins shook his head. "I wonder what Brody must think of his mother's confession. It's not the kind of thing a fourteen-year-old boy cares to learn about his mother—similar, wouldn't you say, to your own thoughts about me? A bit uncharitable."

Gabe tightened his hold on Riley. There wasn't much he could say in answer, but he could clear up his debts. "Thank you for vouching for me."

"You've done a good job for me despite the rancor of a few of the men, especially Johnson. It's time to set things straight. Your new life together shouldn't begin with lies."

Gabe nearly choked. Rawlins was not going to try to prevent them from marrying? Not that Gabe would have let him...

"So," Rawlins said, his gaze shifting to Riley. "When do you plan to tell your son that Coulter here is his father?"

A strangled noise in the hall drew his attention. Gabe spun around. On the stairs Brody jumped to his feet. His eyes were wide with shock. "Mr. Coulter...is...my father?"

Riley stepped toward him. "Brody...listen..."

He gripped the banister, his knuckles white. "All this time you could have told me and you didn't?"

"It was for your own good! He was in prison! I didn't know what kind of man he was anymore," Riley said quickly. "We...we should talk about this...together. You, me and Gabe."

With that, Brody bolted down the rest of the stairs, slammed through the front door and ran from the house. She hurried after him. "Brody! Stop! Let's talk about this!"

He ignored her. Throwing open the corral gate, he jumped onto Gabe's palomino and reined it through the open gate. No bridle! No saddle! With the little bit of experience he had, Gabe had no idea how the boy managed to stay on. Probably grit and determination and anger all rolled into one.

Gabe raced around Riley and rushed to stop the horse before it dashed by. He waved his arms hoping to stop the beast. "Hold! Hold!" he yelled, but the palomino simply swerved and galloped down the lane, dust and dirt flying. Without taking a breath, Gabe raced to the stable and bridled the gelding. Swinging up onto its bare back, he reined it around and galloped after his son.

The palomino's tracks down the lane and across the meadow were easy to trace. Dirt clods littered the trail along with broken branches. It amazed Gabe that Brody hadn't fallen off immediately. Actually made him proud. Twice the horse had jumped over small boulders in its path and Brody had managed to stay astride.

It was the third jump over a small creek that finally dislodged the boy.

Gabe came upon him sprawled out on his back in the dirt, half in and half out of the clear water. Gabe jumped down from his mount and rushed over to him. A scrape on Brody's forehead oozed blood. He moaned and relief speared through Gabe. He was alive.

"You promised me you wouldn't go running off."

Brody scowled. "And you lied to me!"

He would deal with that in a moment. "Wiggle your feet in those fancy new boots of yours. Now raise your arms."

"Why?"

"So I know you didn't break your neck, boy!"

Grimacing, Brody did as he asked.

"You hurt anywhere?"

Brody gave him a flat look. "Everywhere. Where's the horse?"

With that question, Gabe finally relaxed. Brody was all right. Seemed he just had the wind knocked out of him. Gabe looked around and spotted the palomino. "He stopped farther downstream for a drink."

"Figures."

Gabe almost chuckled with relief. "You did a heck of a job hanging on all this way."

"Looks like I come by it naturally," he said sarcastically.

"By that you must mean your mother."

Brody met Gabe's gaze squarely. "Nope. That's not what I meant."

Gabe recognized the uncertainty there—behind the bravado. Brody looked so much like Gabe felt on the inside. "We'll talk about it, but your mother should be with us when we do."

Brody snorted.

"Whenever you are ready, I'll help you up."

"Why would I want your help?" Brody ground out. "You left us."

Gabe didn't care for the attitude. "That's not how it was. I didn't know you existed until this week. And just so you know…I loved your mother then and that has never changed. I still do."

"Then it's her fault."

"It's easy to place blame—not so easy to be right about it. And in the long run, blame doesn't do anything but twist you up inside. You need to hear her side."

Brody struggled to sit up on his own. When Gabe reached to help, he jerked from his grasp. "I can do it myself." He rubbed the back of his head and then slowly got to his feet. "All right. Let's go hear her side."

Gabe stood and crossed his arms over his chest. "As soon as you catch your horse."

Brody scowled.

"You wanted a riding lesson? This is it. You fall off, you get back on."

Brody hesitated and for a moment Gabe wondered if another tussle would occur, but then the side of his mouth quirked up in a half grin. Brody stuffed his battered hat on his head. "Okay...Pa." He turned away to go after the palomino.

Gabe swallowed past the lump in his throat. He was new at this, but realized the situation called for more. "Wait." He walked over to Brody and studied his face, seeing his own father's mouth and green eyes and the smaller ears of his mother. It was like seeing himself for the first time. In another three years Brody would be the same age he had been when he fell in love with Riley.

He wrapped his arms around the boy in a bear hug. His father had done the same with him at important times in his life. This was one of those times. He had a family, and now Brody had one more person in his life who would stand with him. He closed his eyes and murmured, "My son."

Brody's body stiffened and then slowly he slipped his arms around Gabe's waist. Hesitantly at first, and then tighter and tighter, his son squeezed him back.

Gabe held on. Bone-deep joy coursed through him. For the first time in a long time, he felt grateful. He had something precious to live for. Something precious to fight for. A lump swelled in his throat. He lowered his arms and stepped back, embarrassed that he couldn't talk for a moment. When he glanced at Brody, he realized the boy was struggling with the same feelings. He swallowed. "Now go get that horse."

Chapter Nine

Riley waited on the porch. Would they come back together? Or would there be distance between them and a frozen wall of hurt to get through on Brody's part. Or worse…would Gabe be carrying her son because he was injured?

It was near noon, the sun straight overhead, when the two returned side by side, leading their horses. No one else was in the yard. They led their mounts to the corral—Brody holding on to the gelding's bridle and Gabe having wrapped his shirt around the larger palomino's neck in order to guide him. Gabe latched the gate and then shrugged into his shirt, buttoning it while she crossed the yard to him. She stopped short before reaching Brody. Was he still upset? Would he reject her?

He hung his head and fumbled with the loose bridle in his hands. "I'm okay, Ma. Sorry I took off."

Relieved, she enfolded him in a hug. "No broken parts?" She looked him over, raking back his hair to examine his scrape. "You scared me half to death!"

"Better go clean that scrape," Gabe said.

"Then we will talk? Like you said?" Brody asked.

Gabe nodded. "Hang up the bridle, too."

Brody walked into the stable. She turned back to Gabe. "Thank you. That's twice now you've helped us."

"That's what a family does. They look out for each other." His deep brown eyes searched hers. "You did the same for me."

She placed her hand on his chest, feeling the steady beat of his strong heart. "I loved what you said in there to my father. I want to be a family more than anything. I never want to be separated from you again." Beneath her hand his chest expanded.

"You'd be giving up a lot," he warned.

She smiled. "Are you trying to back out now?"

He shook his head and covered her hand with his. Words weren't necessary. He leaned down and kissed her tenderly.

At the sounds of footsteps approaching from the stable, she wondered what Brody must think of her kissing Gabe…but then everything around her faded and all she could think about was the man who held her. She wanted to be his completely and forever.

When they broke apart, he looked up to the house. "I need to clear something up with your father. He said it was time to set things straight. He's right."

At Gabe's determined tone, she glanced at Brody. His eyes were wide. Together they followed Gabe as he strode to the house and disappeared inside.

* * *

Rawlins was bent over before his small safe, dialing the lock when Gabe entered the study, ready to negotiate. "I need to know exactly what I owe for my family's property."

Rawlins withdrew a wooden box and rose to his feet. "I agree. You do need to know the exact amount." He held out the box.

Gabe took it and smoothed his hand over the rich finish and intricate carved design on the lid. "I remember this. Ma kept it on our mantel. Why do you have it?"

"Ramona gave it to me for safekeeping. Open it."

Gabe unlatched the lid. Inside lay a silver and turquoise cross with a chain—one he'd seen his mother wear for many years. He swallowed hard. He didn't need emotion clogging his thoughts. He was here to discuss his property.

Beneath the cross lay a folded piece of paper. He unfolded it and realized he held the deed to his parents' ranch. He looked up at Rawlins, unsure what to think. Surely the man couldn't be giving it to him.

"Laws here don't allow a Kumeyaay woman to own property. When you ended up in jail, your mother was beside herself for fear that the sheriff would come and force her from her land."

"She came to you?"

Rawlins nodded. "I bought it from her."

So there was more than the property taxes he owed. Gabe braced himself. "How much?"

"A dollar."

"A dollar! I could have paid it off right away!"

"Yes. But there was also the matter of back taxes, which were considerably more. I figured you could work that off. Besides, I needed a good trainer and you needed a job."

Gabe swallowed. Guess he could accept that reasoning.

"I also had to be sure, for your parents' sakes, that you were ready to settle down and take care of it. You've been running for years. I needed to know that you got all that out of you." Rawlins narrowed his crystal-blue eyes. "I expect that you have."

Gabe could barely breathe. What was Rawlins up to now?

"Now, I don't want to see my daughter and grandson or, for that matter, Ramona and Gerald's son, moving away in search of another place to live when there is plenty of land right here."

Gabe looked down at the box, his heart racing with a strange new feeling. He was afraid to hope… "You are giving it to me?"

"No. You owe me a dollar. When you pay me, I'll consider us even."

He still couldn't quite believe it. "You always wanted that patch of land."

Rawlins shrugged. "I have enough land…land that Brody will inherit one day if he learns to run it. What I don't have is family. Or, at the moment, a foreman."

Riley looked up at him, her gray-green eyes shining and full of love. No question there that she hoped he would take her father's offer. Brody, too, looked eager for him to make that choice. He swallowed.

"You've earned it, Mr. Coulter," Rawlins said, extending his hand.

Gabe stared at the man's scarred work hand. Could it really be that simple? He thought back to all that had happened over his life. No...not simple.

"You have a deal, Rawlins." Gabe shook hands with him and felt a new sense of completeness. He thought back to the last time he'd struck a bargain with this man and remembered hating every second of it. He sure hadn't expected anything like this to happen—not in any future he'd envisioned.

Chapter Ten

Gabe stood at the graveside of his parents next to Brody. Over the past week he and his son had spent hours here at the ranch, clearing brush and readying the place for the wedding. Riley had insisted on the old homestead for the ceremony, saying it would feel as if his parents were part of the moment. He only hoped it was a good omen. If his marriage came anywhere close to theirs, he would be happy for the duration.

The sheriff had stopped by two days ago and told him that an itinerant peddler confessed to the crime in town after someone noticed him wearing Odom's handmade neckerchief. He also mentioned that Johnson was working on a spread farther south as a regular ranch hand. Gabe had the feeling that, with the timing of his visit, the sheriff was wrangling for an invitation to the wedding. He didn't quite know what to make of that but invited him just the same. He told his son that for once it couldn't hurt to have the law on his side.

He ran a finger under the scratchy collar of his new shirt and tugged it away from his skin. He couldn't remember the last time he had brand-new clothes. Beside him, Brody mimicked his actions, pulling at his cuffs also. Then they both had to cinch up their bolo ties again.

Hearing the creak of a carriage, he checked the road. Rawlins pulled the horse and rig to a stop in front of the cabin. He'd brought the preacher. Behind him came a wagon carrying the ranch hands and behind them were two more carriages with the nearest neighbors. This was turning into a bigger hullabaloo than Gabe or Riley had wanted.

"Guess it's time," he said to his son.

Brody grinned. "You sure about this?"

"Never been so sure about anything in my life."

Rawlins knocked on the door to the cabin and a moment later, Riley stepped out.

Gabe's breathing ceased. She looked like an angel. She wore an ivory dress with turquoise trim and a lacy turquoise shawl. Her hair was tied up on top of her head with a crown of tiny yellow and blue flowers from the meadow. Wavy strands of honey-colored hair fell this way and that and were looped up and pinned again loosely.

She saw him and smiled, and then took her father's arm.

Unaware he'd even moved, he found himself waiting next to the preacher with his son beside him. When Rawlins placed Riley's hand in his, Gabe realized the man's eyes were moist.

"I'll take good care of her, sir," he promised.

"See that you do."

And then he was holding on to Riley and she was squeezing his hand as they turned to face the preacher.

He felt a persistent tickle at his wrist and glanced down. Brody wrapped the silver and turquoise cross and chain around his hand and Riley's, binding them together. His mother's cross.

Riley laid her other hand on his chest, covering his heart. "I came here hoping for a new start for Brody and myself. Instead, I found you. There has never been anyone else, Gabe. I love you...still. I always will." As she spoke her vows and slipped a gold band on his finger something inside his chest finally loosened all the way and released. He was where he was supposed to be and with the woman he was supposed to be with. He would never let Riley go again.

He said his vows, conscious only of her before him as he slid a ring on her finger. Then he kissed her and hooked the silver chain around her neck. The special look in her eyes touched him...warmed him. He brushed the smooth skin beneath her ear with his fingertips and was rewarded with a shiver. Already he was learning what she liked.

She looked up at him with those pretty gray-green eyes and smiled a smile only for him. *Tonight*, it promised...

Then people—mostly ranch hands—surged forward, shaking his hand and congratulating him. Gabe was astonished at the support he felt. Neighbors he had known as a boy welcomed him back to the area. By the time they all climbed into their respective conveyances and headed to Rawlins's ranch, where Rosaria had cooked up a small celebratory party for everyone, he felt overwhelmed with his good fortune.

Under the large oak at the ranch, a wooden platform had been built for dancing. When he took Riley in his arms and started swaying with the mariachi music, he thought his heart might burst with happiness and pride. A whoop erupted and he and Riley looked up to see Brody grinning broadly from the first branch of the tree.

Gabe pulled Riley close and swept a strand of hair from her face that had loosened in the breeze. The small bouquet of wildflowers she held tickled his neck as he bent down and pressed a kiss on her waiting lips. He held the kiss until he felt her weaken and go limp in his arms.

When he pulled back, her eyes were misty and slightly out of focus, but they held complete trust…and a promise that she was his. It hadn't been easy to get here, to this place. He felt as though he'd been through a long dark tunnel and was finally stepping into the light of a new dawn. "You wanted a new start…"

She sighed. "And spring *is* the best time of year to begin…"

He grinned. She was so easy to love. "Ready for forever, Mrs. Coulter?"

"With you? Always…"

And she kissed him.

* * * * *

WHEN A COWBOY SAYS
I DO

Lauri Robinson

Dear Reader,

I love spring—don't you? The trees are budding out, new shoots of grass pop up in order to send down roots and draw water during the summer months, the southern birds return, hibernating animals reappear and show off their young ones, and the days grow longer and longer. It's a time of new beginnings—which makes it the perfect time for weddings!

Several years ago my husband planted fruit trees along our driveway—plum, cherry and crabapple—and I absolutely adore it when they are all blossoming. There is a big bush of wild roses there as well, and the air smells so good I've been known to stop and just smell the roses.

I hope you enjoy reading *When a Cowboy Says I Do*, and that you like Dal and Ellie's journey as they venture through a final snowstorm before arriving at their spring wedding!

Lauri Robinson

Dedicated to Dallas and Liz
for loaning Dal and Ellie their names.
Love you both! Mom.

Chapter One

Buckley, Kansas
1884

Dal Roberts pinched the bridge of his nose and drew in a deep breath, trying in earnest to control his temper. Being an older brother was hard enough, but at times like this, when he was more of a parent than a sibling, he wished to high heaven their mother and father were still alive. He wished that at other times, of course, just not as reverently or as selfishly as he did right now.

"Clara," he said slowly.

"Please, Dal?" she interrupted. "With sugar and cherries on top? I won't have my dress in time if you don't."

"You have a hundred dresses upstairs."

"Not a wedding dress," she argued. "Ellie is sewing one for me, and she knows exactly what to buy. She's never gone to Wichita, never been on a train, and she's so excited to go. And…"

Dal braced himself. There were always several *ands* when it came to Clara, and the mere mention of Ellie Alexander's name made his spine stiffen.

"…she can go to the cattlemen's ball, so you won't have to attend that alone."

That tore his final nerve. "I don't care if I attend the cattlemen's ball or not. The only reason I accepted the invitation was because I knew I'd be chaperoning you and Ellie. Now that you can't go, none of us will go."

That, to be truthful, was a great relief. Dal would rather spend six straight months on a cattle drive than one hour with two giggling girls—not that Ellie Alexander was much of a giggler. She rarely cracked a smile. That wasn't *his* fault, but that clearly wasn't the way she saw things.

"You have to go," Clara said. "To the meeting and the ball."

He would regret missing the cattlemen's meeting—the fact that sick cattle were infecting herds statewide needed to be addressed—but he would not regret missing the ball. That was the cattlemen's wives' idea, giving them a reason to tag along with their husbands to the city. He hadn't enjoyed a single one of their frivolous events over the years, and this one wouldn't be any better.

"No, I don't," he argued. He could send a wire to make sure his points were addressed.

Clara's big blue eyes filled with something as close to compassion as he'd ever seen. "Yes, you do. You have to go so Caroline will know she didn't break your heart by marrying Ed Mansel."

Ten minutes ago he had been concerned that his younger sister's injury might be life threatening and now he wanted to strangle her! Which was often how things were. He loved her to death, even while she drove him crazy.

"A meaningless ball is the least of my worries. I agreed to go because you wanted to go. And Caroline did not break my heart by marrying Mansel," he said seriously. "I'm glad she married him."

He'd had no intention of marrying Caroline or anyone else. Having one woman around the house was a handful—throw in the nosiest housekeeper this side of the Rockies, and he had more than enough women telling him what to do. That wasn't going to change anytime soon. Especially as Clara wasn't moving anywhere even after marrying Bill, which was fine by Dal. The Rocking R Ranch was as much hers as it was his.

"And that's why you have to go," Clara said. "Everyone from here to Wichita thought you two would marry, and now they think she broke your heart."

A sigh built in his lungs, mainly because she was right. At least she was right about the part where everyone seemed to believe he was heartbroken. "What other people think is of no concern to me."

"Yes, it is," she persisted. "It always has been." Meeting his gaze, she added, "And you have to go to the meeting. The Texas fever epidemic is getting closer every day."

No one had to remind him of that. He lived and breathed for the cattle on the Rocking R. But Dal was done arguing, so he crossed his arms and changed the subject. "How does the foot feel?"

Clara shook her head at the way he'd changed the subject but knew better than to push too hard. "It hurts, but Doc says I'll be fine by my wedding day." Her bottom lip started to quiver. "If I have a gown, that is."

Dal clamped his back teeth together and prepared to stand his ground, but he was spared having to say anything more as Doc Fisher returned to the room.

"That's not exactly what I said, young lady," the doctor said to Clara before turning to address him. "Dal, this little gal cannot, and I repeat, *cannot* walk on this leg. Not for six weeks. She broke two bones in her ankle. I set them, but the slightest pressure could shift them and she'd be lame. Of course, I could always try to rebreak them if that happens, but—"

"Rebreak them?"

Clara's gasp sent a shiver up Dal's spine, just like Doc Fisher's statement had, but it was the tears in his sister's eyes that stung his heart. He knelt down beside the sofa she was lying on in the front parlor to say softly, "He won't have to rebreak them."

"If she stays off her feet."

Dal shot a glare toward the doctor, letting the man know they both had heard him the first time. When he turned back to Clara, his stomach hit the floor. He'd never been able to say no to her, and today was no different.

He was going to Wichita.

With Ellie Alexander.

A woman who blamed him for the death of her father, despite the fact that her father had been the one at fault. What had the man expected when he chose to rustle Rocking R cattle?

Chapter Two

The shrill whistle of the number 1917 was still fading when Jamison Linkletter shouted a warning that the train would be departing in five minutes. The volume of the conductor's announcement wasn't necessary. She was the only one at the depot.

The excitement that had filled Ellie for the past few days was no longer there. It had disappeared shortly after she'd arrived at the train station. The empty train station. Clara was nowhere to be seen. Neither was her older brother, Dal. He was the reason Ellie had walked to town rather than accepting Clara's offer to pick her up in their carriage. Clara had seen the Alexander house, but Ellie didn't want Dal to see it. Not ever. The sod shanty was home, and she was thankful for the protection it offered, but Dal already looked down his arrogant nose at her. He didn't need any more ammunition.

As steam hissed out of the train's engine, Ellie surmised that all those hours she'd spent worrying about him seeing her home and about being in his company for four days had been a waste of time. Those worries had eaten at her insides and had been the reason why she'd tried to get out of going, even though saying no to Clara Roberts had been hard.

So hard, in fact, that it hadn't worked. Clara had come up with an answer to every excuse Ellie had provided. Including her lack of funds.

Wrapping the front folds of her coat, which was several sizes too large, tighter around her, Ellie glanced at the short road that led from the depot through the heart of Buckley and then farther west, all the way to the Rocking R Ranch. There was quite a bit of traffic—horses and buggies, people in wagons and those traveling afoot. There was no sight of Clara or her brother.

Ellie couldn't deny the sense of disappointment rising up inside her. As much as she hadn't wanted to go to Wichita, she'd secretly relished the idea of seeing the city. She'd looked forward to the shops, the people, staying in a hotel with running water and real beds. She'd been looking forward to the train ride, too. As a person who went everywhere she needed to go on foot, a train ride would have been a thrill she'd never forget. Dal had probably put his foot down and said no, he wouldn't pay for Clara to take a friend with them. Especially not *her*.

After giving a final glance up the road, and emptying her lungs into the chilly March air, Ellie bent down and picked up the tattered traveling valise that held the best of her meager clothing. It was just as well she wasn't going. She wouldn't have fit in in Wichita any more than in Buckley, or anywhere else other than the sod shanty with no windows and its dirt floor. Her brothers were right when they said that weeds can grow in flower gardens, but sooner or later, they get pulled out and tossed aside. Unwanted.

She might as well dream about changing the moon into the sun instead of becoming someone other than Ellie Alexander—a cattle rustler's daughter.

"Hold up there, Jamison!"

The shout echoed amid the shrill screech of the whistle, and Ellie snapped upright at the sound of Dal Roberts's voice. It was a commanding voice, one that was listened to in Buckley.

His horse, a huge palomino, was breathing hard as its hooves slid to a stop next to the platform. "And find someone to take Trigger to the livery for me," Dal added, swinging a leg over the saddle. Once on the ground, he untied two large leather bags. Spinning toward her with a bag in each hand, he nodded at the train. "We best get aboard, Miss Alexander."

It took a moment for Ellie to regain her senses, and her brain didn't actually start to function until he stood right beside her, making her heart thud. "Wh-where's Clara?"

"She's unable to accompany us," he said. "Getting out of the house without her took longer than getting out of the house with her."

"Why—why isn't she coming?" Without waiting for an answer, Ellie added, "I can't go without Clara."

"I'm afraid we don't have a choice. Move along, now," he said urgently, once again gesturing toward the train with his chin. "I'll explain on the train."

Ellie opened her mouth to protest, only to hear the train whistle sound again. Dal shifted his bags into one hand, and took her arm, pulling her toward the metal steps. He was a tall man, and strong, but she might have been able to dodge his hold if her mind had been functioning. It wasn't. The next thing she knew they were in the passenger car, stumbling down the aisle as the train jerked forward.

There were a few others on the train, including a woman with two children, an old man with a big nose and watery eyes, an older couple sitting side by side, and a man with his hat pulled over his eyes and his boots resting on the seat across from him.

Dal propelled her toward the back of the car where there were several open seats. Walking was awkward with the train's unstable movements and she more or less fell onto one of the wooden benches as soon as he released her arm.

After tossing their bags onto the floor between them, Dal sat down across from her. Set upon averting her gaze in order to get her nerves under control, she pretended to examine the car's soot-coated windows and mud-covered floor as the train's jerky movement became smoother. The rumbling and hissing quieted, leaving just the sounds of the car rattling as they rolled along.

"Clara broke her ankle."

Dal got her full attention with that.

"What?" she asked. "Broke her ankle? How?"

"Running down the stairs," he answered.

"Oh, heavens. When?"

"'Bout four hours ago. Doc says if she walks on it at all, she could wind up lame."

Concern leaped inside Ellie's chest as her heart sank at such an idea. Clara was the dearest person. She was kind to everyone, and generous, and about the most beautiful woman one would ever see. Her eyes were the deepest blue, and sparkled so brightly when she spoke that people couldn't help but smile, and her brown hair was naturally curly and so thick she could poke a flower behind her ear and it would stay there all day even without a pin.

"Lame?" Ellie repeated softly. "Dear me. She must be so distraught, so..." Her thoughts shifted slightly. "What are we doing leaving her? You should be there to take care of her, and I—"

"She has Mrs. King taking care of her, as well as Bill. He's never far from hand."

Mrs. King was the housekeeper at the Rocking R and Bill Thorson was the man who Clara was so excited to be marrying. Those two were truly and sincerely in love. Bill was a ranch hand who had grown up on the Rocking R right alongside Clara. At least, that was how Clara had explained it. Ellie couldn't imagine ever experiencing the kind of feelings Clara had for Bill, but then again, it wasn't likely she ever would. Marriage was not in her future. She'd had enough of taking care of men with just her two brothers. She'd been catering to them, it seemed, since the day she'd been born, and that wasn't about to end anytime soon. They couldn't so much as boil water. It was just as well, as it wasn't likely any man would ever want to marry a cattle rustler's daughter.

Swallowing around the lump that formed in her throat, she focused her wandering thoughts back on her friend. "Without Clara, there is no reason for me to go to Wichita."

"She says there is," Dal answered. "She says you're sewing her wedding dress and must make this trip in order to have it done by her wedding day."

"That is true," Ellie said. "I will sew her dress once I have the material, and I will have it done by her wedding day, but I could have given you a list of items, and—"

"No," he interrupted. "I'm not traipsing in and out of dress shops to buy silk and lace or anything else." He leaned back and looked at her thoughtfully for a long moment. "Why didn't you just order what you needed from Silas?"

"I suggested that, but Clara didn't want to. She said Mr. Thatcher would probably get the order wrong, and that she wanted to go shopping for the material, not just settle on whatever he managed to get in."

Dal nodded. "She's right that Silas might get it wrong. It took him three tries to get in the perfume I ordered for Clara for Christmas. It almost didn't arrive in time."

"She really likes that perfume," Ellie answered.

"I know she does. It's the same one my father always bought for my mother."

The lump in her throat returned—or maybe it

had never left. It was always there when she was around Dal. "Yes, she mentioned that," Ellie managed to answer.

He glanced out the window briefly before turning back to her. "Well, Miss Alexander, I hope you are up for completing Clara's list on your own."

Having never stepped foot in a store other than Silas Thatcher's, Ellie had no idea what she was in for, but she unabashedly answered, "Of course I'm up for it."

"Good, because Clara's counting on you." Leveling his stare at her until she felt it right at the center of her bones, he added, "I will not allow my sister to be disappointed, so I'm counting on you, too."

His blue eyes, which were the same shade as Clara's, were so intent, so serious, that Ellie couldn't have spoken if her life depended on it, but she did muster up a slight nod of acknowledgment.

"While we are on that subject," he continued, "if your sewing skills are not up to the standard Clara believes them to be, please tell me now."

Ellie opened her mouth to tell him she'd been sewing for years, but the words wouldn't come out. Shirts made for her brothers held little comparison to a wedding gown. This was her first attempt at something so intricate, something so important, but if Clara's dress was half as gorgeous as how she pictured it in her mind, the entire town would be talking about it, and she'd finally have a way to make money. Enough money that someday the sod shanty would be but a memory.

"As I said, I won't have my sister disappointed,"

Dal repeated. "She's been dreaming of marrying Bill since she was no more than ten. Making her wait until she turned eighteen was not an easy feat. But she's done it, and she'll have the wedding I promised her."

Thankfully Ellie's voice had returned—at least she hoped it wouldn't fail her a second time. "I would not want to disappoint Clara any more than you would, Mr. Roberts. I am fully aware of how much this wedding means to her, and also how much her wedding gown means to her."

"But can you sew it?"

His arrogance, that attitude he had whenever she was around, grated on her nerves. She had no idea whether he was the same with others—she'd barely seen him except for the few times she'd visited the Rocking R at Clara's invitation. He might be far richer than she, and an extremely handsome man who left girls giggling in his wake, but in her eyes he was nothing more than a cowboy. A man who cared more about cows than people. The very kind of man she never wanted anything to do with. He might think he was something special, but he wasn't. He wasn't some sort of supreme being, put there by the Almighty to look down upon others. She understood all of that very clearly. He, it seemed, did not.

"Yes, Mr. Roberts," she answered. "I can sew it."

The gaze that roamed over her and spent a significant amount of time on her old and much-too-large coat and the skirt of her well-faded dress said he clearly had his doubts.

"I'll believe that when I see it."

Although he'd barely uttered the words, she'd heard them and they stung. Anger zipped up her spine faster than a bee could sting. Insults were not new to her, and living with two brothers had taught her how to fling gibes back as fast as she could sling rocks. "Excuse me?"

Chapter Three

Dal rarely regretted anything he said, but right now he did. She was to blame. Every time he got within ten feet of Ellie Alexander he felt like a greenhorn tossed upon a saddle for the first time. That was why he tried to stay as far away from her as possible. There was no logical reason for him to feel that way, and he was a very logical man, which was why it irritated him so badly.

Knowing crow was better eaten warm than cold, he drew a breath and apologized, "I beg your forgiveness, Miss Alexander. I'm afraid Clara's mishap has left me rather irritated. I should not have taken it out on you. You have my word I won't do it again. If Clara wants you to sew her dress, then you are the one who will sew it." If that meant he would have to oversee every stitch she made in order for the dress to be up to his standards, he would do that, too. Clara and Bill had obeyed his rules as promised, and he'd fulfill his promise to them by providing the most elaborate wedding Buckley had ever seen.

If the blush on Ellie's face was any indication, he'd guess his apology had caught her off guard.

Which could be a good thing. He had a feeling that keeping her off guard might be his best approach.

"Th-thank you," she stammered. "In turn," she continued, with her voice gaining more stability, "I promise that I will not disappoint either Clara or you with my sewing abilities. Her dress will be precisely what she wants."

Her chin had risen as she spoke, and whether he wanted to or not he had to appreciate her resilience. Much like he did her beauty. With eyes as brown as coffee and her long, straight hair so black it literally shone, there were few more lovely than Ellie. That, too, had concerned him recently. With her living out in the middle of nowhere with her two brothers, Dal wondered about her safety every time she left the ranch. He wondered who knew where the little sod shanty was located. And how many hours her brothers left her alone out there with no protection other than a dog the size of a horse. At least he assumed she still had that dog. It had been years since he'd ventured out to the shanty shortly after her father had died.

Lester Alexander had been caught red-handed stealing cattle, and had been hanged on the spot, along with his brother, Ellie's uncle Alfred. Dal's father had been among the men who'd hanged the brothers, but Dal's mother had been the one who'd taken food to the Alexanders afterward. His father had been mad that she'd hauled Dal along with her. At the time, Dal hadn't liked it much himself, but over the years he'd come to understand his mother had been teaching him a lesson in life. That there are two sides to every story and the outcomes of every action ripple out to far more people than just those directly involved.

He'd been ten when his mother had taken him to that sod shanty, which meant it had been sixteen years ago.

Dogs didn't live that long. He looked up. "Whatever happened to your aunt?"

As her eyes widened and she swallowed hard, he realized he'd asked aloud the question that had shot into his mind. The way her teeth sank deep into her bottom lip had regret floundering about inside him again. Damn, he was a greenhorn when it came to her. The next four days were going to be the longest of his life. That idea didn't please him in the least, and when things didn't please Dal, he always tried to change them. Surely today should be no different.

"We're going to be spending a considerable amount of time together the next few days, Miss Alexander," he said. It was time to face the topic that was always just below the surface when she was near. It couldn't stay buried that long. "We might as well accept that, and how uncomfortable we make each other."

Both of her dark eyebrows rose into perfect arches. "Uncomfortable?"

"Yes," he answered. "Uncomfortable. It's quite obvious you don't like me, and that's understandable, considering the history between our families." He paused briefly before saying, "Yet, you've befriended Clara."

"It's impossible not to befriend Clara," she pointed out.

"That is true. She's a very likable person."

"And an honest one." She appeared to relax a bit then, sitting back in her seat rather than perching on the edge as she had been. "Evidently, that runs in your family."

"Evidently?"

She nodded. "You're right, I don't like you, but it has nothing to do with the history between our families."

"Oh? Then why is it?"

Glancing around the car before slowly leaning forward, she hissed, "Because you are an arrogant ass."

Dal couldn't stop himself. His roar of laughter had all the other passengers looking their way, including the old cowboy who lifted a corner of his hat to peek out beneath the rim.

"I guess we're now even," he said.

She removed the hand she'd thrown over her mouth to ask, "Even?"

"Yes, one insult for another." He released another chuckle as he shook his head. Ellie Alexander had more guts than he'd given her credit for.

Her cheeks were bright red, but her eyes turned dark. "You find that funny?"

"I think I find it admirable, Miss Alexander."

"Admirable?"

"Yes. I'm aware that some people have described me just as you stated, but none have had the courage to say it to my face."

"I may not like you, Mr. Roberts," she said with a hint of nervousness, "but you do not scare me."

He had to wonder if she'd said that to convince herself more than him. Whatever the case, he said, "You do not scare me, either."

"Then again," she said smartly, "we're even."

Dal wasn't sure he would say that, but he leaned back and relaxed. Taking off his hat, he laid it on the seat beside him. "So, whatever happened to your aunt?"

Ellie wondered if she should answer. Keeping quiet truly seemed to be the best option as the less Dal knew about her and her family the better. But a knot forming in her stomach didn't completely agree. It told her he already knew anything there was to know.

"How about that dog you had?" he asked.

The softening in her chest had her responding without thinking. "Samson?" She'd cried for weeks after the dog had died, but now his memory brought nothing but fondness. "He died a few years ago," she said. "Of old age."

"That's too bad," Dal said with enough sincerity that she believed him. "I'd never seen a dog that big. Haven't since."

"Since when?" she asked. "When would you have seen Samson?"

"Shortly after your father died," he answered. "I went to your place with my mother. Your brothers were there, and your aunt."

"I must have been there, too," Ellie said. "My mother died a few days after my father." At two, she'd been too young to remember the event, but had been told the tale often enough that it was now seared in her memory as if she did recall every minor detail. How Mrs. Roberts had brought over baskets of food, and how her mother and the baby she'd been carrying had died that same day. In the bed Ellie still slept upon every night. However, she hadn't been told that Dal had been with his mother.

"I didn't know that was when your mother died."

Ellie lifted her head. "Few did. Considering the circumstances."

"I can't be blamed for your father's death. Only he can be blamed for that."

"I never said I blame anyone." And she didn't. But James and Daniel, her brothers, certainly did. Aged five and six, they had been old enough to remember everything, and to this day they still held responsible anyone who had anything to do with the Rocking R for the death of their father.

"You don't need to say it."

Ellie leveled her gaze on him. "No, I don't. Do I?" If that was what he wanted to believe, it was fine with her. She wasn't here to make friends with him. She was here because of Clara, her one and only true friend.

They stared at each other for a length of time. Long enough that the rumbling of the wheels and the rattling of the carriage no longer echoed in her ears because all of her thoughts shifted to focus on why she should care if he thought she blamed him or not.

"What happened to your aunt?"

It was a moment before she realized he'd spoken, and by then, her mouth had already started to answer. "She left five years ago."

"Left?"

That event she did remember. "A drifter came through looking for work, to earn enough money to further him along. The next morning he was gone and so was Aunt Jenny. Along with the small amount of money we'd had." Ellie let out a sigh, mainly to release the thoughts that surfaced when she thought of her aunt. She didn't begrudge her. It was more that she envied her. Aunt Jenny had had the courage to walk away. She didn't.

"Do you ever hear from her?" he asked.

"She wrote once," Ellie said, clearly recalling how Aunt Jenny had written that a person just knows when it's time to move on.

"How old were you when she left?"

"Thirteen. James was sixteen and Daniel seventeen, so we were plenty old enough to take care of ourselves." Lifting her chin, she added, "And we have."

"Thirteen," he repeated. "The same age Clara was when our parents died."

Ellie remembered the Sunday both Mr. and Mrs. Roberts had been shot while riding home from church in their buggy. The posse tracking down the killer had stopped at their place, wanting to know where Daniel and James had been that morning. They had been at home but the sheriff hadn't believed that, not until he had tracked down the shooter—the son of another man who had been hanged for rustling Rocking R cattle.

Unlike when her own parents had died, the entire community had turned out for Dal's parents' funeral.

Wanting to avoid any more animosity, Ellie said, "And like you've done for Clara, my older brothers have provided for me."

He made no comment or acknowledgment. Granted, her brothers didn't make the kind of money that Dal did, but they worked from sunup to sundown and kept paying the taxes on their ten-acre plot. Dick Weston, the farmer they worked for, couldn't afford to give them the kind of wages the Rocking R paid, but her brothers didn't want to work with cows. They preferred farming the land. That didn't remind them of their father and how his theft of Rocking R cattle had led to their whole lives being stolen from them.

"The sun will be setting soon," Dal said. "We should see what Mrs. King packed for us to eat while we still can."

Ellie's cheeks grew warm again. The jerky and biscuits she'd packed for herself would pale in comparison to anything Mrs. King had made. The lunches she'd eaten while visiting Clara had been extraordinarily delicious.

Dal opened one of the leather bags near his feet and pulled out a red-and-white-checkered bundle. It might have been her imagination, but Ellie swore she smelled freshly baked bread and her mouth began to water.

Opening the neatly folded package, he said, "Looks like ham."

Ellie managed to swallow a moan before it sounded.

"Here," he said, holding out a thick sandwich.

Ellie turned away. "No, thank you."

"Clara will be sorely disappointed," he said. "She insisted that Mrs. King pack a sandwich for you."

"That was kind of her, but not necessary. I packed my own," she said, "and will eat later."

"It'll be dark later," he said.

She kept her eyes locked on the window. From past travelers, there were smudges in the soot that distorted the view of the passing landscape, but it didn't matter. She wasn't looking at anything in particular. She was just trying to keep her mind off that sandwich.

"I missed lunch," he said, "and no restaurants will be open by the time we arrive, so I hope you don't mind if I eat."

"Not at all." To her embarrassment, her stomach growled loudly enough that the sleeping cowboy probably heard it.

Chapter Four

Dal smiled to himself. She was a stubborn one, but she was also proud. Whether she wanted to eat, whether she was hungry or not, shouldn't be any of his concern. Neither should whether or not she did blame him, or at least his family, for the life she now led. Dal couldn't be blamed for what had happened in the past. His mother had taken him out to the Alexander's home so he would see that the men who had been hanged had families, just like they did, and that there were better ways to solve problems than killing people. She'd never believed in the vigilante lifestyle of those days. It had taken her life, too.

The ham sandwich, which a moment before had been tasteful, turned to sawdust in his mouth. Damn it. Laws were laws, and people needed to obey them. Needed to understand the consequences of breaking them. Her father should have considered them before he stole his father's cattle. Lester Alexander had died because he'd broken the law. And he and his brother hadn't been the only ones. Being the largest cattle ranch for miles around, the Rocking R had been a target back then—still was—and it took a plethora of watchful eyes to make sure every cow carrying the Rocking R brand was accounted for at all times.

There were far better ways to make a living than by stealing that which belonged to someone else, and why some thought that was an easier way to go about things, Dal would never know. He'd never understand why the children of such men thought that way, too. Tag Evert had found out the hard way that stealing wasn't the solution. But only after he'd killed Dal's folks. Dal had been part of the posse that had hunted the killer down. His bullet hadn't taken Evert's life, but he'd been prepared to fire. Protecting what was his was in his blood. And always would be.

"I'm terribly sorry."

Dal looked up at the stranger standing beside his seat. "Excuse me?"

"My cat," an older woman said, pointing toward the fluffy orange animal sniffing at the checkered napkin on the seat beside Ellie. "She smells your food. If you'll excuse me, I'll fetch her."

Dal shifted his legs for the woman to step between his and Ellie's seats. At the same time, Ellie reached down and scooped up the cat. Holding the critter with both hands, she leaned forward and touched her nose to the cat's.

"My, but you are a pretty thing, aren't you?"

The cat meowed in return, and the sound of delight coming from Ellie stirred something inside Dal. He handed the rest of his sandwich to the older passenger. "Here, it can have this."

"Oh, but I couldn't," the woman exclaimed.

"Yes, you can," Dal said. "I'm finished."

"Why, thank you," she said, taking the sandwich. "We are going to Wichita to see our daughter and couldn't leave Miss Priss home alone. Heaven knows what sort of trouble she'd get into."

"So you're not only lovely, you're mischievous," Ellie said to the cat.

"Mildred, you've disturbed these young people long enough," an older man said, arriving at the woman's side.

"I'm just collecting Miss Priss, Henry." The woman handed the man the sandwich. "This nice young man gave her the rest of his meal."

"Hoping you'd collect your cat and go and sit back down," Henry replied.

Dal silently agreed, but the glance he received from Ellie as she handed Mildred the cat instantly had him regretting the thought. He reached out a hand to the older man. "Dal Roberts."

"Of the Rocking R?" the man asked, shaking Dal's hand. "Henry Krantz. This is my wife, Mildred. We've heard of you. Eat your beef regularly. Get it at Walt Smith's place in Redville."

"That's where we live," Mildred added. "Redville. It's quite a distance west of Buckley, but a nice town. A real nice town. Isn't it, Henry? Henry here has a barber shop there, but he closed up shop for a week so we could go and see our daughter and her family." Leaning closer to Ellie, she said, "Our granddaughter is singing in church this Sunday and we are going to watch her."

"Come along now, Mildred," Henry said. "Nice

meeting you, Mr. Roberts." The man then nodded toward Ellie. "Mrs. Roberts."

She nodded, then quickly shook her head. "I'm not—"

But Henry had already spun Mildred around and was saying, "I told you we should have left that cat at home."

"Miss Priss would have starved to death being alone that long," Mildred argued.

"She's too fat to starve to death," Henry answered. "Besides, she's a cat, she could've caught herself a mouse or something."

"There are no mice in my house, Henry, not one I…"

Their voices faded as they walked farther down the aisle, and Dal turned to Ellie. "I'd say Miss Priss already ate all the mice. That's one fat cat."

"Miss Priss is about to have a litter of kittens," Ellie said, pulling her gaze off the couple. "I do hope it's not before we get to Wichita."

Dal couldn't stop from turning about to glance at the older couple no doubt still discussing their cat. Twisting back to Ellie he asked, "How do you know?"

The look she gave him, accompanied by a sigh, told him she wasn't about to elaborate.

"Poor Henry," he muttered.

"Poor Miss Priss," Ellie answered.

Dal didn't feel the need to agree or disagree, but he did take one final glance over his shoulder. "Here."

Turning, he shook his head when he saw the

sandwich still wrapped in the napkin that she held out. "No, that one is yours."

"I have—"

"I know you have your own food, but that's yours, too. Besides, I'm no longer hungry."

"You said you missed lunch."

"It's not the first time, nor will it be the last," he answered.

She didn't say anything at first as she placed the sandwich back on the seat beside her, but then, as she pushed it away from the edge, she said, "That was kind of you."

"Clara had Mrs. King make—"

"I'm referring to the sandwich you gave Miss Priss."

"Oh, well, I'm just a generous sort of guy," he said, half-embarrassed.

She laughed as if truly delighted by the thought. "Says who?"

He grinned and shrugged. "All sorts of people. Haven't you heard that about me?"

"Never," she answered.

Liking the sight of her grin, and knowing it would disappear if the topic didn't change, he asked, "Do you have a cat?"

A part of Ellie wanted to tell him that people who could barely feed themselves shouldn't have animals—it wasn't fair to the pet—but instead she simply replied, "No."

"Dog?"

"Not since Samson."

"Horse then? Pig? Sheep?"

Flustered and a bit tickled by the teasing glint in his eyes, she said, "No, no, no."

"Ostrich?"

"Ostrich?" she repeated.

He shrugged.

His expression, full of mischief and wit, made his features seem softer, younger-looking. She fought the smile trying to grow on her lips, and said, "No, I've never even seen an ostrich."

"Me, neither," he admitted with a chuckle. "Then how'd you know Miss Priss is…in the family way?"

Still attempting, but failing to hold back a smile, she said, "It's obvious."

"If it's obvious to you, why isn't it obvious to Mr. or Mrs. Krantz?"

"Because they see Miss Priss every day, they haven't noticed the weight she's gaining is…" Heat flushed into her cheeks. This was not a topic of conversation for mixed company. "Why do you care so much about a cat?"

"I don't," he said. "I'm just making conversation. It'll be hours yet before we get to Wichita."

Ellie glanced toward Mr. and Mrs. Krantz, truly hoping Miss Priss didn't go into labor within the next few hours. She shifted her gaze back to him. "There are many other things we could discuss."

"Like?"

She opened her mouth, but an idea wouldn't form in her head. Flustered, she sighed. "I don't know. The weather?"

"It's Kansas," he answered. "The weather changes at the drop of a hat."

That was true. Even though it was only the first of March, yesterday had been extremely warm, and yet today, the chill in the air had numbed her cheeks while she'd walked the hours it had taken to get to town. Following the direction of her shifting thoughts, she said, "You could tell me about Clara's accident. Did the doctor really say she could become lame?"

"Yes, he did. She tripped rushing down the stairs and her foot twisted beneath her. Luckily that was all that happened. She could have broken her neck."

"Don't say such things," Ellie said swiftly. Years ago she'd convinced herself that if she didn't want bad things to happen, then it was best not to think about them. Or to utter a word concerning such events.

"Well, she could have," Dal said. "She tumbled all the way to the bottom. Good thing Doc was already out at our place. He'd stopped to see how one of our cowboys was getting along. Slim Marks had taken a nasty fall off a horse last week and broke a couple of ribs. Doc had just gone to the house for coffee with Mrs. King when Clara fell."

"The poor dear," Ellie offered sincerely. Clara had been nothing shy of an angel from the time the two of them had met last summer. Although they both had known the other existed, they had never met until Clara, driving her awning-covered buggy, happened upon Ellie walking to town for a few supplies. Clara had insisted she get in the buggy, and after they'd both completed their shopping, had been just as insistent about driving her all the way home.

Ellie's brothers hadn't been happy about that, but later, when the friendship between her and Clara had continued to grow, they had given up complaining. She figured it had happened much the same way at the Rocking R—that Dal had finally stopped insisting the two of them couldn't be friends. Clara had never made mention of such things. There had been no need. Dal's attitude, and the way he glared every time he'd see Ellie in their parlor, had said it all.

"I do feel bad for her," he said. "And I must admit, I'm glad you have become such a good friend to her. The ranch has been a lonely place for her. The opportunity to have friendships with other girls her age has been limited."

"Everyone in town adores her," Ellie said.

"That may be true," he agreed, "but until she was old enough to travel to town alone, she had few opportunities to visit friends. Unfortunately, by that time, most of the girls she knew were getting married, or already married and having children."

Ellie took a moment to look beyond the man who had irritated her so deeply in the past to see one who genuinely loved his sister. It was clear in his blue eyes and on his rugged, yet overly handsome, face. The fact that Caroline Barnett had married Ed Mansel instead of Dal had confused many and had infuriated Clara. Clara insisted that she hadn't wanted Caroline as a sister-in-law but had been very upset by the way the woman had tossed aside her brother for the much older and rather homely Ed. Ellie's brother Daniel had said it was because Mansel had more money than Dal. She had never met either Caroline or Ed, yet she didn't agree with her brother. Few people had more money than the Roberts family. Furthermore, some things were more important than money. Even she, who craved many things money could buy—like real floors and windows, and a full pantry—knew money wasn't the answer to everything.

"What is it?" he asked, frowning.

She blinked and swallowed. "Nothing." Shrugging, she added, "Just that you must sincerely love your sister."

"Of course I do. Don't you love your brothers?"

Ellie didn't answer right away. She was attempting to figure out what made Dal so handsome. His dark hair was brushed back from his forehead and the ends were slightly curled from where his hat had sat upon it. There were a few faint wrinkles at the corners of his eyes, along his forehead and between his brows. They were more like crinkles than wrinkles, she thought, moving her gaze to the lower half of his face. His lower cheeks, upper lip, jaw and chin were darker due to the whiskers that he must not have shaved this morning. Or maybe he had and they were already growing back.

All in all, there wasn't one thing in particular that stood out, yet he was handsome. One of the most handsome men she'd seen to date. Then again, in truth, she hadn't seen too many men.

Tossing aside any further thoughts, for there was no telling where such lines of thinking could go, she said, "Of course I love them, and they love me."

"But…" he said expectantly.

"But nothing." She withheld the fact that no one in her family talked much about love.

"Then why are you amazed that I love Clara?"

"I'm not amazed," she disputed.

"Surprised then?"

"Perhaps."

He grinned slightly. "Because an arrogant ass couldn't love anyone besides himself?"

She rolled her lips between her teeth to keep herself from speaking and smiling.

He lifted one eyebrow.

"You said it," she said. "I didn't."

Chapter Five

By the time the train arrived in Wichita, Ellie had begun to think Dal wasn't nearly as conceited and arrogant as she might have once assumed, and she also was very glad she'd worn her old, oversize coat. The temperature had dropped considerably. Although the porter had lit the lamps and the oil-burning stove in the back of the car, the heat it gave out couldn't begin to take the chill from the air.

She was also glad it was dark. That way the driver of the lush enclosed carriage that Dal had hired to take them to the hotel couldn't see the shabbiness of her coat. However, the people of the very elegant hotel Dal escorted her into could, and she'd never felt quite so ashamed as when the clerk had looked her up and down with a scornful leer.

It took Dal all of thirty seconds to be completely annoyed. Glancing at the keys the man held out over the large desk, he clenched his teeth. "I asked for two of your best rooms."

"I assumed that was for you and your sister," the man said with a sideways glance at Ellie, "not—"

"We'll go somewhere else," Dal interrupted, reaching out to take Ellie's elbow.

"No you won't."

Dal let his breath out slowly at the sound of a second man's voice. He shifted his stance to acknowledge the man walking down the main staircase.

"You will not go elsewhere, Dal. This is the only place you ever stay in Wichita. What's the problem?" Jake Reynolds, the hotel owner, asked.

"Your clerk gave me only one suite," Dal pointed out. The second key the man had held out had not been for a private room. Every hotel had cheaper *common* rooms with multiple beds, and he wasn't about to have Ellie sharing a room with strangers. "We need two."

"I reserved the best two for you myself," Jake said. "And I've just lit the lamps in them, knowing you were arriving on the 1917." Rounding the huge desk, Jake elbowed the clerk. "Step aside Oscar."

"I—uh—" Astonished, the clerk stopped talking and dropped the keys from his hand into a wooden box beside the registrar book.

"There're two rooms noted right here, with your name on them," Jake said.

"I'm glad to hear that," Dal replied, giving Oscar the clerk a glare. Turning back to Jake, he added, "The train ride here was sooty and we both smell of kerosene. I should have been as wise as Miss Alexander and worn old clothes." Why he had felt the need to create an excuse for her shabby coat, he wasn't sure, other than the fact he didn't want anyone else looking at her the way Oscar had.

"They do need to do something about that train, Miss Alexander," Jake said to Ellie, gathering up the correct keys. "I'm Jacob Reynolds, the proprietor of this hotel, and I sincerely hope the trip was otherwise enjoyable. Your suite does have its own bathing chamber for your convenience."

Ellie lifted her chin and an elegant smile appeared on her face. "Thank you, Mr. Reynolds, and the train ride was most enjoyable."

"Except it was very cold," Dal said, fully aware of how Jake saw past Ellie's ragged old coat to the beautiful woman beneath. He held out his hand for the keys. "We'd like to get settled in."

"Oscar, get their bags," Jake directed the clerk before he turned to Ellie, dropping the keys in Dal's hand. "If there is anything you need, Miss Alexander, don't hesitate to ask. We are at your disposal and wish for you to enjoy your time here."

The blush on her cheeks enhanced her dark brown eyes, and the zip that created in Dal's bloodstream had him silently claiming he must be more tired than he realized. She was an attractive girl, but *beautiful* had never been a word he'd used for any woman. Until now. And by the look on his face, Jake was thinking the same thing.

"Thank you," she said softly.

Dal twisted her about and headed toward the stairs. Jake could look all he wanted. His redheaded wife, Sara, who managed the hotel kitchen would tear Jake apart if he did more than look. That piece of information released some of the tension that had settled in Dal's neck as he led Ellie up the staircase and down the hall.

He opened her door first and waited for Oscar

to set down her bag. "That will be all," Dal said, taking the other two bags from the clerk. The man could wait until he turned to dust before Dal would give him a tip.

Oscar must have understood that because he bowed at the waist, and then quickly backed out the door.

"I'll be across the hall," Dal said to Ellie, setting down one of the two bags in his hands.

As he turned away, she said, "Your other bag."

He didn't turn around. The sight of the big bed in the room behind her had his blood heating up far faster than the warmth from those little kerosene heaters on the train. "That is yours. Clara sent it. I'll see you in the morning." He shut Ellie's door behind him and marched across the hall. He'd barely closed the door to his own room, and was still staring at the big bed identical to the one across the hall, when a knock sounded.

Holding in the air in his lungs was impossible. Letting it out in one breath, he spun and opened the door. A maid with a tray supporting a decanter of what he assumed was brandy and a glass smiled up at him. "Mr. Reynolds said this should warm you."

As Dal waved a hand for her to enter and to set the tray on a table, he noticed another maid across the hall, at Ellie's door. That tray, which Ellie was graciously accepting from the maid, held a porcelain teapot and cup. Dal grinned and gave Ellie a nod before he turned to the maid leaving his room. Pulling out his money clip, he separated out two bills. "Here, give one to the maid across the hall, please."

"Certainly, sir," the girl said.

Ellie had already closed her door. Dal shut his and walked over to the table, taking a shot of brandy, which did a nice job of warming him and settling his nerves.

Until he climbed into the big bed, that was.

Ellie had never seen such elegance and was afraid to touch anything. Her hands had trembled so badly she'd feared the teapot on the tray would fall off and break before she'd set the tray on the table. That had been several minutes ago. The tea would most likely be cold by now, and her hands were still shaking no matter how briskly she rubbed them together. Her entire home could almost fit in this room. The bed was twice as big as any she'd seen, and there was a table with two chairs, a dresser with a mirror and another chair over near the curtains that hung clear to the floor. There was also the separate bathing chamber just as Mr. Reynolds had said.

Pivoting in the doorway of the bathing chamber—something she'd truly never seen before, nor had ever imagined existed—she scanned the rest of the hotel room again. The bed was covered with a shimmering white quilt that looked as thick and soft as clouds. Biting her bottom lip, she slowly crossed the room and then laid a hand on the bed. It was as soft as she'd imagined, maybe softer.

Ellie took another look around as excitement began to bubble in her stomach. Unable to control herself, she turned and threw herself backward to land on the bed. It bounced slightly, but silently, as she sank into the softness.

"Oh, my," she whispered, closing her eyes to fully experience the luxury completely surrounding her. She, Ellie Alexander, was lying on a cloud of softness, surrounded by luxury—

She shot upright and flung herself off the bed. Spinning about, she scanned the white material for any dirt or grime from her coat. Thankfully there wasn't a mark to be seen. She removed her coat, and sniffed it, wondering if it did smell like kerosene as Dal had said. After hanging it on a hook by the door, she paused near the table holding the tea. She supposed it would be terrible for it to go to waste, so she poured a cupful and sipped it.

By the time the cup was empty, she'd wandered up and down the room one more time. It was like a fairy tale, a dream. Upon setting the cup back down carefully on the table, she pinched herself just to make sure she wasn't actually dreaming.

As she rubbed her arm, easing the sting of her own pinch, her gaze landed on the bag Dal had left. It wasn't a dream. She was here to buy the items for Clara's wedding gown, and she needed to get her head out of the clouds.

Ellie picked up the bag Clara had sent with Dal. That hadn't surprised her. One of her excuses not to go had been the condition of her wardrobe. In that case, too, Clara had been relentless, insisting that she would loan her clothes.

Thankful that Clara, even injured, had remembered that, Ellie set the bag down on one of the chairs and opened the hatch. On the top rested an envelope, bearing her name. She set it on the table in order to first examine the rest of the bag's contents.

The bag wasn't very large, but here, Clara had performed a miracle. There were three dresses. Lovely dresses. A blue one with covered buttons, a pale orange one with white stripes and a mint-green one with delicate lace trim. There was also a gray cape with black frogs. It was the cape that made Ellie's heart soar clear to the heavens above. Dal's comment about her wearing old clothes because of the train had been a kind thing for him to say, but it had made her fear tomorrow morning and more of the clerk's scathing looks at her coat.

"Thank you, Clara," she said softly to the air. "You are truly the best friend I've ever had. Will ever have."

Ellie hugged the cape one last time before she draped it over the back of the chair. Then she proceeded to hang up the other dresses, removing her old coat from one of the hooks in the process. She folded the coat and placed it in one of the dresser drawers, along with the extra undergarments she'd brought from home. She also tucked her traveling bag and the leather one of Clara's in the bottom drawer before going back to the table.

Settled on a chair, with another cup of tepid tea

sitting before her, she gently unsealed the envelope. This was the first letter she'd had addressed to only her. Even though it hadn't arrived by post, she treasured knowing that the words inside were meant for her alone.

Unable to stop herself, she read the neatly penned note quickly. By the end of the message, her heart was racing. Taking a deep breath, she read it again, and then closed her eyes.

"Oh, heavens, Clara," she whispered. "How could you ask that of me?"

Chapter Six

Dal had bathed and shaved, and wasted a good amount of time listening and checking for movement across the hall. For the hundredth time since crawling into the bed last night, he wished his sister had been able to join them on this trip. Then he would be able to go about his business without having to wait for a woman.

Having believed that Clara and Ellie would be shopping together, he'd set up a few appointments for himself, including visiting the carriage company. Clara's buggy didn't have a backseat, and Dal had a feeling she and Bill would be starting a family soon. They would therefore soon need something larger. He'd planned on ordering one as a wedding gift while in town.

Letting out a growl, he marched for the door. It had been late when they'd arrived, but Ellie should be up by now. If she wasn't, he'd wake her.

His knuckles were about to rap on her door when he pulled his hand back. He could leave a message at the front desk for her. But then she probably didn't know where any of the shops were. Although they weren't hard to find, and the clerk could direct her.

Hell. He didn't want Oscar talking to her, not after the way he'd sneered last night. For that matter, he didn't want Jake ogling her, either.

"Oh, for tarnation," he muttered and rapped on the door before he changed his mind again.

It opened almost instantly, and what he saw made *him* ogle. His eyes were glued to her and wouldn't move.

"Good morning," she said. "I was hoping you'd rise soon. I've read the paper three times."

"You— I—" He bit his tongue to keep it from flapping. The white-and-orange-striped dress fit her as perfectly as his favorite gloves covered his hands. He could believe running his hands down her sides, over her hips, would be just as— Stopping that thought before it could fully form, he asked, "Are you ready for breakfast?"

Her smile was amused. "Breakfast? I already ate."

"You did? Where?" He peeked around her to see the room as neat and tidy as it had been the previous night.

"I brought things with me," she said. "And had tea left over from last night."

He'd been wasting hours, ignoring the growling in his stomach, while she'd been eating cold food from home and drinking leftover tea?

"Well, I'm hungry," he said. "So you'll have to eat again."

The snap of his words stung even him, as did her startled look.

"All right," she said softly. "I didn't mean to upset you."

Guilt, something he rarely felt, burned in his stomach. He scratched his head with fingers that still tingled from his earlier wayward thoughts. "You didn't upset me. I'm just hungry."

"I'll gather my cape," she said, "so I can leave after we eat."

He nodded and waited for her to drape a gray cape he recognized as his sister's over her arm before she stepped into the hallway. Now that he thought about it, he recognized the dress that fit her so perfectly was Clara's, too.

"Did you sleep well?" he asked, trying to keep his eyes and mind on things other than that dress.

"Yes, you?" she asked as they started for the staircase.

He nodded and let out a grunt of sorts. The air around him had picked up a subtle sent, like the smell of sunshine after rain.

"I never dreamed a bed could be so soft."

At her words, a sting struck him low down, and caused him to stiffen. Clearing his throat, and stopping his thoughts from going off-kilter again, he said, "Jake prides himself on having the most comfortable rooms in the city. He's built quite a reputation for it. People from all over the nation have stayed here."

"It's certainly lovely," she said.

"So are you." Dal bit his tongue, but the words were already out.

Her gaze snapped his way, but then away again just as fast.

He held his breath as they started down the stairs. Maybe she hadn't heard him, or understood what he'd said. He could hope that was the case.

"Good morning," Jake greeted them from behind the desk. "Sara still has breakfast on the stove, and I have a table ready for you." He stepped around the high counter. "Miss Alexander, dare I say you are as glorious as the sun today? I do hope you slept well."

"Very well, Mr. Reynolds. Thank you."

"Come," Jake said, taking her elbow. "I told my Sara I would introduce you this morning."

"Is Sara your wife?" she asked.

"Yes, the other most beautiful woman in the world."

Following behind, Dal clamped his back teeth together. He no longer felt like a greenhorn, but he wasn't willing to acknowledge that the green in him now was more the shade of jealousy. That would be ridiculous, and he was not a ridiculous man. Or a jealous one.

After seating them at a table near the windows, Jake went to locate Sara.

"Is his wife as gracious as he?" Ellie asked quietly once they were alone.

Ready to snap that *gracious* wasn't the word he'd use, Dal pinched his lips together, but his muscles loosened as his gaze met hers. There was trepidation in Ellie's eyes. He'd forgotten this was her first trip to the city, her first trip anywhere.

"Yes," he answered. "Sara is a very nice woman, and an excellent cook." Nodding in the direction over Ellie's shoulder, he said, "Here she comes now."

Sara was as welcoming as ever, and quickly left to make their breakfast orders. Dal found himself relaxing and enjoying Ellie's company. Her eyes never stopped taking in their surroundings and the sights out the window, and he didn't mind answering her questions.

When Sara returned to their table to deliver an appetizing meal of steak and eggs, Ellie's eyes widened.

"We only serve Rocking R beef. It's the best there is," Sara said.

Ellie nodded, but waited for Sara to leave before she whispered, "I'll never be able to eat all this."

"Then just eat until you're full," Dal said, already slicing into his steak.

After a couple of bites, she asked, "Does all of Kansas eat Rocking R beef?"

"No," he said. "Just half of it."

Her eyes widened again before a smile spread across her lips. "You're teasing."

He nodded. "Eat. You have a lot of shopping to do today."

She took a couple more bites and then asked, "What are you going to do today?"

"I have a list of things to see to," he answered after swallowing.

"Me, too," she said. "Clara's list is long, but luckily I read the paper this morning."

Dal stopped the fork near his mouth. "Luckily?"

She chewed and swallowed while nodding. "Yes. There were numerous sales advertised in the paper. I was able to find everything on the list, and I made a list of where I'll find each item. On sale no less." Her eyes lit up even brighter. "Oh, and remember Mr. and Mrs. Krantz?"

His answering nod wasn't really needed, as she continued talking.

"And how their granddaughter is singing in church this Sunday? Well, my goodness, but Wichita has as many churches as you have cows. I believe their granddaughter will be performing at the Methodist church. That is the one having a children's day on Sunday. The Presbyterian and the Universalist churches are providing sermons on character and the Baptist, the AME church, the Catholic church and several other city churches are having regular services and Sabbath school."

"How do you know that?"

"It was all listed in the paper. There was also an article about the new bank being built and one about a terrible robbery of a grocery store as well as a story about how several people were arrested during a political debate in one of the saloons."

Dal highly doubted that it had been a political debate. Having eaten his fill, he wiped his mouth with his napkin. "Remind me to tell Jake not to deliver you a newspaper tomorrow morning."

"Why?"

"So you don't memorize the entire thing and quote it to me over breakfast."

She set down her fork with a clank. "Well, if you hadn't slept so late, I wouldn't—"

"I didn't sleep late," he interrupted. "I was waiting for you to get up."

Crossing her arms, she leaned back in her chair. "I had been up for hours."

Biting back a smile at the way her eyes snapped at his teasing, he stood. "Then you must be ready to go shopping."

"I am," she agreed, and jumped to her feet before he made it around the table to pull out her chair.

He waited until she put on her cape before taking her by the elbow to lead her out of the dining room. "Where are we off to first?"

A frown took over her entire face. "We?"

He nodded.

She shook her head slowly. "I thought you didn't want to go shopping for silk and lace. That's what you said on the train."

"I'm not going shopping for those things," he explained. "I'll simply escort you and wait while you complete your purchases."

Pulling a slip of paper out of the cuff of one sleeve, she said, "There's no need for that. I jotted down the stores and their addresses."

He took the piece of paper, and instantly recognized the name of a store close to the carriage shop. The others he'd never heard of, but the addresses suggested they were across the river, in a part of town he didn't want her wandering off to alone. "We'll start with this one," he said, pointing to the one he'd recognized. "It will have most everything on this list."

"It might," she said, "but other places have things on sale."

Dal chose to hold back his sharp answer. He wasn't opposed to saving money, but he wasn't willing to forgo her safety in order to save a dime.

"Shall we?" he asked, opening the hotel's front door and gesturing for her to exit in front of him.

"This really isn't necessary," she said over her shoulder while walking out of the door.

"We'll have to agree to disagree on that," he said.

"Agree to disagree?"

He nodded.

"Why?"

"Because I promised Clara I'd make sure you got everything you needed, and I never break a promise."

"You don't?"

There was skepticism in her eyes and in her tone. "No, I don't," he answered. He could add that it was because he was a Roberts and no Roberts ever broke a promise, but a sinking sensation told him she'd find fault in that. So instead he added, "A cowboy never breaks a promise."

Something in his statement made Ellie stumble slightly. She caught herself, but was flustered all the same. "Who says?"

He shrugged. "Cowboys I guess, but it's true.

Years ago, when they were driving cattle north out of Texas, cowboys swore to deliver the cattle to the railhead no matter what, and they did."

"You didn't," she pointed out.

"No, I didn't, but I work cattle from sunup to sundown, no different than the way they did. I'm just on a ranch rather than the open prairie. Some call us cattlemen, but I like the sound of cowboy better, and I keep my promises."

Ellie could believe Dal kept his promises, especially those he'd made to his sister, but she didn't believe that was the case with all cowboys. At least not those who thought more of the cattle they managed than people.

She wasn't too sure she wanted to be in this man's company all day, either. He was too likable. She'd started to feel comfortable around him, and that was a bit frightening. If she returned home liking Dal Roberts, her brothers would never let her leave the shanty ever again. They couldn't stop her of course. Except, she had nowhere else to go.

"This way," Dal said. "Let's cross while it's clear."

She glanced both ways as he hurried her across the street and onto the boardwalk on the other side. Wichita was far larger than Buckley. People were everywhere. She'd never seen this many at one time, and it felt as if her lungs were tightening inside her chest. When a man rushing past them bumped her shoulder, she flinched and stepped closer to Dal.

"It's always busy downtown," he said. "And

it's easy to get lost, or turned around when you've never been here before."

She hadn't thought of that and glanced up to nod at him, but the sincerity in his eyes made her swallow instead.

"Which is why I will escort you to wherever you need to go," he said.

This time she did manage to nod, and silently accepted the idea as a good one. She was also glad she'd made a list. Right now, with all the hustle and bustle going on around them, she couldn't remember a single thing she needed or the addresses of the stores.

Before long they arrived at a shop with windows full of dress forms wearing beautiful gowns. The sight of them sent her heart plummeting. Would she truly be able to create something even close to these? To what Clara wanted?

"Here we are," Dal said. "I'll speak with the owner, tell them to have everything billed to me and delivered to the hotel."

"And then?" she asked, feeling a bit insecure about being left alone.

"Don't worry," he said. "I won't interrupt your purchasing, or hurry you along. I have some things to see to next door at the carriage shop."

Ellie took a deep breath for fortitude and then nodded. She'd never questioned her abilities before and now wasn't the time to start. While Dal went to speak to the woman behind the long counter, Ellie pulled out her list again, telling herself this shop was just like Silas's store in Buckley, only bigger, and grander.

She managed to get a hold on herself and was slowly making her way around a large table holding bolts of cloth when Dal returned to her side. "All's set," he said. "Just sign your name at the bottom of the slip of purchases."

"All right," she agreed. "Thank you."

He eyed her cautiously for a moment. "I need you to promise me something."

Ellie stilled. She had no intention of spending frivolously, but purchasing everything on Clara's list was going to be expensive. "I'll try my best to keep it reasonable."

A frown flashed across his face before he smiled. "Don't worry about the cost. Buy everything Clara asked for and whatever else you see that she may have overlooked." He touched her beneath the chin with one finger, forcing her to look at him. "That's not the promise I'm going to ask."

"Then what is?"

Chapter Seven

"That you stay here until I return. Even if you don't find everything you need, stay here. I don't want you wandering about alone."

A sigh pushed upward, but caught in her throat and stayed there. He sounded as if he was worried about her. "I won't," she said, a bit breathless, her lungs burning. "I promise."

"Good girl," he said. "I won't be long." He started for the door, but paused little more than a step away to turn back around. "And, Ellie…"

She held her gaze on his, wondering, yet unable to think of anything else he might need to say.

"Enjoy yourself." Then he tipped the brim of his hat to her with one hand and walked out of the door.

The air rushed out of Ellie's lungs with such force that she had to brace herself by placing a hand on the table full of material. She stood there for a moment, sucking in breaths to refill her lungs and staring at Dal as he walked past the window. What was wrong with her? She'd never been so lightheaded and her heart had never beaten so hard, not ever. Well, maybe once before, when she'd thought she'd stepped on a rattlesnake.

"Did you find anything to your liking?"

Ellie tore her gaze away from the window to face the woman beside her and flinched slightly at the burning sensation in her cheeks.

"If not, I have more bolts in the back room," the woman said. "And everything else you'll need for the most beautiful wedding gown ever."

Flustered and feeling as uprooted as a discarded weed, Ellie thrust out her hand. "I have a list."

Abigail Hollingsworth turned out to be exactly what Ellie needed. The woman was not only the shop owner, but an excellent seamstress who graciously took it upon herself to explain exactly how to recreate one of the gowns in the window. Abigail was also willing to strike a bargain when she learned things were on sale elsewhere. Ellie's good-sense had returned, and her focus was once again on Clara's dress, which meant she now clearly remembered the advertisements she'd read in the newspaper.

She'd completed her shopping, and was just about to sign the bottom of the slip when someone tapped her on the shoulder.

"Excuse me, dear. I called your name but you must not have heard me. It's me, Mildred Krantz from the train. Remember?"

Turning, Ellie smiled at the familiar face. "I'm sorry, Mrs. Krantz, of course I remember you, I—"

"You were too busy with your purchase," Mildred finished for her. "I see that. I just wanted to tell you our wonderful news. You aren't going to believe this. Oh, it's just so wonderful!"

Mildred grabbed Ellie's shoulders and pulled her

into a hug so swiftly the pencil slipped from Ellie's fingers and rolled across the floor.

"Last night, shortly after we arrived at our daughter's house, Miss Priss had a litter of kittens."

Excitement lit up the older woman's face, and Ellie couldn't bring herself to say she'd expected as much. "Really? How delightful." After returning the other woman's hug, Ellie stepped back. "I do hope Miss Priss is doing well."

"Oh, yes, very well, and so are the babies, all five of them. Henry and I are just beside ourselves with happiness."

Ellie sort of doubted that Henry was overjoyed, but she wasn't about to breathe a word of that, either. "I'm sure you are. Congratulations."

"Oh, thank you, dear," Mildred said. "I recognized you through the window and said to my daughter, 'Oh, there's Mrs. Roberts from the train, I have to tell her about Miss Priss.' I knew you would want to know."

Ellie held her breath, prepared to point out the woman's mistake in thinking she was Dal's wife, but Mildred was still talking.

"Henry says this will not delay our trip home, but I told him that if Miss Priss isn't up to traveling, we aren't leaving. I told you our granddaughter is singing in church on Sunday and—"

"Excuse me," another woman interrupted, elbowing her way alongside Mildred.

Assuming she was Mildred's daughter, Ellie smiled at the woman. "Hello."

"Did I hear her call you Mrs. Roberts?" the woman asked.

Mildred answered before Ellie could. "Yes. Mrs. Dal Roberts of the Rocking R. We met on the train. I'm Mildred Krantz, and you are?"

"None of your business," the woman said, pushing Mildred aside so roughly that she stumbled. "You can't be married to Dal Roberts."

The anger that had rushed up inside Ellie at the way the woman treated Mildred floundered as her stomach fell, yet she still couldn't find her voice to agree with the stranger—she wasn't Dal's wife.

"Yes, she is," Mildred insisted.

"No, she's not," the woman snapped.

"Yes, she is," Mildred said. "I told you, my husband and I met them on the train from Buckley yesterday and—"

"Dal Roberts would never be married to the likes of her!" the woman hissed.

"That will be enough," Abigail exclaimed. "I'm going to have to ask you to leave if—"

"Shut up, both of you!" the woman spat out as her burning glare closed in on Ellie. "You are not married to Dal. Admit it! Speak up! Or are you deaf and mute?"

At that point, it wouldn't have mattered if the woman had been asking if Ellie was married to the President of the United States. No one had the right to be that rude, or insulting. Ellie stepped forward, planting her nose right before the other woman's. "Deaf and mute? No, I'm not deaf or mute, and I'm not mean and nasty, either."

"You little strumpet." The woman seethed with anger. "Why, I ought to—"

"Ought to what?" While the other woman huffed and turned redder, Ellie continued, "Cat got your tongue? Don't worry, it'll spit it out. Cats don't eat rotten meat."

The woman actually hissed, and Ellie's natural instincts kicked in. She'd learned plenty from scrapping with her brothers over the years and intuition had her ducking. The woman's hand didn't connect with anything, but Ellie felt it swoosh over her head and heard a screech of dissatisfaction. She took a step back before lifting her head and then she brought up both fists, ready to pop the woman on the nose. To her disappointment, the other woman was being pushed away from the counter by a man. She was still shouting some sort of gibberish, and Ellie was about to respond when she noticed a second man coming through the shop's doorway.

Her stomach dropped all the way to the floor while her heart clawed its way up her throat like a cat caught in a dried-up well.

Dal didn't even glance toward the man and the woman making all the ruckus. Instead, his gaze remained solely on her. Realizing her hands were still raised, Ellie dropped them to her sides and wished she could disappear. Completely disappear.

While the other man pushed the still-struggling woman toward the doorway, Dal moved forward. "Are you finished?"

Biting her lip until it hurt, Ellie nodded.

He kept walking closer. "Your purchases will be delivered to the hotel?"

She nodded again.

Once at her side, he took her elbow. It was a gentle hold, but Ellie imagined that would change as soon as they stepped outside.

"Excuse me, Mr. Roberts, your wife didn't have a chance to sign the slip yet."

Ellie couldn't blame Abigail. The woman didn't know she wasn't Dal's wife, just like Mildred, who seemed to have disappeared. It was all a simple misunderstanding. One Dal most likely wouldn't understand. He might realize Mildred's mistake, as he'd heard her on the train, but when it came to Abigail and the other woman, that was her fault. She should have said something right away.

"I'll sign it," he said.

"I'm so sorry about what happened," Abigail said, glancing toward the empty doorway. "I have no idea who that woman is. I've never seen her before. And I must say, I hope I never do again. I hope it won't stop you from shopping here again."

"You can't control who walks through your doors," Dal said. "I'm sure Ellie will shop here on each of her trips to Wichita."

The chances of her ever visiting Wichita again were next to nil, yet Ellie nodded. The shopkeeper had been extremely helpful, and deserved her thanks. She found her voice. "I appreciate all of your assistance, Abigail, and I'm sorry to have caused such a scene."

"You didn't cause anything but pleasure," Abigail said. "It was all that other woman. I look forward to seeing you again."

"Good day," Dal said, steering Ellie toward the door.

He'd heard and seen enough to know exactly what had happened, and was trying his darnedest to figure out what to do about it. Of course he'd known that Caroline and Ed would be in town for the cattlemen's meeting and the ball, but he hadn't expected this mess. None of it would have happened if he'd told Henry and Mildred on the train that Ellie wasn't his wife, but it had seemed a minor issue then.

It wasn't now.

"I'm sorry," Ellie said as they walked down the boardwalk. "One minute Mildred was telling me about Miss Priss's kittens and the next minute that nasty woman was shouting at both Mildred and Abigail to shut up and calling me names. I lost my temper, and I shouldn't have. I should have—"

"Miss Priss had her kittens, did she?" Dal asked, grateful to change the subject.

"Yes, five kittens, last night."

He nodded, glancing around. Caroline and Ed were nowhere in sight. It had taken him longer than he'd expected to finish his business at the carriage shop. If he'd been there a little earlier, the entire escapade would have been avoided. He'd heard the shouting while walking up the street, and had started to run when he'd seen Ed enter the shop at full speed. He'd arrived in time to see Ellie duck a blow from Caroline, and then Ed pulling her away. It was a good thing Ed had been there, as he wouldn't have been so gentle.

He'd figured Ellie was a scrapper, having been raised with her two brothers, but when she had come up, fists barred, he'd had to bite back a chuckle. Of the two women, he'd place his money on Ellie if it came to a fistfight, but that wasn't the way Caroline fought. She was mean and vengeful. That was what scared him. Learning that Ellie wasn't his wife would make Caroline the winner, but she'd take things further—she'd make sure that everyone knew.

Letting out a sigh, he asked, "Where to now?"

"Actually," Ellie said, "Abigail had everything I, or Clara, I should say, need. Except for the shoes."

"We can buy those later," he said, "if you want to return to the hotel."

Her sigh echoed his. A moment later, she turned to look up at him. "This isn't all my fault you know."

"What?"

She gave him a grimace that said she knew he knew.

"I never said anything was your fault," he told her while taking her arm to keep her close as a group of women approached.

"You never told Henry and Mildred Krantz I wasn't your wife, and you could have," she hissed near his ear.

He waited until all the women were past them before saying, "You could have, too."

She sighed again. "That's true, but I didn't want to chase them down the train aisle, nor shout over their arguing."

"I didn't, either."

"I didn't think it would matter," she said quietly. "I didn't think it would come back to haunt me."

"Is the idea of being married to me haunting?" For some unimaginable reason, he found he truly wanted to know her answer.

"When it's completely impossible, yes."

"Why would it be completely impossible?"

She didn't reply. She didn't need to. Not verbally at least. Her eyes said it all. They'd filled with something akin to disgust.

"Nothing's impossible," he said, nodding for them to cross the street while there was a chance.

She stepped off the boardwalk and kept up with his fast pace. "Plenty of things are impossible."

"Name one."

Stepping onto the boardwalk on the other side, she stopped and spun around to look up at him. Her brown eyes were so dark he could almost see his reflection in them, and the dark lashes surrounding them were long, with the tips curled upward. He'd never seen eyes so stunning. They could be called sinful. At least they seemed that way to him, made him think about things that he shouldn't be thinking about.

"You don't seem very upset over what happened," she said. "Why?"

He shrugged. He was trying not to think about what had happened. "Because it doesn't matter."

"Yes, it does. It's a lie, and I don't lie."

"It's not a lie." He took her arm again as they walked to the hotel's front doors. "It's a misunderstanding. Nothing more."

"Well, I don't like misunderstandings any more than I like lies," she said. "And you don't, either."

"How do you know that?"

"I just do, and don't try to tell me I'm wrong, because I'm not."

Dal didn't answer. It wasn't because she was right, but because Oscar had seen them coming and was holding the door open for them. The lobby was filled with plenty of customers, so he guided her directly to the staircase. As they climbed, he said, "I have to meet some people this afternoon, but I do have time for lunch if you're hungry."

"Hungry? Good heavens, we just ate breakfast."

"Three hours ago," he pointed out. "My meetings will take up all of the afternoon."

A frown covered her face.

"I'll be back in time for supper," he explained, feeling a bit unsure. It wasn't his place to tell her to stay in her room. If Clara had been there with her, he wouldn't have had to, but one woman roaming the streets alone, especially one who'd never been to Wichita, was unsafe. He didn't like the idea of her encountering some of the local riffraff. He'd taught Clara how to handle herself and a gun, and while he'd seen Ellie with her fists drawn, he figured her brothers had never taught her how to avoid a confrontation. "If you get hungry while I'm gone, you can have something delivered to your room."

She walked the remainder of the way to their rooms before she stopped and looked up at him. "I have food if I get hungry, and you don't need to worry about me running up and down the streets shouting that I'm married to you."

Anger rolled in his stomach. "That's not what I'm worried about."

She planted both hands on her hips. "I can't think of any other reason why you want me locked in my room."

"I never said—"

"You didn't have to. It's evident you don't want me traipsing around without you at my side. Why? What are you afraid I'll do? Rob the place?"

"No."

She lifted both brows.

"Wichita is a tough town, and while you are here, you're my responsibility."

"I'm no one's responsibility." Anger shimmered in her eyes as her glare narrowed. "I can take care of myself."

"Not here you can't."

She spun around and stuck the key to her room in the lock.

The animosity filling the air caused Dal to sigh. "Ellie, I didn't mean to upset you, I just—"

"Just what?" She opened the door and spun around in the frame to face him. "Want me to know my place? Trust me, I do."

The door slammed shut before he could spit out a word.

Chapter Eight

Ellie paced the room much like she had last night, but this time anger drove her footsteps. She couldn't exactly say why. The mishap at Abigail's store wasn't completely her fault. And it wasn't Dal's, either. As he had pointed out, it was a misunderstanding. And she had no desire to go traipsing about town. She had seen enough ruffians leaning against the buildings for her to know walking around alone wouldn't be a good idea. Still, she didn't like the thought of being banished to her room.

But it wasn't as if Dal had done that, either.

So then, what was wrong with her?

Catching her image in the mirror above the dresser, she stopped pacing.

"I'll tell you what's wrong, Ellie Alexander. You're what's wrong." Stepping closer, she stared at her reflection. "You spent the morning buying everything needed to sew a spectacular wedding gown, and the entire time you were wishing it was your gown. Wishing that you were planning a spring wedding for yourself. That was foolish. So foolish a complete stranger pointed out Dal would never marry someone like you."

Spinning about, she plopped onto the bed. "I

don't want to be married to Dal or anyone else," she said softly to herself. "It never even crossed my mind until that nasty woman said I couldn't be."

Ellie stood and once again glanced in the mirror. She'd never claim to be beautiful, but with her hair pinned back and wearing Clara's clothes, she didn't look like her normal pauper self. As a matter of fact, there was no reason why she couldn't be married to Dal. It wasn't as if she was homely or ignorant. What it came down to was the fact that he'd never *want* to be married to her. She didn't even like him, so why should that matter?

It didn't. Not at all. Letting out a growl, she mumbled, "I should never have come on this trip. Never."

But she had, and there wasn't anything she could do about it.

Spinning away from the mirror, she spied the gray cape she'd carelessly tossed upon the bed after entering the room.

Or is there? She was here for Clara, not herself or Dal, and she had to remember that.

Ellie picked up the cape and flipped it over her shoulders as she headed for the door.

Just as Dal had imagined, the meeting with several other cattlemen concerning the Texas fever epidemic took all afternoon. They'd created a quarantine proposal for the entire association to vote upon tomorrow, but in truth, Dal couldn't remember much of the conversation. Cattle were his livelihood, and keeping those Texas longhorns from infecting his herds should have been foremost in his mind, but thoughts of Ellie kept overriding everything else.

At first he'd assumed it was because curious glances at the meeting told him Ed Mansel had already spread the word that Caroline thought Ellie was Mrs. Dal Roberts. He'd considered explaining the misunderstanding, but the more he thought about it, the less he cared what Caroline or Ed or anyone else thought. His mind had turned solely to Ellie. Besides her embarrassment, he'd wondered about her being stuck in the hotel all afternoon. She had to be bored out of her wits. He knew she wasn't the type to sit around doing nothing. It was more than a three-mile walk for her to come to the ranch to see Clara, and more than five miles from her shanty to Buckley, closer to six, yet she walked it, there and back, a couple of times a month from what Clara had said, and she visited his sister more often than that.

"Oh, Mr. Roberts, I'm sorry, Ellie has already left."

Dal glanced up, not realizing he was passing the shop they had visited that morning.

"She must not have known you were coming to walk her back to the hotel. She asked if my assistant could, knowing you'd be upset if she walked it alone," Abigail Hollingsworth said.

"I would be," Dal admitted.

"She said as much, and please allow me to apologize for what happened earlier today," Abigail continued. "Ellie explained the misunderstanding on the train with the older couple, but I must say, that still didn't give that woman reason to be so rude. If I discover who she is, I will never allow her in my store again."

"I agree." Dal was more concerned about Ellie going back to the store than Caroline's behavior. He'd witnessed how rude Caroline could be long ago and he didn't envy Ed in the least. "Did Ellie get everything she needed?"

"Oh, she bought everything this morning. This afternoon she borrowed my back room to start sewing your sister's wedding dress. She's an excellent seamstress. I tried hiring her on the spot, but she said she couldn't move away from Buckley until after Clara's wedding. I do plan on hiring her then. She's exactly what I need."

A hard knot formed in Dal's stomach.

"If you'll excuse me," Abigail said. "I have to lock up and get home to make supper for my family."

Dal nodded and his pace increased as he headed for the hotel.

Chapter Nine

The food was delicious, but the silence from across the table meant anything Ellie attempted to swallow needed to be washed down with gulps of water. Finally, laying down her fork, she asked, "Did your meeting this afternoon not go well?"

"It went fine."

Dal's tone was as sharp as the knife he'd used to cut his steak, which caused her hands to tremble slightly. He was upset about something, and she was inclined to believe it included her. "That's good."

"How was your afternoon at Abigail Hollingsworth's store?"

She flinched inwardly but held her chin up to meet the icy glare in his blue eyes. "It was very nice, and productive. I made a good start on Clara's dress." Drawing in a breath of fortitude, she continued, "You have no cause to be upset about that. Mr. Reynolds allowed one of his clerks to escort me to the shop and Abigail's assistant walked me back. I couldn't just sit around here doing nothing all day."

"So you decided to snag yourself a job."

"Snag a job?"

He set his fork down and leaned back in his chair. "Yes, sewing for Abigail."

"I sewed Clara's dress, and plan to do the same tomorrow."

"And made plans to move to Wichita after the wedding."

It was a statement, not a question, yet she answered, "Perhaps. I will need to talk with James and Daniel, but it is what I've always wanted to do."

"Work for a dressmaker?"

"To begin with. Someday I'd like to have my own shop, just like Aunt Jenny used to talk about. But that will take money."

"The same aunt who stole your money and ran away with the drifter." He folded his arms across his chest.

Angered by his attitude, she glared across the table.

"What about Clara?" he asked.

Goose bumps rose on her arms. "What about her?"

"Have you considered how she'll feel if you move to Wichita?"

Abigail's offer had surprised Ellie, and she'd immediately refused, at first. But afterward, while she'd worked more on the dress, she'd thought about it. Seriously. "I told Abigail I couldn't consider her offer until after Clara's wedding."

"She'll still need friends after the wedding. The ranch is a lonely place."

Ellie knew all there was to know about loneliness, and she had considered Clara's feelings. She'd considered a lot of people. She always did.

Her swirling thoughts stopped abruptly when Dal pushed away from the table.

"We should return to our rooms," he said.

For the first time, the tightness of his lips and the glint in his blue eyes saddened her more than irritated her. "I didn't mean to upset you."

He waited until they were crossing through the arched threshold that led from the dining room to the hotel lobby before he said, "Then you should have stayed in your room rather than going job seeking."

Irritation zipped up her spine. He was back to being his arrogant self, a fact which shouldn't surprise her. "Why are you upset that Abigail offered me a job? It's none of your business." The glare he cast her way was more than insufferable. "It's not," she insisted. "I'll finish Clara's gown before deciding, so you don't have to worry that she'll be disappointed."

"I know she won't," he said sternly. "I'll make sure of that."

Hitching her skirt higher in order to take the steps faster, she said, "Then we have nothing to argue about, do we?"

"I believe we do." He marched up the stairs just as fast. "I didn't agree to bring you to Wichita in order for you to sell your wares."

"Sell my wares?" Her irritation was fast turning into full blown fury. "I'm not selling my wares, but even if I was, you would have no say about it. You have no say in what I do at all."

"As long as you are in my care, I do."

"I'm not in your care."

Taking hold of her arm, he propelled them both down the hall toward their rooms. "I beg to differ. As long as I'm paying your way, you are in my care."

There had been a million times when she'd wished to have money, but right now, she'd practically sell her soul to have enough to be able to pay her own way. A sense of pride, the small amount she did have, made her want to explain.

"I'd much rather have stayed home. I only came because Clara insisted upon it." Pulling the key from her pocket, she shoved it in the lock. "I'm sewing her gown for free, in exchange for my share of the costs of this trip."

As his hold on her arm lessened at her words, she shot into the room and spun around to slam the door shut.

Dal stopped himself from grabbing the door before it closed with a bang that rattled the wall, and his hand balled into a fist. Damn it. He shouldn't care if she wanted to move to Wichita and work for Abigail or anyone else, but he did. The depth of his anger said his feelings had little to do with Clara's dress. It was more that Ellie knew nothing about living in the city. Nothing about the dangers. There were far more of those here than in her isolated sod shanty.

It irked him, too, that she'd wasted no time in

making sure Abigail knew about the misunderstanding of them being married.

He turned about, but rather than entering his own room, he headed for the stairway. Several of the men in town for the cattlemen's meeting would be gathered across the river in the Delano district, which didn't have to abide by Wichita's gambling and prostitution ordinances. Dal supposed there was no reason why he shouldn't join them.

Ellie was still on Dal's mind as he entered the Mulberry Tree Saloon—named after the landmark that used to signal the end of the trail for the cattle drives. The place was known for an attraction that used to bring in droves of men. The Running of the Doves had been a regular event put on by the saloons in the area. Wagon loads of doves, or saloon girls, were taken to the river where the cowboys who were fresh off the trail stopped to bathe. The doves would strip naked and at the sound of a gun, race back to the saloons with the cowboys, whooping and hollering, running behind them. The walls of the Mulberry hosted pictures of the naked winners.

"Dal Roberts!"

He turned at the sound of his name and moved toward a table surrounded by several men who had been at the meeting that afternoon.

"Didn't expect to see you here," Joe Thomas said. "Figured you'd be busy with the feisty little filly Mansel said you'd got hitched to."

Chapter Ten

Ellie's mood wasn't any better in the morning than when she'd gone to bed, and the pounding on her door told her Dal's wasn't, either. "I'm coming," she muttered, while gathering up Clara's gray cloak. She had half a mind to wear her old coat. Dal would be too embarrassed to walk down the street beside her then. If he still insisted upon escorting her and tried to explain to others that she had worn the old coat to keep from getting dirty, she would correct him by saying it was the only coat she had, and that it was so large because she shared it with her brothers.

Half a mind wasn't enough to convince her, however, so she let the thought go and flipped the gray cloak over her arm before opening the door.

The "good morning" she'd been about to say stuck to her tongue at the sight of Dal's face. One of his eyes was black-and-blue and his bottom lip was split. The anger she'd harbored dissolved. "What on earth…?"

"Don't ask," he mumbled.

"Who—"

"I said, don't ask."

Despite his surly attitude, compassion welled within her. "You need to put something on—"

"I slept with a beefsteak on it," he said. "Are you ready?"

Ellie stepped out of the room, pulled the door closed and locked it, all the while wondering how he'd ended up in such a condition. The how was easy to imagine, but not the why. "I sincerely hope the other man, whoever he was, fared worse."

She cringed at how Dal flinched slightly, but met his somewhat crooked grin with one of her own when he replied, "He did."

"Good." His attitude might anger her at times, but she didn't loathe him and certainly didn't want to see him hurt. "I'm sure I can find the shoe store on my own if you don't feel up to it."

"I'm up to it," he answered. "If I left you alone, knowing you, you'd get a job there, too."

She opened her mouth to protest, but his smile told her he was teasing, therefore she simply said, "I don't know anything about making shoes."

He chuckled. "Well, that's good."

This time, his comment didn't elicit irritation. Instead, heat rushed to her face. She understood he was teasing her, but she couldn't figure out why that pleased her, or exactly what it made shift inside her.

They ate a large breakfast again, and easy conversation flowed between them, not only as they ate, but as they walked the numerous blocks to the shoe store. There she tried on several pairs of shoes until she found the exact pair that would match Clara's dress.

"You're sure those are the right ones?" Dal asked.

"Certain," she answered. "We wear the same size, and these will look perfect with her dress."

"I'll pay for them and have them sent to the hotel."

"Thank you." She handed over the shoes and sat down to put on her boots, which looked all the more worn and tattered surrounded by all the new pairs.

Dal returned to her side just as she stood. "Ready?"

"Yes. That was the final thing on my list."

"Good." He led the way out of the door. "I have some things I need your help with."

"You do?"

"I do."

"What?"

"You'll see."

Their first stop was at a store the likes of which she'd never seen. Besides other expensive merchandise, it had display cases of jewelry. She was in awe of the sparkling jewels, and couldn't fathom where to start when Dal insisted she help him pick out a set of cuff links for Bill and a necklace with matching ear fobs for Clara. In the end, she chose some with blue stones, knowing they would match Clara's eyes. After paying and receiving the assurance his purchases would be delivered to the hotel, Dal ushered her out the door and into the store next door, where he asked her to pick out a new winter cape for Clara.

Once again thinking of her friend, Ellie was drawn to a blue cloak, but Dal had her try on a brown cape with a soft fur collar. It was the loveliest thing she'd ever seen and much heavier and warmer than Clara's gray one, but she still had to point out that the blue would look nicer with Clara's eyes and blond hair.

"That's all right," he said. "I like this one."

"Do you even know if Clara needs a new cloak?" she asked.

"Clara would have bought one if she were here."

Ellie couldn't say that wasn't true. Clara had more clothes than anyone she'd ever known, and most likely would appreciate the brown cape as much as a blue one. Leaving the store, she pulled the gray cloak tighter together at her chin.

"With the way the temperature's dropping, I wouldn't be surprised if it snowed. Here, put this on," Dal said, draping the brown cloak he'd just purchased over her shoulders.

Attempting to pull it off, she said, "I can't. It's brand-new."

Dal's hands held the cloak on her shoulders. "That's right, it is. And it's yours."

"No, it's not."

He stepped around her and fastened the hook beneath her chin. "Yes, it is. I just bought it for you."

"You can't buy—"

"I already did."

Shocked, yet excited at the same time, Ellie couldn't do more than shake her head.

"I'm sorry for being so short with you last night and..." He shuffled his feet as if unsure of what to say.

A shiver tickled her spine. "And?"

"And I want you to have a nice coat to wear to the ball tonight."

Her stomach plummeted. The note Clara had left for her had gone beyond asking to actually begging Ellie to attend the ball with Dal. Ellie had hoped, as Clara's note had suggested, that Dal would forgo the ball. That way she could tell Clara he'd refused and that she hadn't been able to change his mind. She knew nothing about galas, and though a part of her was excited to see such an event, a larger part dreaded the prospect.

He urged her forward with a hand on her back. "We just have one more stop."

"Where's that?"

"Abigail's. I know Clara sent a dress for you to wear, but I thought you'd like your own."

"Not really," she said. "One of Clara's will do fine."

"Well, I want you to have a new one," he answered. "Call it payment for going with me."

If she had been back home, she would have refused both the dress and going to the ball, but here in Wichita, she didn't have a reason to refuse, not one she could justify anyway, so she forced herself to walk beside him down the boardwalk.

To her dismay, as well as a gorgeous gown made

of yellow silk, he instructed Abigail to send a new set of undergarments, right down to the stockings, to the hotel, along with all of the sewing things she'd left there the day before.

Ellie found it impossible to protest, perhaps because the look on Dal's face asked her not to. Or maybe it was because deep down she wanted to go to the ball. Just one time in her life she wanted to know what it would be like to be part of a world she'd only dreamed about.

Her thoughts were twirling around in her head as they walked back to the hotel. After she declined lunch, stating she was still full from breakfast— which was true—he left her alone in her room. Shortly afterwards, packages started being delivered to her room by a young cleaning girl.

On her third trip, the girl asked, "Are you going to the cattlemen's ball tonight?"

Ellie nodded, but her attention was on the dress Dal had purchased. The yellow satin was so soft and beautiful—too beautiful, and beyond anything she'd ever dreamed of wearing.

"I could help you get ready," the girl said. "And do your hair. I'm very good at it."

Gently setting the dress on the bed, Ellie's hands went to her hair. She hadn't thought about fixing it. All she ever did was twist it into a bun, and that had only been for the past two days. Usually she just tied it away from her face with a piece of string.

"It would be my pleasure," the girl said. "Truly, it would."

Ellie turned, and though her eyes settled on the

girl, her mind didn't. All she could think about was how, deep down, she'd been lying herself. For years she had dreamed of something like this happening to her. She'd dreamed of getting all dressed up and going out in public—showing the world she wasn't just a shameful cattle rustler's daughter that people pointed their fingers at. She was a real person with feelings, and full of hopes and dreams.

Swallowing the lump in her throat, she said, "I wouldn't want to impose."

"Oh, you wouldn't be," the girl said with excitement. "I have everything we need. I'll just go and get it."

Chapter Eleven

Once again, Dal felt like a greenhorn. He knew he shouldn't. He'd been to enough of these events over the years to be an old hand. The difference was, this time he wanted to go. He wanted to walk into the ballroom and watch jaws drop. That's what would happen when everyone saw Ellie dressed in her finery.

Stepping closer to the mirror, he fiddled with his string tie, making sure it was centered and then glanced up. His lip looked better, and didn't smart nearly as much as it had this morning, but his eye had definitely seen better days. The swelling had gone down, but it would be black for a few days yet. He didn't mind that. To him it was a statement. *Mess with mine, and you mess with me.*

Some little corner of his mind chose to point out that Ellie wasn't his, but he disputed this, telling himself just what he'd told her—as long as he was paying her way, she was his responsibility. Knowing himself well enough to know he could stand there arguing with himself all night, he spun away from the mirror and headed for the door.

Across the hall, standing outside Ellie's room, he took a deep breath before knocking. He'd have to warn her, tell her what had happened last night so she wouldn't…

His brain stopped working, as did his lungs, when a servant girl opened the door and stepped aside to reveal Ellie. He'd seen stunning before, but nothing had ever compared to the black-haired beauty looking back at him.

"Isn't she beautiful?"

Dal blinked and swallowed and then nodded toward the girl still holding the door open. "Yes, she is."

"Lottie did my hair," Ellie said quietly.

"She did a wonderful job," Dal answered, glad his voice was working. The rest of him seemed to have frozen stiff. Willing his hands to move, he dug into his pocket and pulled out a bill. Without looking at the denomination, as it didn't matter, he handed it to the girl. "Thank you."

"Thank you, sir," she answered. "Is there anything else you need, Ellie?"

"I don't think so," she replied. "Thank you, Lottie."

Dal found his senses when he realized he had to move for the girl to exit. He stepped into the room and in need of something to do, picked up the cape he'd purchased for Ellie in the morning. His hands balled into the material as she walked closer. Once again, sheer will alone made his muscles move enough to drape the cape over her shoulders. Her hair had been pinned up and curled, but several long ringlets caught beneath the cape's collar. He slid his hands around her neck to gently ease the hair out from the beneath the cape. The action along with the sweet flowery scent filling his nostrils and the proximity of their bodies together caused a rather chaotic rush that shot from his toes to his head and back down again. It left him as out of breath and jarred as being bucked off a horse ever had.

"I've never worn anything so beautiful." Her cheeks blushed red. "Or so many brand-new things all at once."

In the moment their eyes met, Dal realized something else. He'd never made eye contact with another woman the way he did with her. That was what had been so different about her right from the start. Since the first time he'd seen her in his parlor, whenever his eyes had found hers, they hadn't wanted to look anywhere else. And tonight he wasn't going to make them look away.

"The dress is just material, Ellie. You are what makes it beautiful."

She bowed her head bashfully and stepped back. "You look beautiful, too." Her cheeks turned redder. "I—I mean handsome. You look handsome in your suit."

"Even with a black eye?" he asked, hoping to ease her stiff posture.

She grinned. "I hardly notice it."

"Maybe I should have bought you a pair of glasses."

"Oh, no, there is nothing wrong with my eyes," she said. "And there will be no more buying of things. I promise to not get a speck of dirt on this dress so we can return everything before leaving tomorrow."

"We can't return them."

"Yes, we can. Lottie said—"

"We won't be returning anything," he interrupted, not caring what the servant girl might have said.

She walked toward the still-open door. "It would be a waste for me to keep such a dress. After tonight, I'll never have a reason to wear it again."

He followed her out and closed the door behind them. Taking the key from her outstretched hand, he suggested, "You could wear it to Clara's wedding." After locking the door, he pocketed the key. "On second thought, you can't wear that to Clara's wedding. Everyone would think you were the bride." That idea made his heart skip, and he quickly changed the subject. "They are serving a full meal before the ball, but we could eat here if you'd prefer."

"To be perfectly honest, I'm so nervous I don't know that I can eat at all."

"Nervous? Why?"

She sighed. "This isn't something I do every day."

Once again resorting to teasing in order to ease her uncertainty, he asked, "What? Be in the company of a handsome man?"

She shook her head, but grinned. "That, too."

"I'll let you in on a secret," he said, leaning down to speak softly into her ear.

Her sideways glance held skepticism, but it was also curious. "What?"

"I don't bite."

"Really?" she answered drily. "I'll try to remember that."

He kept one hand on the small of her back, liking the way it felt, as they walked down the steps and out of the front door. The wind had picked up and carried a biting chill. Leave it to Kansas to be as cold in March as it had been in January. He instantly instructed Ellie to go back inside to wait while he summoned a carriage.

"Is it that far?" she asked.

"No, but it's that cold, and it could start raining."

Neither of them had had time to step back inside when someone shouted his name and a buggy rolled to a stop across the street.

"Can we offer you a lift?" Walter Hagen asked.

"We'd be obliged," he shouted to Walter before hurrying Ellie across the street. While assisting her into the backseat of the buggy, he made the introductions. "This is Walter and Edith Hagen."

"And you must be Ellie," Edith supplied, twisting about on the front seat to smile at her. "Walter told me I'd get to meet you tonight."

That was when Dal realized he'd never explained to Ellie what had happened the previous night.

With a laugh and a shake of her head, Edith continued, "As you can see from Walter's face, he was in the same saloon as Dal. It happens every time we come to Wichita. Someone starts a fight and every cowboy in town has to get in the mix, throwing punches like they are boys in a schoolyard rather than men who should know better."

As Ellie arranged her skirt, giving Dal room on the seat beside her, he saw her eyes move from him to Edith and then to Walter, who had one eye as black-and-blue as his own.

"Men are like that," Edith said. "I don't believe they ever grow up, but I'm so glad to meet you. Are you enjoying your trip to Wichita?"

"Yes, thank you," Ellie answered. "And it's nice to meet you, too. Both of you."

"I'm sure Dal has told you about us. We knew his parents, and we just got our invitation to Clara's wedding before we left home. Oh, there is nothing like a spring wedding. It's the only time to get married. That's when Walter and I were married. Of course we lived over in Missouri then. It was a beautiful day and the cherry trees were full of blossoms. Remember that, Walter? How Momma's cherry trees were blooming?"

"Yes, dear, I remember," Walter answered as he pulled the buggy back into the line of traffic.

Until a sharp pain struck him, Dal hadn't been aware he was gnawing on his bottom lip. He had no way of knowing how much Walter had said to Edith about last night.

A completely different train of thought had him wondering if Walter really remembered the cherry blossoms or not. Probably not. Weddings were for women. Men just showed up because they had to.

"I also remember how pretty you looked that

day, dear," Walter said. "Almost as pretty as you do now."

"Oh, you," Edith said, her cheeks flushing pink. "You are just saying that so I'll forget you were in a fight last night."

"Is it working?" Walter asked.

Dal didn't hear Edith's answer. His attention had turned to Ellie, who was giggling behind her hand. He gave her a wink and smiled when her cheeks turned as pink as Edith's.

Edith monopolized the conversation, talking about their four children who ranged in age from eight to sixteen and were all back at the ranch, which was about fifty miles south of the Rocking R. Dal kept one ear tuned in at all times, ready to change the subject if Edith brought up the fact that Walter had been with his pa when Ellie's father had been hanged. The subject had come up last night and was a major part of what had caused the all-out fist fight that had left the Mulberry Tree Saloon with more broken tables and chairs than unbroken ones.

By the time they arrived at the community hall hosting the ball, Dal was no longer worried about Edith mentioning the past. She was a lot like his mother had been, and was most likely glad to see that Ellie wasn't being blamed for what her father had done. However, he did wonder what a few others might say, and he pulled Ellie aside as soon as she stepped down from the buggy.

Edith, however, had other plans. "Come along,

dear. We'll go inside to wait while the men see to the horses. Hurry now, before we get windblown."

The caution in Ellie's eyes said she understood something was up but not what, and the way she was holding one hand to her head told him she was also afraid the blustery wind would ruin her hair.

"Go on," he said. "I'll be in shortly."

Ellie couldn't deny the sinking feeling in her stomach as she hurried up the steps of the large building. Dal was nervous and it seemed to have nothing to do with the ball. Well, it both did and didn't. He was clearly nervous about bringing her here, and rightfully so. Wearing a new dress or not, she was a weed in a flower garden and always would be.

"Goodness that wind is fierce," Edith said once they were inside. "We'll wait here for the men."

Ellie nodded, but her eyes were on the large room. Tables covered with tablecloths were arranged near the back wall, leaving much of the floor open for dancing. She'd never danced, other than skipping around the front yard when something had made her giddy with silliness. With fear bubbling inside her, she spun toward the door, but found it crowded with others rushing in to get out of the wind.

Edith tugged on her arm, pulling her farther into the room. "There's Charlotte Wyman, I'll introduce you."

Ellie stepped closer to Edith, but shook her head. "I'd prefer to wait for Dal, if you don't mind."

"All right," Edith agreed.

The more people who stepped through the door, the more nervous Ellie became. She had never been fond of crowds, probably because she'd never been in them, at least not one like this. When Dal finally walked through the door, she had to stop herself from rushing forward.

"Let's find some chairs before they are all taken," Walter said, taking Edith's arm.

Ellie was glad to move away from the crowds, but even more glad to be able to glue herself to Dal's side. "Goodness," she whispered, "I didn't think there would be this many people."

"They come from around the state for the annual meeting," he said.

"Is that where you were all afternoon?"

"Yes."

"What was it about?"

"Cattle."

"I figured that much. What about them?"

"We've had a lot of issues with diseases this year, and cows being brought up from Texas are the culprits, so most of the discussion was about quarantining them."

"How can you do that?"

"Not let them cross the state line," he answered.

"I never thought of cows getting sick."

"They do," he said. "And it can quickly take over an entire herd."

"What happens then?"

"They die."

She truly hadn't thought of such issues. "Do you eat them then?"

"No. We can't. Anything that eats the meat could get sick, too. We can't have that, so we bury the dead or, if there's a lot, burn them."

"Raising cattle is a lot of work, isn't it?" she asked.

"Yes, but it has its rewards, too."

They arrived at a table where Walter and Edith were taking off their coats. Ellie glanced at the other occupants. All of the men hosted bruises of some sort. She turned to Dal. "Was everyone from the Cattlemen's Club in a fight last night?"

"Most of them," he answered, reaching over to help her with her cloak.

It was warmer on this side of the room. Either that, or Dal's presence heated her insides enough that she didn't notice the cold, not even when he lifted the cape from her shoulders. He handed it to a man who was holding several other cloaks and then he pulled out a chair for her to sit on.

Between him and Edith, who sat on her other side, Ellie was introduced to everyone at the table and several others who stopped to visit momentarily before moving on to other tables. She would never be able to remember so many names, and after the first few, gave up trying. The guests at the table were friendly, and she relaxed enough to eat a portion of the food put in front of her. Once again the servings were more than she usually ate in an entire day, or even two at times.

During the meal, several men stood behind a

podium to talk about votes and the quarantine Dal had mentioned. Overall, she found their speeches interesting, which surprised her. Cattle had always been a sore spot for her, which now seemed silly. They were animals that needed to be taken care of and protected by their owners. They were expensive, too—something else she'd learned and had never thought about before.

Shortly after the meal ended, several men with instruments gathered along the wall. Even before they started playing, couples left their tables and walked to the center of the floor in preparation. Once the music started, Ellie watched, a bit in awe at the way the men and women moved together.

When Edith and Walter left the table to join the dancers, Dal turned to her. "Do you want to dance?"

Ellie shook her head.

"Do you want to leave?"

She turned him. "Do you?"

"Not if you don't."

She leaned back to examine him more thoroughly. "You didn't want to come in the first place."

"At first, but I changed my mind."

"Why?"

"Well…" He scratched the side of his neck. "Last night—"

"Imagine that, Dal Roberts bringing someone besides his sister to the ball."

A chill rippled over Ellie's shoulders. She'd heard that voice someplace before and shifted in her chair to turn around enough to see who it was.

Her heart stumbled at the sight of the woman who had caused the commotion in the dress shop.

"Imagine that," Dal said. "I finally met someone I don't mind taking out in public."

Ellie almost choked on her own saliva, and spun around to gape at Dal. He sounded like the arrogant Dal again, not the man who moments ago had been acting nervous, or the one who had been so charming and pleasant all day.

"Come on, Ellie, let's dance."

He stood and pulled her to her feet. Though she didn't want to dance, had no idea how to dance, she did want to get away from that woman.

Dal led her among the other dancers, and copying what the other women were doing, she put one hand on his shoulder while he clasped her other one.

"Just let your feet follow mine," he said.

It took her a few clumsy steps, but finally she understood what he meant, and soon they were gliding across the floor as elegantly as the other couples. Those people faded away and so did all her other thoughts as Dal guided her. He was smiling down at her, and she couldn't look away. He did that to her—could catch her gaze so deeply she felt as if he could see right inside her. This time, that didn't even scare her, not like it usually did, and she didn't mind not looking away. As a matter of fact, there wasn't anywhere else she wanted to look. Not even when the music ended and they parted in order to applaud.

As the clapping stopped, someone pushed her

from behind. Ellie caught herself from tripping by planting both hands on Dal's chest. He gripped her waist and, secure in the strength of his hold, she looked over her shoulder.

It was that woman again. Only this time a man was with her, who with two black eyes was almost unrecognizable as the man who had been at the dressmaker's shop.

"Caroline, come on," he said, pulling on the woman's arm.

"But, Ed, I want to introduce you to— No, wait, that's right," the woman said loudly while pointing a finger at Ellie. "You aren't Dal's wife, you were just pretending." Twisting about, she said into the crowd, "She was just pretending."

Ellie's spine stiffened as her stomach sank.

Beside her, Dal growled, "Mansel, I told you last night to control your wife."

The man's name clicked in Ellie's mind, and suddenly so did Caroline's. Was this the Caroline who had broken Dal's heart? That seemed impossible. And the man beside her certainly wasn't more handsome than Dal, not in any way.

"I'm sorry, Dal," the man said while grimacing. "I—"

"You're sorry?" the woman interrupted. "For what?"

"For your behavior," the man replied.

"My behavior?" Caroline screeched.

"Yes. Do you think I don't know you only agreed to marry me in order to make Dal jealous? It didn't work, Caroline."

Stomping a foot, Caroline shouted, "She's the one running around town claiming to be married to him."

"No, she didn't," Dal said.

"Oh, shut up!" she snapped before spinning toward her husband. "He stands up for a lying little tramp, and you—"

"That's enough, Caroline," the man said.

"No, it's not enough!" Spinning back around, Caroline shouted, "She shouldn't even be allowed at this ball. Her father was a cattle rustler, and he's a stupid fool for thinking—

Ellie didn't hear the rest of Caroline's words, nor did she take the time to think through her reaction. Anger filled her and rather than duck as she had at the dress shop, when the woman came at her this time, Ellie swung a punch. "Dal isn't stupid, or a fool!"

It wasn't until Caroline hit the floor, blood coming out of her nose, that Ellie realized what she'd done.

Shouts sounded and people rushed forward, and Ellie wanted to disappear. Knowing that was impossible, she looked at Ed Mansel, who was kneeling beside his wife. "I'm sorry. I—I— So sorry."

He waved a hand, and Ellie spun around to Dal.

"I'm sorry, but she had no right to call you a stupid fool."

Dal did the most unexpected thing. He didn't shout or stomp away. Instead, he pulled her close and kissed her square on the lips.

Ellie went into complete shock. At least that was

what she assumed had happened. Why else would her knees want to buckle and bees be buzzing in her ears? Dal's hold kept her upright as he continued to kiss her. She gasped for air when his lips left hers, and her head fell forward. Dal kissed her on the forehead before pulling her against his chest.

His arms around her felt so wonderful, she stood there until her senses returned enough that she could comprehend the rumble coming from his chest was laughter. The rest of her off-kilter senses returned, and she snapped up her head.

"What are you laughing at?"

"I think that was the best right hook I've ever seen."

Ellie stepped back and rubbed the knuckles on her right hand, which were throbbing. Thinking about what she'd just done, she glanced about gingerly. People were still gathered near, but no one was pointing. They were grinning and nodding, and one man even winked at her. Peering back up at Dal, she asked, "Where's Caroline?"

"Ed carried her out the door," he answered. "You want some ice for that hand?"

She shook her head. "No, it'll be fine. I've punched my brothers harder than that."

When the piano player hit the keys, Dal took her hand. "In that case, let's dance."

Chapter Twelve

As Ellie carefully wrapped the beautiful yellow dress in the paper it had arrived in, she wished she didn't have to give it back. But knew she did. Last night would forever live in her mind as the dream that really had come true. She didn't need a dress she would never wear again to remind her of dancing with Dal. Of laughing like she'd never laughed before. Of feeling as if she wasn't an outsider, a weed among flowers.

She set the package on the table with the others as a knock sounded on her door. Drawing in a deep breath, she placed a hand on her chest in an attempt to slow the commotion of her heart. Dal had only kissed her that once, right after she'd punched Caroline, but when he'd said good-night, she'd thought he had been about to kiss her again and had bolted into her room, only to regret having done so. In fact, she had regretted it so much, she'd lain awake most of the night.

Disappointment flooded her system when she opened the door and found it wasn't Dal on the other side.

"Mr. Roberts sent me to haul your luggage down

to the lobby," Oscar said. "The carriage will be around to get you shortly."

"Thank you," she said. "It's all right there. Lottie knows where those packages go."

He nodded. "Mr. Roberts—"

"Is right here."

Her heart somersaulted at the sound of Dal's voice.

"Good morning," he said. "Did you sleep well?"

The commotion inside her continued, but she managed to say, "Yes, thank you. You?"

"Yes, you wore me out. I haven't danced that much in years."

As usual, his teasing calmed her nerves and gave her the courage to retort. "Well, I've never danced that much, so we're even."

"I hope I don't have blisters. Do you?"

"Do I what? Have blisters or hope that you do?"

Dal chuckled and took her arm to lead her out of the room. "New boots can cause blisters."

"Not those ones," she said, referring to the pair that had been delivered to her room yesterday before the ball. They hadn't been the pair of shoes she'd picked out for Clara; those were packed and ready to be delivered back to Buckley. She'd packed up the new boots, too, along with her dress, in order for them to be returned to the shoe store, but she'd never forget them. Not only had they been extremely soft and comfortable, they'd been embroidered with yellow flowers that had perfectly matched the dress she'd worn. "I packaged them up. Lottie knows where to return them."

"I heard you tell Oscar that," he said. "Ready for breakfast? You'll want to eat as much as possible. I think we're in for a long day of traveling. The snow is really coming down out there."

"I noticed that from the window," she answered. "So much for an early spring." She hadn't meant to say that aloud, but the gloomy sky on the other side of the window was depressing. As if she'd needed a reminder that her future wasn't full of sunshine and trees covered with blossoms. "It won't slow the train, will it?" she asked.

"Anxious to get home?"

They were walking down the stairs, and she feigned interest in her steps. She wasn't the least bit anxious to get home, but she certainly couldn't tell him that.

"Don't worry, trains can travel through the snow."

Of course they could. Nothing as simple as the weather could prevent her from returning to the world in which she belonged. "I know," she answered. "I hear their whistles all the time. Even when it's snowing." She held in a sigh, thinking about all the times she'd heard those whistles, wishing she was on one of those trains and not in her sod shanty sparingly burning twists of grass and tree roots to keep from freezing.

They ate a large breakfast, thanked Sara for the wonderful meal and the basket of food she'd packed for their day of traveling and then climbed into the enclosed carriage that would take them to the train station. Ellie was surprised at the amount of snow that had fallen, and was glad she didn't have on the embroidered boots or the cape with the fur collar. The wet snow would have damaged them. Her worn boots and old coat were much more suited to this weather. Much more suited to her life.

Once she and Dal were seated across from each other on the train's hard seats with only the basket from Sara on the floor, she asked, "Where are our bags?"

"I had them put in the baggage car along with the things we bought for Clara."

She nodded and glanced around. "There are more people on the train this time."

He scanned the car before agreeing. "A few, but I don't see a cat."

"You didn't see Miss Priss until she wanted your sandwich."

"You're right, I didn't." He scanned the car again, this time leaning down to glance under the benches.

"Oh, stop it," she said, tickled by his actions.

"Hopefully Sara packed enough to share."

She frowned. "Why? Did you see a cat?"

"No, but as you pointed out, I didn't last time, either."

The train jerked and jolted a few times before it began to roll more smoothly. Through the falling snow, Ellie watched buildings roll past the window until the last one had disappeared completely. She couldn't stop the sigh that left her lungs.

"Did you have a good time?" Dal asked.

There was no reason to deny it. "Actually, I did. Did you?"

"Actually, I did, too."

She grinned at how he teased her, and then bit her bottom lip, unable to think of anything else to say. The trip would soon be over, and things would return to the way they'd always been. The way they were supposed to be.

Dal stood and turned around, sitting down beside her on the bench. "I have something for you."

Finding she wasn't in the least disturbed by his closeness, she asked, "What?"

He reached inside his brown coat and pulled out a newspaper. "It's today's." Snapping it open, he said, "We can read it together."

The trip would end soon, but until it was over, there was no reason why she couldn't enjoy the friendship they'd formed. "All right." She leaned closer to his shoulder and he put one arm around her, holding the paper wide-open in front of both of them. By page three, or maybe four, the words turned into nothing but blurry smudges, and she stifled a yawn. The slow movement of the train was like a rocking chair lulling her to sleep. Well, that and being snuggled against Dal.

When Ellie's head landed on his shoulder, Dal folded up the paper and tossed it onto the opposite bench before he rested his head on top of hers and closed his eyes. Not kissing her good-night at her door had kept him awake half the night. Or maybe it had been kissing her at the dance. For it had been the lingering taste of her kiss that had eaten away at him until the wee hours of the morning.

As well as the flashing image of the solid right hook she'd laid into Caroline. Ellie had the same attitude as him—*mess with mine, and you'll be sorry.* Caroline had deserved that punch. It seemed everyone had thought so, and said he'd landed quite a catch when it came to Ellie. He'd admitted that the couple from the train had been wrong in assuming that they were married, but he'd never once protested against him and Ellie being a couple. He couldn't say why, but that idea didn't bother him. Not in the least.

Dal couldn't say how long he'd slept, but when he awoke, the desire to taste Ellie's lips again was stronger than ever. Especially when she stirred slightly and lifted her eyelids, looking at him with sleep-filled eyes.

He'd been wrong yesterday. She'd been stunning all dressed up for the ball, but right now, with those shimmering sleepy eyes, she was by far the most beautiful woman on earth. Without further ado, he leaned down and pressed his lips to hers.

It took Ellie a moment to realize she wasn't still dreaming, and another to remember she was on a train, headed home. It was that final thought that made her snap her head back, breaking the kiss. Her heart raced and her lips tingled. She pressed three fingers against them and refused to glance toward Dal.

Her breathing was still haphazard when he asked, "Did you have a good nap?"

She nodded, but feeling the need to change the subject, she pointed out how slow the train was traveling. "I hope we make it to Buckley before dark."

"We will," Dal answered.

Ellie bit her lip and tried hard not to think about how her mouth was still tingling, along with other parts of her.

"Don't worry," he said.

"I'm not worried."

"Good." His tone said he didn't believe her.

"I'm not," she insisted.

"It was snowing the first time I rode on a train," he said.

With a mixture of interest and skepticism, she asked, "It was?"

"Yes, I was eight and..."

He easily drew her into a story of visiting his grandparents, and that led to another and another. She enjoyed learning things about him, and to her surprise, shared things about her own childhood while they ate from the lunch basket. Afterward, Dal invited her to join him in a walk through the car to share their leftovers with the other passengers. Everyone was thankful for the food, and she felt a sense of pride like she'd never known.

By the time the train pulled into the Buckley depot, evening was well upon them. As Ellie walked down the steps she wondered how to say goodbye to Dal. She knew it should be a trivial issue, but somehow it wasn't.

Sheriff Herber met them on the snow-covered platform. "I'm sorry, folks, but the train will be held up here. The snow storm's too dangerous for any traveling. The hotel is full, but we have families who have agreed to take you all in for the night. Hopefully the storm will be over by morning and you can continue your travels."

The biting wind and snow, as well as the passengers hurrying along, created a chaos that matched what was happening inside Ellie as Dal hurried her away from the train station. The weather had truly become her enemy today. Not only was it now delaying her separation from Dal—something she was already struggling with—but it put her in a very precarious position. The sheriff had directed them to his house. *Her*, Ellie Alexander, a rustler's daughter, staying with the town lawman didn't seem right. Where was spring when she needed it?

It turned out her fears were unfounded. The sheriff and his wife were friendly and welcoming, and their three young sons were utterly charming, especially the way they joked around with Dal. Her time at the sheriff's home turned out to be as enchanting as the ball had been, minus Dal's kiss, which filled her mind again that night while lying in Rupert's bed. Rupert was the sheriff's youngest son, aged only five, and he'd been thrilled at the prospect of sleeping with his mother and father— which brought teasing from his older brothers until

Dal pointed out that they used to like sleeping with their mother and father, too. They'd agreed he was right when he'd admitted that he had liked sleeping in his parents' bed when he was young.

His words must have stuck in her mind, because that night she dreamed about being snuggled in a big, soft bed with Dal and a tiny child. That dream, or the memory of Dal's kisses, didn't lessen in the morning. They stayed in her mind long after she had risen and dressed.

The weather seemed to take pity upon her, too. The storm had stopped during the night and the bright sunshine was melting the snow as fast as it had fallen the day before. Dal refused to allow her to walk and insisted upon renting a buggy to take them both home.

"Do you want to stop at the ranch and see Clara?" Dal asked after they'd traveled some distance.

As much as she would have liked to, and understanding Dal was surely anxious to see how his sister was doing, Ellie shook her head. It was time for her to get home and return to being a weed, just like the ones sprouting up alongside the road despite the melting snow. Those weeds were her homecoming. They were signs that she was back where she belonged. But it had been a wonderful four days, full of more fun and adventures than she'd ever even dreamed about.

"You're awfully quiet this morning," he said.

She nodded. He'd been doing that since they'd left town—trying to engage her in conversation—

but she held her tongue. She couldn't be sure of what might slip out if she opened her mouth. The dreams and memories filling her head left her discontented, and she felt it far more strongly than ever before. It had been easy to believe things could be different while in the city, but back here, where every bump and corner was familiar, she had to face the fact that nothing had changed. She was still Ellie Alexander, a rustler's daughter. People in Wichita hadn't all known that, and therefore had accepted her being at Dal's side, but that wouldn't happen back here in Buckley. Here they would point out she didn't belong at his side. Didn't belong anywhere near him. And no one would be more certain of that than her brothers.

When Dal pulled the wagon up next to the sod shanty, she quickly climbed down and grabbed her traveling bag out of the back. "Thank you for the lift home and tell Clara I'll be over to see her later this week," she said, heading for the door.

He'd already climbed down from his seat and stopped her before she got all the way to the house. "Whoa up. There's other stuff in the back that belongs to you."

She held her bag up a bit higher. "No, there's not."

"The things I bought for you are yours. They weren't returned."

Ellie's stomach churned as if she was about to be sick, and her eyes burned. She sincerely didn't need any reminders of what couldn't be. "Thank you, but I have no need for them."

He stiffened and she looked away, unable to meet the anger that flashed in his eyes, and blinked away the tears in hers.

"What about the material for Clara's wedding dress?"

She'd forgotten about that—the very reason she'd gone on the trip—and suddenly realized not visiting the ranch any more than was necessary would serve her best. "I—I'll sew it here. I'll put my bag away and come and get it."

"I'll carry it in."

Her insides quivered, yet she knew protesting wouldn't stop him.

The interior of the shanty was dark and gloomy. Thankfully James and Daniel, who must have left hours before, hadn't left things in disarray, but it was still a sod shanty. This little shack seemed the epitome of her life. Of who she was.

"You can just set it by the door." Although her back was to him, she felt the moment Dal stepped over the threshold.

She closed her eyes against the sting of tears, which only made the sound of him setting things down that much louder. The stinging grew as he grasped her shoulders and spun her around.

Ellie didn't have time to open her eyes before his lips landed on hers. This kiss was far more ardent than his others, and some inner will she couldn't control had her responding eagerly. When his tongue slipped inside her mouth, she grasped the sides of his coat, wishing she would never have to let go.

She knew she had to, though, and battled against herself until she found enough will to break the kiss and spin around. Her heart was racing and breaking at the same time. The past few days had been wonderful, and a time she'd never forget, but she was home now. Someday things might be different, but today wasn't someday.

"Ellie—"

"Goodbye, Dal," she said firmly. "Goodbye."

Chapter Thirteen

Spring arrived with such force it was hard to believe that a foot of snow had covered the ground what seemed like only days before. Although, actually, it hadn't been days, but weeks. The fields had turned completely green, the trees had budded out and birds greeted each morning with more happiness than Ellie could stand.

"Would you like me to borrow a wagon from Mr. Weston again so you can take Clara her dress?" James asked as they ate breakfast.

He had done that for her shortly after she'd returned home. Clara had been very happy to see her, and excited about the dress, but had been so full of questions about the trip to Wichita and the cattlemen's ball that Ellie dreaded the idea of visiting again. Dal hadn't been at home, and fearing he might be on her next trip had made her put off another visit.

"Her wedding is only a few days away," James said.

"I know when her wedding is." Ellie flinched slightly. She hadn't meant to snap at him.

"You sure haven't been yourself since you got

home, Ellie," Daniel said. "What happened in Wichita?"

Ellie drew a deep breath. The discontentment that had settled deep and hard inside her was so suffocating it hurt to breathe at times. "If you must know," she said, looking for a reason herself, "I was offered a job while in Wichita."

"Doing what?" James asked.

"Sewing. The woman who owns the shop where I got the material for Clara's dress wanted to hire me on the spot. Said I had a job waiting there whenever I wanted it."

"That's great, Ellie," James said.

His excitement surprised her.

"You've always wanted to be a seamstress," he continued. "Are you going to take her up on her offer?"

Ellie glanced from him to Daniel. "Who would take care of you two?"

They both laughed. "We are plenty capable of taking care of ourselves," Daniel said.

"Besides," James replied, glancing at them and shrugging, "you both know Bonnie Weston and I have been sweet on each other for some time. Well, Bonnie wants to get married this spring. It seems there's something about spring weddings. Anyway, I agreed to it but wasn't sure how to tell you."

Ellie was a bit stunned. "Tell me?"

"Yes, you've been moping around since you got home. Now that I know it's because you had to come home to sew Clara's dress, I can see why. I'm sure you would have rather stayed in Wichita."

Ellie couldn't say that was true. "You wouldn't mind if I moved? Wouldn't miss me?"

"Oh, we'd miss you," Daniel said, "but we can't all live here together forever."

Dumbfounded, she turned to him.

"Do you have plans to get married, too?"

A sliver of anger struck her. She'd had all the spring wedding talk she could handle. It must be some sort of fever that hit at this time of year. While sewing Clara's dress, she'd even fantasized about her own spring wedding—and who the groom would be.

"No," Daniel said with a laugh. "But I do have plans." He glanced at James and waited for a nod before he said, "I talked to Jamison at the depot, and he's willing to take me on as an apprentice."

"At the railroad?" she asked.

"Yep. Every time I hear a train whistle blow, I feel like it's calling to me." He shrugged. "But I couldn't leave you here alone, not with James getting married."

"Now that you have a job in Wichita, we can all move on," James added.

"Move on?" she repeated. "What about this place?"

"Considering it butts up against Dal Roberts's land, I'm hoping he'll be interested in buying it," James said. "That would give us each a bit of starting money."

Her heart skipped a beat at just the sound of Dal's name. "You'd sell this place to Dal?" she asked. "I thought you hated him."

"I don't hate Dal," James said. "There's no reason to. We can't blame him for his father hanging ours. That was Pa's fault, not ours, or Dal's."

"But—"

"It's long past time for all of us to move out from under the dark cloud Pa left hanging over us," Daniel said. "I think selling this place would be the best thing."

"Think about it, Ellie," James said, pushing away from the table. "We can talk about it tonight."

She hadn't come up with a response before they'd both left for work, and still wasn't sure what she thought about it long after the breakfast dishes had been washed and put away. The shanty had been the only home she'd ever known, and while she'd claimed to hate it, she wasn't ready to leave. Or maybe she just wasn't ready to move to Wichita.

Opening the door to toss out the dishwater, she stumbled at the sight of the man standing on the stoop. The dishpan jostled in her hand, and though both she and Dal fumbled to catch it, the pan toppled, sloshing both him and her in the process.

He laughed as he picked it up. "I didn't mean to scare you."

"You didn't scare me," she said, instantly defensive.

"All right, I didn't mean to startle you."

Her heart was already thudding, but the beat doubled when she saw the shine in Dal's blue eyes. She took the pan from him and spun about to carry it inside to the table. "What are you doing here?"

Once again, her entire body felt the moment he crossed the threshold.

"Well, I could say Clara sent me to check on her dress, but that would be a lie."

Ellie turned about, prepared to tell him the dress was finished, but her breath caught in the back of her throat, making speech impossible. He was moving closer and all she could think about was the last time he'd been here. The last time she'd seen him. The kiss they'd shared.

"Truth is, Ellie, I've missed you. Missed you like I've never missed anyone, and I'm tired of it."

A bout of trembles overtook her. "T-t-tired of it?"

Dal had known seeing her would send his insides on a wild ride, but he could handle that. What he couldn't handle was not seeing her. "Yep," he said. "And I'm tired of hearing about spring weddings and how every girl wants one."

He reached out and took hold of the hands she was wringing together. Feeling how they trembled, he held them more firmly. "Is it true?" he asked.

She frowned slightly and bit her bottom lip before lifting her head to meet his gaze. "Is what true?"

"That every girl wants a spring wedding?"

Shrugging slightly, she answered, "It seems so."

"Do you?"

She took a step back and Dal followed, pinning her between the table and him. He'd mulled over his options for far too long and wasn't about to let her get away. Over the past few weeks he'd come to understand why Ellie had always made him feel like a greenhorn, why he'd jumped at the opportunity to defend her when someone had remarked on who her father was at the Mulberry Tree Saloon, why he'd been so upset about Abigail offering her a job and why he hadn't gotten a good night's rest since they'd arrived home from Wichita. If there ever had been a man in love, it was him.

"Do you, Ellie?" he repeated.

"Do I what?"

"Want a spring wedding?"

She glanced left and right, avoiding making eye contact.

He leaned closer, forcing her to look at him. "I do, and when a cowboy says *I do*, he means it from the bottom of his boots."

"What? You—"

"I want a spring wedding, and years from now, I want my wife to ask me if I remember how the cherry trees were blooming so I can tell her that I do and that I remember how beautiful she was that day. And how beautiful she still is and will always be. Do you want to know who I want that woman to be?"

Her eyelids closed and her lips trembled as she pressed them together.

"You, Ellie," he whispered, his insides chaotic. He'd never bared his soul before, but he'd bare more than his soul for her. "I want to marry you, and I'm hoping beyond all I've ever hoped for that you want to marry me."

Her eyes snapped open and the light that shone from them lit up his insides until she sighed and bowed her head. Holding his breath, he waited for the moment he'd feared.

"You can't want to marry me, Dal."

"Yes, I can, and I do."

"I'm Ellie Alexander," she said. "My father—"

"I know who you are, and I know who your father was. I just hope you can forgive me for who my father was."

She frowned. "Forgive *you*? Your father—"

"What my father did to yours was far worse than what yours did to him," Dal said, voicing another thing he'd come to understand and accept. "I'm hoping we can move past that, Ellie. Neither of us had anything to do with anything that happened back then."

"I know we didn't," she said, "but you don't even like me."

"Yes, I do. I have for a very long time." Knowing she'd argue until the moon turned blue, he said, "Matter of fact, I love you. Now will you marry me or not?"

Pinching her lips together she whispered, "People will—"

"What other people think has never concerned me," he said. "You know that, but let me assure you, no one questions my actions. And they won't this time, either. This is between you and me, Ellie, not our fathers, or anyone else."

She appeared taken aback, so he clarified, "Will you marry me? Yes or no?" Then, taking it a step further, he said, "Yes, and I kiss you, no, and I walk away."

Her features softened as a smile tilted the edges of her mouth upward. "You'll walk away?"

His insides jolted briefly, until he realized she'd seen though his bluff as she most likely always would. "No," he admitted, "I'll get on my knees and beg."

She shook her head slightly and then stretched upward. Moments before she pressed her lips to his, she whispered, "You Robertses are impossible to say no to."

"Good," he replied, and pulled her into a kiss neither of them would ever forget.

Chapter Fourteen

$\mathcal{Y}$ears from now Ellie knew she would remember how handsome Dal looked, and how happy she felt walking down the aisle toward him. The sun was shining, but at that moment, she knew that made little difference. It could have been cloudy or raining or snowing. The sunshine was inside her.

She and Dal said their I dos alongside Clara and Bill, something Clara had insisted upon, and this time, Ellie had had no desire to argue or say no. Clara wore the gown Ellie had sewn, and Ellie wore the one Dal had bought in Wichita. He'd offered to buy her another one, but this was the one she wanted to wear again—although the dress mattered little to her. The man she was marrying was all she cared about, and when he vowed to love her, she felt the strength of his words clear to her toes.

How he affirmed that promise with a breath-stealing kiss at the end of the ceremony sent a fiery thrill through her. When the kiss ended, he murmured against her mouth, "This is just the beginning, darling."

The mischief in his eyes made her giggle. "Promise?"

"Oh, I promise."

The excitement that ensued barely allowed her to keep her feet on the ground, and the anticipation of what was yet to come had her wishing the festivities were over.

It appeared Dal thought the same, because shortly after they had received a swell of congratulations and well-wishing, he whispered in her ear, "Ready to make our exit?"

She nodded, and neither of them looked back as they hurried toward the ranch house. At the front door, Dal paused long enough to sweep her into his arms, and a wail of whoops and hollers from their guests followed them from afar as he carried her over the threshold. A heated blush flooded her system, for the guests surely knew what she and Dal were about to do, but it wasn't enough to quell the eagerness flowing through her veins. Besides, he had been right—no one questioned his actions.

For the past few days, while making the final preparations for the wedding, she and Clara had giggled and gossiped about what their wedding nights would bring—the full initiation into womanhood. Those discussions had left Ellie giddy, but also a bit nervous.

Dal carried her all the way up the long stairway and down the hall to his room before setting her down. As if reading her thoughts, he said, "Don't be frightened, Ellie. I'll never hurt you."

She looped her arms around his neck. "It's not you I'm frightened of," she whispered. "It's me. I'm dying to become your wife in every way. It's as if all of my dreams are coming true, and I'm afraid I'm going to do something, make a mistake—"

He stilled her words with a gentle, sincere kiss that filled her heart so completely it swelled in her chest.

"No mistake will ever make me stop loving you," he murmured against her lips. "Nothing will ever do that."

Tears welled in her eyes. "I hope not, Dal. I love you so much, I don't want to disappoint you, not ever."

He'd leaned back and held her face with both hands. "Say that again."

"I don't want to—"

"No," he said. "The 'I love you' part. It's the first time you've said it."

Taken aback, she shook her head. "It is?"

"Yes, I was starting to worry—"

Alarmed, she pressed one hand to his mouth. "That I didn't love you?"

He nodded.

"Why would I marry you if I didn't love you?"

"There are all sorts of reasons people get married," he said. "I was willing to take whatever I could get."

If Ellie hadn't already realized she loved him more than this world could understand, she would have known for sure at that moment. She had to sniff as the tears on her cheeks made her nose itch. "No one in my family ever said *I love you*," she whispered. "So it's a bit foreign to me, but I assumed you knew how deeply I love you."

"I do now," he replied softly, "and I'm ready to show you just how deeply I love you."

He undressed her slowly, as if her dress was made of some fragile fabric that one had to be extra cautious with. It was insanely and incredibly wonderful, and though she felt a hint of shyness when she was completely bare, she also felt powerful. He loved her, and she him, and she never wanted him to doubt that ever again.

His fingertips barely touched her skin as he slid his hands down both of her arms and back up. "You are so beautiful. So breathtakingly beautiful."

"That's a bit like *I love you*," she said, stepping closer to him. "They're foreign words to me, but I like hearing you say them." Liking the smile on his lips, she kissed his chin. "Now quit fooling around cowboy and kick off your boots."

He laughed and swung her into his arms, holding her only long enough to drop her onto the bed. "Whatever you say, darling."

She twisted to pull the covers out from beneath her and then plumped up the pillows. He was kicking off his undergarments when she turned to lie back against the pillows. After sweeping a gaze from his bare toes up to his overly handsome face, she held out both arms. "I'm waiting."

His passion was as powerful as his strength, and his teasing nature even more prominent as he set about introducing her to the marriage bed. Between his lips and hands, Ellie was soon beside herself, reaching a desperation she'd never expected. Dal was taking his time, exploring every minute part of her body with such thoroughness she feared she might burst. She repeated his name over and over and her hips rose off the bed as his hands and lips created an intensely burning need so powerful she could barely breathe.

"Dear heavens," she mumbled between gasps, "what are you doing to me?"

"Loving you," he replied.

"Well, for land's sake," she all but shouted, "don't stop."

"I won't, darling," he replied. "I won't."

The moment, the one she hadn't realized she'd been waiting for until it happened, arrived when Dal slowly slid inside her. Her entire being tensed momentarily at a snap, but then her breathing quickened at the pleasure of raising her hips to meet his.

"Oh," she whispered. "Oh, Dal."

"Hello, Mrs. Roberts," he said as his mouth met hers. Their tongues played a game of hide-and-seek while their bodies united in a ritual so spectacular she didn't want it to ever end. They moved together, as one, rising and falling, all the time kissing and whispering words of pleasure and love.

All the wildest dreams in the world could never have prepared her for all of this. The love, the passion, the need, the finality. Like a bubble blown too big, all of a sudden she seemed to pop, and it was the most satisfying, beautiful thing that had ever occurred inside her.

Then she realized Dal was holding her close and breathing as hard as she was, and they were both covered in a sheen of sweat, and she loved every detail.

"Are you all right?" he asked.

"I've never...been more...all right...in my life," she responded, still trying to catch her breath.

Dal rolled off her to lie on his side, watching her closely. "Me, neither."

She closed her eyes, still a bit stunned and a whole lot happier. "Goodness." Taking in a deep breath in order to speak without gasping, she said, "I guess I didn't do anything wrong."

Dal chuckled and kissed the end of her nose. "You, Mrs. Roberts, are amazing." Plucking out one of the yellow blossoms she'd pinned in her hair, he said, "As amazing and beautiful as a flower in full bloom."

Content and fulfilled, Ellie closed her eyes and smiled. "I am, aren't I?"

* * * * *

MILLS & BOON®

Helen Bianchin v Regency Collection!

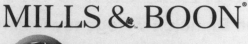

MILLS & BOON®

HISTORICAL

AWAKEN THE ROMANCE OF THE PAST

A sneak peek at next month's titles...

In stores from 21st April 2016:

- **In Bed with the Duke** – Annie Burrows
- **More Than a Lover** – Ann Lethbridge
- **Playing the Duke's Mistress** – Eliza Redgold
- **The Blacksmith's Wife** – Elisabeth Hobbes
- **That Despicable Rogue** – Virginia Heath
- **Printer in Petticoats** – Lynna Banning

Available at WHSmith, Tesco, Asda, Eason, Amazon and Apple

Just can't wait?
Buy our books online a month before they hit the shops!
visit www.millsandboon.co.uk

These books are also available in eBook format!